CW01346858

Long Odds

H. Rider Haggard

Kessinger Publishing's Rare Reprints

Thousands of Scarce and Hard-to-Find Books on These and other Subjects!

- Americana
- Ancient Mysteries
- Animals
- Anthropology
- Architecture
- Arts
- Astrology
- Bibliographies
- Biographies & Memoirs
- Body, Mind & Spirit
- Business & Investing
- Children & Young Adult
- Collectibles
- Comparative Religions
- Crafts & Hobbies
- Earth Sciences
- Education
- Ephemera
- Fiction
- Folklore
- Geography
- Health & Diet
- History
- Hobbies & Leisure
- Humor
- Illustrated Books
- Language & Culture
- Law
- Life Sciences
- Literature
- Medicine & Pharmacy
- Metaphysical
- Music
- Mystery & Crime
- Mythology
- Natural History
- Outdoor & Nature
- Philosophy
- Poetry
- Political Science
- Science
- Psychiatry & Psychology
- Reference
- Religion & Spiritualism
- Rhetoric
- Sacred Books
- Science Fiction
- Science & Technology
- Self-Help
- Social Sciences
- Symbolism
- Theatre & Drama
- Theology
- Travel & Explorations
- War & Military
- Women
- Yoga
- *Plus Much More!*

We kindly invite you to view our catalog list at:
http://www.kessinger.net

THIS ARTICLE WAS EXTRACTED FROM THE BOOK:

The Omnibus of Adventure Volume Two

BY THIS AUTHOR:

H. Rider Haggard

ISBN 1419181335

READ MORE ABOUT THE BOOK AT OUR WEB SITE:

http://www.kessinger.net

OR ORDER THE COMPLETE
BOOK FROM YOUR FAVORITE STORE

ISBN 1419181335

Long Odds

BY H. RIDER HAGGARD
(1856-1925)

THE story which is narrated in the following pages came to me from the lips of my old friend Allan Quatermain, or Hunter Quatermain, as we used to call him in South Africa. He told it to me one evening when I was stopping with him at the place he bought in Yorkshire. Shortly after that, the death of his only son so unsettled him that he immediately left England, accompanied by two companions who were old fellow-voyagers of his, Sir Henry Curtis and Captain Good, and has now utterly vanished into the dark heart of Africa. He is persuaded that a white people, of which he has heard rumours all his life, exists somewhere on the highlands in the vast, still unexplored interior, and his great ambition is to find them before he dies. This is the wild quest upon which he and his companions have departed, and from which I shrewdly suspect they never will return. One letter only have I received from the old gentleman, dated from a mission station high up the Tana, a river on the east coast, about three hundred miles north of Zanzibar; in it he says they have gone through many hardships and adventures, but are alive and well, and have found traces which go far toward making him hope that the results of their wild quest may be a "magnificent and unexampled discovery." I greatly fear, however, that all he has discovered is death; for this letter came a long while ago, and nobody has heard a single word of the party since. They have totally vanished.

It was on the last evening of my stay at his house that he told the ensuing story to me and Captain Good, who was dining with him. He had eaten his dinner and drunk two or three glasses of old port, just to help Good and myself to the end of the second bottle. It was an unusual thing for him to do, for he was a most abstemious man, having conceived, as he used to say, a great horror of drink from observing its effects upon the class of men—hunters, transport-riders, and others—among whom he had passed so many years of his life. Consequently the good wine took more effect on him than it would have done on most men, sending a little flush into his wrinkled cheeks, and making him talk more freely than usual.

Dear old man! I can see him now, as he went limping up and down the vestibule, with his gray hair sticking up in scrubbing-brush fashion, his shrivelled yellow face, and his large dark eyes, that were as keen as any hawk's and yet soft as a buck's. The whole room was hung with trophies of his numerous hunting expeditions, and he had some story about every one of them, if only you could get him to tell them. Generally he would not, for he was not very fond of narrating his own adventures, but tonight the port wine made him more communicative.

"Ah, you brute!" he said, stopping beneath an unusually large skull of a lion, which was fixed just over the mantelpiece, beneath a long row of guns, its jaws distended to their utmost width. "Ah, you brute! you have given me a lot of trouble for the last dozen years, and will, I suppose, to my dying day."

"Tell us the yarn, Quatermain," said Good. "You have often promised to tell me, and you never have."

"You had better not ask me to," he answered, "for it is a longish one."

"All right," I said, "the evening is young and there is some more port."

Thus adjured, he filled his pipe from a jar of coarse-cut Boer tobacco that was always standing on the mantelpiece, and, still walking up and down the room began:

"It was, I think, in the March of '69 that I was up in Sikukuni's country. It was just after old Sequati's time, and Sikukuni had got into power—I forget how. Anyway, I was there. I had heard that the Bapedi people had got down an enormous quantity of ivory from the interior, and so I started with a waggon-load of goods, and came straight away from Middelburg to try and trade some of it. It was a risky thing to go into the country so early, on account of the fever; but I knew that there were one or two others after that lot of ivory, so I determined to have a try for it, and take my chance of fever. I had got so tough from continual knocking about that I did not set it down at much. Well, I got on all right for a while. It is a wonderfully beautiful piece of bush veldt, with great ranges of mountains running through it, and round granite koppies starting up here and there, looking out like sentinels over the rolling waste of bush. But it is very hot,—hot as a stew-pan,—and when I was there that March, which, of course, is autumn in that part of Africa, the whole place reeked of fever. Every morning, as I trekked along down by the Oliphant River, I used to creep out of the waggon at dawn and look out. But there was no river to be seen—only a long line of billows of what looked like the finest cotton-wool tossed up lightly with a pitchfork. It was the fever-mist. Out from among the scrub, too, came little spirals of vapour, as though there were hundreds of tiny fires alight in it—reek rising from thousands of tons of rotting vegetation. It was a beautiful place, but the beauty was the beauty of death; and all those lines and blots of vapour wrote one great word across the surface of the country, and that word was 'fever.'

"It was a dreadful year of illness that. I came, I remember, to one little kraal of knobnoses, and went up to it to see if I could get some *maas* (curdled buttermilk) and a few mealies. As I got near I was struck with the silence of the place. No children began to chatter, and no dogs barked. Nor could I see any native sheep or cattle. The place, though it had evidently been recently inhabited, was as still as the bush round it, and some guinea-fowl got up out of the prickly-pear bushes right at the kraal gate. I remember that I hesitated a little before going in, there was such an air of desolation about the spot. Nature never looks desolate when man has not yet laid his hand upon her breast; she is only lovely. But when man has been, and has passed away, then she looks desolate.

"Well, I passed into the kraal, and went up to the principal hut. In front of the hut was something with an old sheepskin *kaross* (rug) thrown over it. I stooped down and drew off the rug, and then shrank back amazed, for under it was the body of a young woman recently dead. For a moment I thought of turning back, but my curiosity overcame me; so, going past the woman, I went down on my hands and knees and crept into the hut. It was so dark that I could not see anything, though I could smell a great deal; so I lit a match. It was a 'tandstickor' match and burned slowly and dimly, and as the light gradually increased I made out what I thought was a lot of people, men, women, and children, fast asleep. Presently it burned up brightly, and I saw that they too, five of them altogether, were quite dead. One was a baby. I dropped the match in a hurry, and was making my way out of the hut as hard as I could go, when I caught sight of two bright eyes staring out of a corner. Thinking it was a wildcat, or some such animal, I redoubled my haste, when suddenly a voice near the eyes began first to mutter, and then to send up a succession of awful yells. Hastily I lit another match, and perceived that the eyes belonged to an old woman, wrapped up in a greasy leather garment. Taking her by the arm, I dragged her out, for she could not, or would not, come by herself, and the stench was overpowering me. Such a sight as she was—a bag of bones, covered over with black, shrivelled parchment. The only white thing about her was her wool, and she seemed to be pretty well dead except for her eyes and her voice. She thought that I was a devil come to take her, and that was why she yelled so. Well, I got her down to the waggon, and gave her a 'tot' of Cape smoke, and then, as soon as it was ready, poured about a pint of beef-tea down her throat, made from the flesh of a blue vilder-beeste I had killed the day before, and after that she brightened up wonderfully. She could talk Zulu,—indeed, it turned out that she had run away from Zululand in T'Chaka's time,—and she told me that all the people that I had seen had died of fever. When they had died, the other inhabitants of the kraal had taken the cattle and gone away, leaving the poor old woman, who was helpless from age and infirmity, to perish of starvation or disease, as the case might be. She had been sitting there for three days among the bodies when I found her. I took her on to the next kraal, and gave the head man a blanket to look after her, promising him another if I found her well when I came back. I remember that he was much astonished at my parting with two blankets for the sake of such a worthless old creature. Why did I not leave her in the bush? he asked. Those people carry the doctrine of the survival of the fittest to its extreme, you see.

"It was the night after I had got rid of the old woman that I made my first acquaintance with my friend yonder," and he nodded toward the skull that seemed to be grinning down at us in the shadow of the wide mantel-shelf. "I had trekked from dawn till eleven o'clock,—a long trek,—but I wanted to get on; and then had the oxen turned out to graze, sending the voorlooper to look after them, meaning to inspan again about six o'clock, and trek with the moon till ten. Then I got into the waggon and had a good sleep till half-past two or so in the afternoon, when I got up and cooked some meat, and had my dinner, washing it down with a pannikin of black coffee; for it was difficult to get preserved milk in those days. Just as I had finished, and the driver, a man called Tom, was washing up the things, in comes the young scoundrel of a voorlooper, driving one ox before him.

"'Where are the other oxen?' I asked.

"'Koos!' he said, 'koos! [chief] the other oxen have gone away. I turned my back for a minute, and when I looked round again they were all gone except Kaptein, here, who was rubbing his back against a tree.'

"'You mean that you have been asleep, and let them stray, you villain. I will rub your back against a stick,' I answered, feeling very angry, for it was not a pleasant prospect to be stuck up in that fever-trap for a week or so while we were hunting for the oxen. 'Off you go, and you too, Tom, and mind you don't come back till you have found them. They have trekked back along the Middelburg road, and are a dozen miles off by now, I'll be bound. Now, no words; go, both of you.'

"Tom, the driver, swore and caught the lad a hearty kick, which he richly deserved, and then, having tied old Kaptein up to the disselboom with a riem, they got their assegais and sticks, and started. I would have gone too, only I knew that somebody must look after the waggon, and I did not like to leave either of the boys with it at night. I was in a very bad temper, indeed, although I was pretty well used to these sort of occurrences, and soothed myself by taking a rifle and going to kill something. For a couple of hours I poked about without seeing anything that I could get a shot at, but at last, just as I was again within seventy yards of the waggon, I put up an old Impala ram from behind a mimosa-thorn. He ran straight for the waggon, and it was not till he was passing within a few feet of it that I could get a decent shot at him. Then I pulled, and caught him half-way down the spine; over he went, dead as a door-nail, and a pretty shot it was, though I ought not to say it. This little incident put me into rather a better temper, especially as the buck had rolled over right against the after part of the waggon, so I had only to gut him, fix a riem round his legs, and haul him up. By the time I had done this the sun was down, and the full moon was up, and a beautiful moon it was. And then there came down that wonderful hush that sometimes falls over the African bush in the early hours of the night. No beast was moving, and no bird called. Not a breath of air stirred the quiet trees, and the shadows did not even quiver; they only grew. It was very oppressive and very lonely, for there was not a sign of the cattle or the boys. I was quite thankful for the society of old Kaptein, who was lying down contentedly against the disselboom, chewing the cud with a good conscience.

"Presently, however, Kaptein began to get restless. First he snorted, then he got up and snorted again. I could not make it out, so, like a fool, I got down off the waggon-box to have a look round, thinking it might be the lost oxen coming.

"Next instant I regretted it, for all of a sudden I heard an awful roar and saw something yellow flash past me and light on poor Kaptein. Then came a bellow of agony from the ox, and a crunch as the lion put his teeth through the poor brute's neck, and I began to realise what had happened. My rifle was in the waggon, and my first thought was to get hold of it, and I turned and made a bolt for it. I got my foot on the wheel and flung my body forward on to the waggon, and there I stopped as if I were frozen, and no wonder, for as I was about to spring up I heard the lion behind me, and next second I felt the brute, ay, as plainly as I can feel this table. I felt him, I say, sniffing at my left leg that was hanging down.

"My word! I did feel queer; I don't think that I ever felt so queer before. I dared not move for the life of me, and the odd thing was that I seemed to lose power over my leg, which had an insane sort of inclination to kick out of its own mere motion—just as hysterical people want to laugh when they ought to be particularly solemn. Well, the lion sniffed and sniffed, beginning at my ankle and slowly nosing away up to my thigh. I thought that he was going to get hold then, but he did not. He only growled softly, and went back to the ox. Shifting my head a little I got a full view of him. He was the biggest lion I ever saw,—and I have seen a great many,—and he had a most tremendous black mane. What his teeth were like you can see—look there, pretty big ones, ain't they? Altogether he was a magnificent animal, and, as I lay there sprawling on the fore tongue of the waggon, it occurred to me that he would look uncommonly well in a cage. He stood there by the carcass of poor Kaptein, and deliberately disembowelled him as neatly as a butcher could have done. All this while I dared not move, for he kept lifting his head and keeping an eye on me as he licked his bloody chops. When he had cleaned Kaptein out, he opened his mouth and roared, and I am not exaggerating when I say that the sound shook the waggon. Instantly there came back an answering roar.

" 'Heavens!' I thought, 'there is his mate.'

"Hardly was the thought out of my head when I caught sight in the moonlight of the lioness bounding along through the long grass, and after her a couple of cubs about the size of mastiffs. She stopped within a few feet of my head, and stood, and waved her tail, and fixed me with her glowing yellow eyes; but just as I thought that it was all over she turned, and began to feed on Kaptein, and so did the cubs. There were the four of them within eight feet of me, growling and quarrelling, rending and tearing and crunching poor Kaptein's bones; and there I lay shaking with terror, and the cold perspiration pouring out of me, feeling like another Daniel come to judgment in a new sense of the phrase. Presently the cubs had eaten their fill, and began to get restless. One went round to the back of the waggon and pulled at the Impala buck that hung there, and the other came round my way and began the sniffing game at my leg. Indeed, he did more than that, for, my trouser being hitched up a little, he began to lick the bare skin with his rough tongue. The more he licked the more he liked it, to judge from his increased vigour and the loud purring noise he made. Then I knew that the end had come, for in another second his file-like tongue would have rasped through the skin of my leg—which was luckily pretty tough—and have got to the blood, and then there would be no chance for me. So I just lay there and thought of my sins, and prayed to the Almighty, and thought that, after all, life was a very enjoyable thing.

"And then all of a sudden I heard a crashing of bushes and the shouting and whistling of men, and there were the two boys coming back with the cattle, which they had found trekking along all together. The lions lifted their heads and listened, and then without a sound bounded off—and I fainted.

"The lions came back no more that night, and by the next morning my nerves had got pretty straight again; but I was full of wrath when

I thought of all that I had gone through at the hands, or rather noses, of those four lions, and of the fate of my after-ox Kaptein. He was a splendid ox, and I was very fond of him. So wroth was I that, like a fool, I determined to go for the whole family of them. It was worthy of a greenhorn out on his first hunting-trip; but I did it nevertheless. Accordingly after breakfast, having rubbed some oil upon my leg, which was very sore from the cub's tongue, I took the driver, Tom, who did not half like the job, and having armed myself with an ordinary double No. 12 smooth-bore, the first breech-loader I ever had, I started. I took the smooth-bore because it shot a bullet very well; and my experience has been that a round ball from a smooth-bore is quite as effective against a lion as an express bullet. The lion is soft and not a difficult animal to finish if you hit him anywhere in the body. A buck takes far more killing.

"Well, I started, and the first thing I set to work to do was to try to make out whereabouts the brutes lay up for the day. About three hundred yards from the waggon was the crest of a rise covered with single mimosa-trees, dotted about in a park-like fashion, and beyond this was a stretch of open plain running down to a dry pan, or waterhole, which covered about an acre of ground, and was densely clothed with reeds, now in the sear and yellow leaf. From the farther edge of this pan the ground sloped up again to the great cleft, or nullah, which had been cut out by the action of water, and was pretty thickly sprinkled with bush, among which grew some large trees, I forget of what sort.

"It at once struck me that the dry pan would be a likely place to find my friends in, as there is nothing a lion is fonder of than lying up in reeds, through which he can see things without being seen himself. Accordingly thither I went and prospected. Before I had got half-way round the pan I found the remains of a blue vilder-beeste that had evidently been killed within the last three or four days and partially devoured by lions; and from other indications about I was soon assured that if the family were not in the pan that day, they spent a good deal of their spare time there. But if there, the question was how to get them out; for it was clearly impossible to think of going in after them unless one was quite determined to commit suicide. Now there was a strong wind blowing from the direction of the waggon, across the reedy pan, toward the bush-clad kloof or donga, and this first gave me the idea of firing the reeds, which, as I think I told you, were pretty dry. Accordingly Tom took some matches and began starting little fires to the left, and I did the same to the right. But the reeds were still green at the bottom, and we should never have got them well alight had it not been for the wind, which got stronger and stronger as the sun got higher, and forced the fire into them. At last, after half an hour's trouble, the flames got a hold, and began to spread out like a fan, whereupon I got round to the farther side of the pan to wait for the lions, standing well out in the open, as we stood at the copse today where you shot the woodcock. It was a rather risky thing to do, but I used to be so sure of my shooting in those days that I did not so much mind the risk. Scarcely had I got round when I heard the reeds parting before the onward rush of some animal. 'Now for it,' said I. On it came. I could see that it was yellow, and prepared for action, when instead of a lion out bounded a beautiful rietbok which had been lying in the shelter of the pan. It must, by the way, have been a rietbok of a peculiarly confiding nature to lay itself down with the lion like the lamb of prophecy, but I suppose that the reeds were thick, and that it kept a long way off.

"Well, I let the rietbok go, and it went like the wind, and kept my eyes fixed upon the reeds. The fire was burning like a furnace now; the flames crackling and roaring as they bit into the reeds, sending spouts of fire twenty feet and more into the air, and making the hot air dance above it in a way that was perfectly dazzling. But the reeds were still half green, and created an enormous quantity of smoke, which came rolling toward me like a curtain, lying very low on account of the wind. Presently, above the crackling of the fire, I heard a startled roar, and then another and another. So the lions were at home.

"I was beginning to get excited now, for, as you fellows know, there is nothing in experience to warm up your nerves like a lion at close quarters, unless it is a wounded buffalo; and I got still more so when I made out through the smoke that the lions were all moving about on the extreme edge of the reeds. Occasionally they would pop their heads out like rabbits from a burrow, and then, catching sight of me standing about fifty yards out, draw them back again. I knew that it must be getting pretty warm behind them, and that they could not keep the game up for long; and I was not mistaken, for suddenly all four of them broke cover together, the old black-maned lion leading by a few yards. I never saw a more splendid sight in all my hunting experience than those four lions bounding across the veldt, overshadowed by the dense pall of smoke and backed by the fiery furnace of the burning reeds.

"I reckoned that they would pass, on their road to the bushy kloof, within about five and twenty yards of me; so, taking a long breath, I got my gun well on to the lion's shoulder—the black-maned one—so as to allow for an inch or two of motion, and catch him through the heart. I was on, dead on, and my finger was just beginning to tighten on the trigger, when suddenly I went blind—a bit of reed-ash had drifted into my right eye. I danced and rubbed, and got it more or less clear just in time to see the tail of the last lion vanishing round the bushes up the kloof.

"If ever a man was mad I was that man. It was too bad; and such a shot in the open, too! However, I was not going to be beaten, so I just turned and marched for the kloof. Tom, the driver, begged and implored me not to go; but though as a general rule I never pretended to be very brave (which I am not), I was determined that I would either kill those lions or they should kill me. So I told Tom that he need not come unless he liked, but I was going; and being a plucky fellow, a Swazi by birth, he shrugged his shoulders, muttered that I was mad or bewitched, and followed doggedly in my tracks.

"We soon got to the kloof, which was about three hundred yards in length and but sparsely wooded, and then the real fun began. There might be a lion behind every bush—there certainly were four lions somewhere; the delicate question was, where. I peeped and poked and looked in every possible direction, with my heart in my mouth, and was at last rewarded by catching a glimpse of something yellow moving behind a bush. A the same moment, from another bush opposite me out burst one of the cubs and galloped back toward the burned-out pan. I whipped round and let drive a snap-shot that tipped him head over heels, breaking his back within two inches of the root of the tail, and there he lay helpless but glaring. Tom afterward killed him with his assegai. I opened the breech of the gun and hurriedly pulled out the old case, which, to judge from what ensued, must, I suppose, have burst and left a portion of its fabric sticking to the barrel. At any rate, when I tried to get in the new case it would only enter half-way; and—would you believe it?—this was the moment that the lioness, attracted no doubt by the outcry of her cub, chose to put in an appearance. There she stood, twenty paces or so from me, lashing her tail and looking just as wicked as it is possible to conceive. Slowly I stepped backward, trying to push in the new case, and as I did so she moved on in little runs, dropping down after each run. The danger was imminent, and the case woud not go in. At the moment I oddly enough thought of the cartridge-maker, whose name I will not mention, and earnestly hoped that if the lion got me some condign punishment would overtake him. It would not go in, so I tried to pull it out. It would not come out, either, and my gun was useless if I could not shut it to use the other barrel. I might as well have had no gun. Meanwhile I was walking backward, keeping my eye on the lioness, who was creeping forward on her belly without a sound, but lashing her tail and keeping her eye on me; and in it I saw that she was coming in a few seconds more. I dashed my wrist and the palm of my hand against the brass rim of the cartridge till the blood poured from them—look, there are the scars of it to this day!"

Here Quatermain held up his right hand to the light and showed us seven or eight white cicatrices just where the wrist is set into the hand.

"But it was not of the slightest use," he went on; "the cartridge would not move. I only hope that no other man will ever be put in such an awful position. The lioness gathered herself together, and I gave myself up for lost, when suddenly Tom shouted out from somewhere in my rear:

" 'You are walking on to the wounded cub; turn to the right.'

"I had the sense, dazed as I was, to take the hint, and slewing round at right angles, but still keeping my eyes on the lioness, I continued my backward walk.

"To my intense relief, with a low growl she straightened herself, turned, and bounded off farther up the kloof.

" 'Come on, inkoos,' said Tom; 'let's get back to the waggon.'

" 'All right, Tom,' I answered. 'I will when I have killed those three other lions,' for by this time I was bent on shooting them as I never remember being bent on anything before or since. 'You can go if you like, or you can get up a tree.'

"He considered the position a little, and then he very wisely got up a tree. I wish that I had done the same.

"Meanwhile I had got out my knife, which had an extractor in it, and succeeded after some difficulty in hauling out the case which had so nearly been the cause of my death, and removing the obstruction in the barrel. It was very little thicker than a postage-stamp; certainly not thicker than a piece of writing-paper. This done I loaded the gun, bound my handkerchief round my wrist and hand to stanch the flowing of the blood, and started on again.

"I had noticed that the lioness went into a thick green bush, or rather cluster of bushes, growing near the water; for there was a little stream running down the kloof, about fifty yards higher up, and for this I made. When I got there, however, I could see nothing, so I took up a big stone and threw it into the bushes. I believe that it hit the other cub, for out it came with a rush, giving me a broadside shot of which I promptly availed myself, knocking it over dead. Out, too, came the lioness like a flash of light, but quick as she went I managed to put the other bullet into her ribs, so that she rolled right over three times like a shot rabbit. I instantly got two more cartridges into the gun, and as I did so the lioness got up again and came crawling toward me on her fore paws, roaring and groaning, and with such an expression of diabolical fury on her countenance as I have not often seen. I shot her again through the chest, and she fell over on her side quite dead.

"That was the first and last time that I ever killed a brace of lions right and left, and, what is more, I never heard of anybody else doing it. Naturally I was considerably pleased with myself, and, having again loaded up, went on to look for the black-maned beauty who had killed Kaptein. Slowly and with the greatest care I proceeded up the kloof, searching every bush and tuft of grass as I went. It was wonderfully exciting work, for I never was sure from one moment to another but that he would be on me. I took comfort, however, from the reflection that a lion rarely attacks a man,—rarely, I say; sometimes he does, as you will see,—unless he is cornered or wounded. I must have been nearly an hour hunting after the lion. Once I thought I saw something move in a clump of tambouki grass, but I could not be sure, and when I trod out the grass I could not find him.

"At last I got up to the head of the kloof, which made a cul-de-sac. It was formed of a wall of rock about fifty feet high. Down this rock trickled a little waterfall, and in front of it, some seventy feet from its face, was a great piled-up mass of boulders, in the crevices and on the top of which grew ferns and grass and stunted bushes. This mass was about twenty-five feet high. The sides of the kloof here were also very steep. Well, I got up to the top of the nullah and looked all round. No signs of the lion. Evidently I had either over-looked him farther down, or he had escaped right away. It was very vexatious; but still three lions were not a bad bag for one gun before dinner, and I was fain to be content. Accordingly I departed back again, making my way round the isolated pillar of boulders, and beginning to feel that I was pretty well done up with excitement and fatigue, and should be more so before I had skinned those three lions. When I had got, as nearly as I could judge, about eighteen yards past the pillar or mass of boulders, I turned to have another look round. I have a pretty sharp eye, but I could see nothing at all.

"Then, on a sudden, I saw something sufficiently alarming. On the top of the mass of boulders, opposite to me, standing out clear against the rock beyond, was the huge black-maned lion. He had been crouching there, and now arose as though by magic. There he stood lashing his tail, just like a statue of the animal on the gateway of Northumberland House that I have seen a picture of. But he did not stand long. Before I could fire—before I could do more than get the gun to my shoulder—he sprang straight up and out from the rock, and, driven by the impetus of that one mighty bound, came hurtling through the air toward me.

"Heavens! how grand he looked, and how awful! High into the air he flew, describing a great arch. Just as he touched the highest point of his spring I fired. I did not dare to wait, for I saw that he would clear the whole space and land right upon me. Without a sight, almost without aim, I fired, as one would fire a snap-shot at a snipe. The bullet told, for I distinctly heard its thud above the rushing sound caused by the passage of the lion through the air. Next second I was swept to the ground (luckily I fell into a low, creeper-clad bush, which broke the shock), and the lion was on the top of me, and the next those great white teeth of his had met in my thigh—I heard them grate against the bone. I yelled out in agony, for I did not feel in the least benumbed and happy, like Dr. Livingstone,—whom, by the way, I knew very well,—and gave myself up for dead. But suddenly, as I did so, the lion's grip on my thigh loosened, and he stood over me, swaying to and fro, his huge mouth, from which the blood was gushing, wide opened. Then he roared, and the sound shook the rocks.

"To and fro he swung, and suddenly the great head dropped on me, knocking all the breath from my body, and he was dead. My bullet had entered in the centre of his chest and passed out on the right side of the spine about half-way down the back.

"The pain of my wound kept me from fainting, and as soon as I got my breath I managed to drag myself from under him. Thank heavens, his great teeth had not crushed my thigh-bone; but I was losing a great deal of blood, and had it not been for the timely arrival of Tom, with whose aid I got the handkerchief off my wrist and tied it round my leg, twisting it tight with a stick, I think I should have bled to death.

"Well, it was a just reward for my folly in trying to tackle a family of lions single-handed. The odds were too long. I have been lame ever since, and shall be to my dying day; in the month of March the wound always troubles me a great deal, and every three years it breaks out raw. I need scarcely add that I never traded the lot of ivory at Sikukuni's. Another man got it—a German—and made five hundred pounds out of it after paying expenses. I spent the next month on the broad of my back, and was a cripple for six months after that. And now I've told you the yarn, so I will have a drop of hollands and go to bed."

This is the end of this publication.

Any remaining blank pages are for our book binding requirements and are blank on purpose.

To search thousands of interesting publications like this one, please remember to visit our website at:

http://www.kessinger.net

Social England Series
Edited by KENELM D. COTES, M.A., Oxon.

THE EVOLUTION
OF THE
ENGLISH HOUSE

BY

SIDNEY OLDALL ADDY, M.A.

WITH 42 ILLUSTRATIONS

LONDON
SWAN SONNENSCHEIN & CO., LIM.
NEW YORK: THE MACMILLAN CO., LIM.
1898

In the interest of creating a more extensive selection of rare historical book reprints, we have chosen to reproduce this title even though it may possibly have occasional imperfections such as missing and blurred pages, missing text, poor pictures, markings, dark backgrounds and other reproduction issues beyond our control. Because this work is culturally important, we have made it available as a part of our commitment to protecting, preserving and promoting the world's literature. Thank you for your understanding.

EDITORIAL PREFACE

IN introducing an old subject with some variety of form, it is easy to be brief and at the same time clear, because the reader supplies from previous knowledge so much that is left unsaid; but in stepping quite out of the beaten track nothing perhaps but actually treading the new path can make the goal that it is intended to reach plainly visible. It is not desirable that the whole object of a new series of books written on a new plan should be capable of being condensed into a few pages; this can be done only for subjects whose scope is already well defined, where there are and have been many previous books written on the same lines, though perhaps from slightly different points of view, and in which the only novelty to be looked for is in the style of writing and in the arrangement and amount of matter.

A New Subject.

Undoubted as is the influence of personality upon history, the attention directed to it has hitherto been rather one-sided; the entire course of national life cannot be summed up in a few great names, and the attempt to do so is to confuse biography with history. This narrow view, besides ignoring other causes, leads to the overrating of details, and since a cause must

Personality.

be found somewhere, personal character becomes everything. The stability of law that is seen in a large number of instances cannot be discovered by watching single lives, however exalted; and history with no intention of discovering the condition of events becomes the sport of accident, resting in great measure for its interest on anecdote and rhetoric.

Politics. The case is not much bettered by long accounts of acts of parliament, with summaries of debates, and numbering of divisions, and more lives of statesmen, eminent and mediocre. The details of parliament no more than the details of biographies afford sufficient data for scientific observation, if the forces of the society that surround them are omitted. Neither does the addition of military detail help much in the comprehension of the course of events; one battle is much like another, except when treated by the professional soldier or sailor, or at all events in the light of professional books; and victories or defeats depend upon something else besides the position of the ground or the plans of the moment. It has been reserved for a naval expert of another power to point this out to the multitudinous writers of the history of the great naval power of the world.

Social Questions. Social questions are to-day taking the foremost place in public interest; the power behind the statesman is seen to be greater in controlling contemporary history than the eloquence or experience of any single man. We see this to be so now, and our knowledge of the present suggests the question whether it has not always been so; and whether the life of society, though it has not had the same comparative weight, has not always been a more important factor than the life of the individual.

The "Social England" Series. The "Social England" series rests upon the conviction that it is possible to make a successful attempt to give an account not merely of politics and wars, but also of religion, commerce, art, literature, law, science, agriculture, and all that follows from their inclusion, and that without a due knowledge of the last we have no real explanation of any of the number.

Not as an Appendix. But the causes that direct the course of events will become no clearer if to one-third politics and one-third wars we add another third, consisting of small portions of other subjects, side by side, but yet apart from one another.

The Central Idea. The central idea is that the greatness or weakness of a nation does not depend on the greatness or weakness of any one man or body of men, and that the odd millions have always had their part to play. To understand how great that was and is, we must understand the way in which they spent their lives, what they really cared for, what they fought for, and, in a word, what they lived for. To leave out nine-tenths of the national life, and to call the rest a history of the nation, is misleading. It is so misleading that, treated in this mutilated manner, history has no pretension to be a science: it becomes a ponderous chronicle, full of details which, in the absence of any other guiding principle, are held together by chronology. Writers of great name and power escape from this limitation, which, however, holds sway for the most part in the books that reach the great majority of readers, that is those who have not time to read an epoch in several volumes.

The Carrying Out of the Idea. It is not necessary, in seeing a famous town, to visit every public building and private house, and so for the carrying out of this plan it has been determined that adequate treatment can be secured of certain subjects in a series of books that should be popular not only in style, but also in the demands they make upon the reader's time.

Specialists. It would be useless for any one writer to pretend to accomplish this task, though when the way is cleared a social history connecting more closely and summarizing the work of all the contributors will be possible; but at present it is intended to ask each of them to bring his special knowledge to bear upon the explanation of social life, and, in treating his portion of the work, to look at original authorities to see not merely what light they throw on his own branch separately, but how they affect its conception considered in relation to the whole, that is, to the development of the life of the English people.

The Possible Limits of the Series. To bring the series to its completion will need the services of many writers. A few of the number of books which might be suggested may be mentioned. The influence upon thought of geographical discovery, of commerce, and of science would form three volumes. The part inventions have played, the main changes in political theories, and, perhaps less commonplace, the main changes in English thought upon great topics, such as the social position of women, of children, and of the church, the treatment of the indigent poor and of the criminal, need all to be studied. The soldier, the sailor, the lawyer, the physician, have still to be written of; the conception of the duties of the noble or the statesman, not in the story of one man's life, but in a general theory, illustrated from the lives of many men, has still to be formulated; the wide range of subjects connected with law—the story of crime, laws made in class interest, laws for the protection of trade and for the regulation of industry—are all to be found in the statutes at large. A more comprehensive sketch of the scope of the series should be found in an introductory volume.

Works already Arranged for. But, apart from the probable extension of the series, sufficient works have already been arranged for to describe some leading features of English social life, and to point out some of the numerous highways which lead to a great centre, passing through different provinces, which all have their local colour, but the lives of whose inhabitants need also to be known if we are to understand the country as a whole, and not merely the court and parliament of the capital.

The King's Place. The king is the centre of this life when war and justice form the chief reason for the loose federation of communities; not merely does he give protection on the frontiers, but among his own subjects it is more and more his duty to enforce peace, and we have to see how step by step the local court or franchise is merged in the strengthening of sovereign justice.

Chivalry. What exactly was the ideal of knighthood? How far did it imply an acquaintance with the learning of the day and with foreign countries? Did it strengthen the feeling of pity for the weak, or purify the love for women? In what are wrongly called the **The Troubadours.** dark ages, was there a vast society of men of culture, who spread over large parts of Northern Europe, to whom we owe the first-fruits of modern literature, the troubadours, who first came from Provence?

The Manor. In the manor is to be found the story of early village life, of domestic manufactures, of the system of agriculture and of the simplest administration of justice, a system the remains of which last **The Working-man.** till to-day; while a sketch of the history of the working-classes helps to complete the picture, and at the same time to place a wider one beside it, to show especially how wages have been regulated, the condition under which the poor have lived, and to see what on the whole is the part they have played in history.

The Rise of the Merchants. Turning from the working-man, we naturally ask when arose the great class of merchants, how their gradual rise affected the condition of the population, whether their appearance synchronised with any other political and social events, and in fact we prepare for the question as to the influence of commerce on politics and society.

The Universities. Those who know the part that commerce plays in civilization are aware that the growth of intercourse will naturally bring larger culture, and the learning of the old world and of the Saracens will be taught in the schools of the West. It will be impossible to rigidly confine the currents of thought to the four seas, or even only to break the barrier here and there by such stories as that of the Roman missionaries. England must be looked on as belonging to the circle of a great civilization. How far Englishmen went abroad, and how far the men of other nations came to England, requires to be set forth.

The Travelled Englishman and the Traveller in England.

Again, to those who believe in the organic connection of all branches of the national life it will be of interest to learn in what way the character of art partook of the nature of life around it, how far its methods or motives can be borrowed, why the fifteenth century gave pause to our art, why at a certain period cathedrals ceased to be built, and when it was we added great names in our turn to the list of painters.

The Fine Arts.

The music of Anglo-Saxon and of Dane will to some make clearer the influence of skald and gleeman; the effect of poetry will be noted, the growth of instruments, and the increasing complexity of music.

Music.

Possibly the change in the landscape might be described: the alteration in the face of the country with the draining of fens, the making of roads, and the clearing of forests; the introduction of fresh trees and plants.

Scenery.

We must recognise that the position of Great Britain, as the known world grew wider, altered for the better; the effect of rivers, mountains, and seas in fixing the boundaries of kingdoms and sub-

The Influence of Geography on Social Life.

kingdoms, in altering or preserving languages, in determining politics and the opinions of districts, and, the chief point of all, in deciding the character of what bids fair to be the language of commerce, and probably of all international communication.

The Homes and Household Implements. As it is important to know where men lived in relation to the world at large in order to understand how they lived, so we should be acquainted with their dwelling-places, whether in town or country, at any period; we should observe the changing styles of building, distinguish the international influence, the part that the facility of obtaining material played, and notice the gradual evolution of the rooms, the way that they were adorned and furnished, to see how far in beds and baths, in the provision for study and privacy, civilization was advancing.

Social England Classics. From their literature we can gather most, for here, with not much thought of history, contemporary spoke to contemporary of what each knew well. In the pre-Elizabethan drama we can see the natural touches that show it was not elaborated as an exercise, but with the intention of possessing a living interest, and in what interested them we discover their attitude, not merely to religion, but to much else besides. By recognising this fact we learn that masterpieces of literature lose their full meaning unless we find in them, besides creative power and command of the technique of art, "the very age and body of the time." Shakespeare's England and Chaucer's England are what Shakespeare and Chaucer knew of life; the outer gallery of pictures the unknown artists drew, from which we pass into the inner rooms whose walls are covered by the groups and figures that the masters painted.

Biography and History. In this widening of history, biography is no longer cramped by being cut off from social life; the great men are not isolated, but take their proper places among their fellow-countrymen, their lives forming fit landmarks, because they are akin to the people among whom they live, their characters not adapted to the century of the commentator, but bearing the impress of the forces round them, whose constant pressure is part of their life. They and those who are lesser than themselves, and the changing conditions that create them and are modified by them, form the great and continuous whole, which constantly alters, as all life alters, coming from the past and linked to the future. It no longer becomes necessary to make all times alike, except for constitutional changes, or improvement in weapons, and the crowning or death of a king, pleading the half-truth that human nature is the same in every age.

AUTHOR'S PREFACE

IN discussing the evolution of the English house we are more concerned with the popular and native art of building than with forms or styles borrowed from other countries.

English writers on domestic architecture have been content for the most part with describing the remains of great villas, or the picturesque timber houses which adorn some of our old cities. Such buildings are more attractive to the casual eye than wattled huts or combinations of dwelling-house and cattle-stall.

And yet, if we would learn how the masses of the English people lived in past times, we must not omit these plainer, but assuredly not less interesting dwellings.

Professor Meitzen, Professor Theodor Siebs, and other German scholars have described still-existing houses in northern Germany which are built, like basilicas or churches, in the form of nave and aisles, with dwelling-rooms, usually three in number, at one end; and Dr. Konrad Lange has shown that these remarkable survivals resemble the peasants' houses described by Galen as existing in Asia Minor in the second century of the Christian era.

At the present day there are no houses in England which resemble the old Greek peasants' houses, or the typical basilica, so nearly as do these German survivals. Our menservants and maidservants no longer sleep in galleries above the aisles of a great farmhouse; and yet we are by no means without traces of the former existence here of similar habitations. We still have examples of barns or "shippons" built in the form of nave and aisles, in which the oxen faced inwardly to the main floor, as they did in the German peasant's house, and at the end of which there is either a small dwelling-house, or, in place of that dwelling-house, a stable, separated from the "shippon" by a threshing-floor.

Taking an ordinary parish church as an illustration of our subject, the main entrance to the German peasant's house was through a pair of large folding-doors at the west end. In the English peasant's house, as now seen in numerous survivals, the main entrance was not in the west end, but in the transept. In one of the outer walls of the transept (or "floor," as it was sometimes called) was a pair of folding-doors, commonly called barn-doors. In the outer wall on the opposite side of the transept was a smaller door, called the winnowing-door. The transept was the "threshold," or threshing-floor. It must not, however, be supposed that these houses were oriented, as the ordinary church is. They may, or may not, have anciently been so, and no assertion on that point is made here.

Although we cannot point to the existence in England of such complete survivals of the ancient "three-naved" house as are found in Germany, we still possess abundant remains of an architectural feature which lies at the root of Gothic architecture.

An example will show best what is meant. The roof of a barn at Upper Midhope, near Penistone, is supported by six thick "forks" of oak, locally known as "crucks," or "crutches." The "forks" stand on little stone pillars, or plinths, embedded in the walls, their bases projecting outside. The "forks" and the little pillars are older than the walls: the pillars are not of the same kind of stone as that which forms the walls. In such a building as this the whole construction from floor to roof is apparent to view. The weight of the roof rests on the stone pillars, which rise a foot or more above the ground. There is no "thrust" on the walls; "the arch which never sleeps" thrusts only on the soil.

"Forks" like these are still abundant in old dwelling-houses. Sometimes they are concealed in the walls, and are all but invisible in the lower story. In barns and rooms where cattle are housed they are either curved or straight. In dwelling-houses they are usually curved or lancet-shaped. The object of the curve was to gain head-room, trees having been chosen which were naturally bent.

You have only to erect a pair of such bent trees on pedestals, however short, of wood or stone, and the Gothic arch of a church or ancient hall, with its subjacent pillars, stands before you in its nascent form.

No living man can now remember the time when "forks" like these were set up, and there are reasons for believing that they have not been used by builders during the last two centuries. But building with "forks" can be traced up the stream of time for at least two thousand years. Such "forks" supported the roofs of Roman cottages in the days of Ovid, and they were regarded by Vitruvius as evidence of the oldest kind of building. In this case, then, we need not look for the past in the present, for traces of this method of construction appear in a long and all but unbroken record.

Anciently buildings supported by "forks" had no vertical side walls; only the two gable ends were upright. Horizontal beams were laid across the "forks," and the slope of the roof extended down to the ground. Hence, when the "forks" were curved or bent, these buildings, more especially when their length was considerable, resembled ships or boats turned upside down.

Complete examples of ship-shaped houses are extremely rare at the present day. But they were once extremely numerous, and if we examine some of the "forks" which support old buildings we shall find that they bear on their outer faces "housings," or cavities, to receive the horizontal beams which were once laid across them.

The addition of projecting tie-beams to the "forks," and of the upright side walls on which the two ends of the tie-beams rested, was an invention of later times.

It was easy to extend a building supported by "forks" by adding to its length; it was not so easy to extend its breadth. Lateral extensions, however, were made, when the occasion required it, by means of an elaborate wooden framework. The building then had wings, or aisles, sometimes called "little bays," on one or both sides. The central room only had the form of an inverted ship, or rather of the skeleton or main timbers of an inverted ship.

Any addition to the ends of such a building, or any extension, whether at the ends or the sides, which did not form an integral part of the great wooden framework, or was shut off from the rest of the building, was called an "outshot" or "outshut." In Old English such an addition was called *gescot*, or "shot." For example, the chancel at the east end of a church is a "shot" or "outshot." The *culacia* at the ends of great barns mentioned in mediaeval documents were probably "outshots."

It must not, however, be supposed that houses supported by "forks" comprehended or included every kind of building in England. Such houses were probably more frequent than any other on account of their cheapness. But wooden houses containing upright columns supporting a middle room or nave, with aisles on both sides, were also common. Extant examples of this basilical type of house are now hardly to be found; their forms have rather to be inferred from records and from similar buildings which now exist in some parts of Germany, and which are known to have existed in Wales and Ireland. The former kind of building was more suitable for the poorest cottages; the latter could be developed, either in wood or stone, into buildings of great splendour.

Nothing is known as to the relative antiquity of these two kinds of buildings. All that can be said is that buildings supported by "forks" are, on account of their simpler construction, probably of an older type than buildings supported by upright columns.

Both these two kinds of buildings were divided into "bays," and again into "half bays," the normal length of the "bay" being sixteen feet. The "bay" became the unit of measurement, and the length of such buildings was estimated by the number of "bays," including "half bays," which they contained.

When, therefore, we read in an ancient survey, or other old document, that such a building was forty feet in length, we know that it must have contained two "bays" and a half. If the building was eighty feet in length it must have contained five "bays."

Consequently the length of such a building, when measured in feet, will be found to be a multiple either of eight or sixteen. If it was a multiple of eight and not a multiple of sixteen—for example, if the building were forty feet in length—it contained a "half bay."

In old Norse buildings, according to Vigfusson, the distance between two posts, or pillars, was known as a *staf-gólf*, or stave-space, and was about two yards, the length of a building being "denoted by its number of *staf-gólf*." Here we are not told what the exact measurement was, but the *staf-gólf* seems to be identical with the English "half bay."

In English ox-houses the "bays" or spaces between the great "forks," or, as the case might be, between the upright pillars, were divided into two equal parts by partitions known as "skell-boosts," the word "skell" being derived from the Old Norse *skilja*, to divide or separate.

The "bay" was just of sufficient length to accommodate a "long yoke" of oxen, or four oxen abreast. The "half bay" was sufficient for a "short yoke," or a pair of oxen. As oxen ploughed the land, and were the labouring cattle of our forefathers, it was considered necessary that they should stand together in the house as they stood together in the field. By standing in pairs or fours in the house they grew more familiar with the accustomed yoke. Moreover, it was necessary that buildings should be so constructed as to hold the greatest number of objects with the least possible waste of timber-work or of space.

The length of the "bay" was identical with the length of the perch or rod in land measurement. Accordingly the normal length of a "bay" of building is equivalent to the breadth of a rod or rood of land.

The necessities or requirements of oxen had more to do with the sizes and forms of our ancient houses than any other factor, for this length of "bay," fixed as it was by the "long yoke" of oxen, became the rule in every kind of domestic building, except mere huts or booths supported by a single pair of "forks."

We learn, then, that the origin of our common architectural forms is not to be sought in arbitrary designs. We must look for it in the simple hut whose roof was held up by a pair of wooden "forks," as well as in the more elaborate wooden house, of which the cathedral is the highest development. The pyramidal outline of the great farmhouse, or peasant's house, which still rises above the plains of northern Germany, and which still, in a less perfect form, may be seen in English villages, is the most striking feature of Gothic architecture. The larger dwelling-house and the great church had this feature in common.

xxiv AUTHOR'S PREFACE

In conclusion, the author offers his best thanks to Mr. Joseph Kenworthy for the interest which he has taken in the present work. With him he has spent happy days in the country examining and measuring old buildings. His thanks are also offered to Mr. Edmund Winder, architect, and to Mr. Barton Wells for their survey and plans of the keep at Castleton; to Professor Meitzen, of Berlin, for leave to make use of illustrations in his books; to Professor Theodor Siebs, of Greifeswald, for a similar kindness; to Mr. E. Sidney Hartland and to Sir George Reresby Sitwell, Bart., for their advice and assistance; to Mr. Thomas Winder, architect, of the Duke of Norfolk's office in Sheffield, for drawings, plans, and other valuable help; to Mr. E. C. Skill, of the same office, for photographs and plans; and to Mr. Charles Macro Wilson for the use of a manuscript in his possession.

As regards the literature of the subject, Dr. Konrad Lange's far-reaching book, entitled *Haus und Halle* (Leipzig, 1885), should be specially mentioned.

Most of the illustrations and plans, etc. in the present work are from photographs and measurements taken and made by the author.

SHEFFIELD, *October*, 1898.

CONTENTS

CHAPTER I.
THE ROUND HOUSE—UNDERGROUND HOUSES . . . 1

CHAPTER II.
THE RECTANGULAR HOUSE IN ITS SIMPLEST FORM . . 16

CHAPTER III.
THE RECTANGULAR HOUSE WITH "OUTSHUTS" . . 42

CHAPTER IV.
THE LARGER RECTANGULAR HOUSE WITH AISLES . . 65

CHAPTER V.
FOREIGN PROTOTYPES: STATEMENTS OF ANCIENT WRITERS 79

CHAPTER VI.
THE TOWN HOUSE 93

CHAPTER VII.
BUILDING MATERIALS — CHIMNEYS — WINDOWS — MURAL DECORATIONS—ROOFS 106

CHAPTER VIII.
THE MANOR HOUSE 129

CHAPTER IX.

	PAGE
The Castle and Watchtower	150

CHAPTER X.

The Church or Lord's House	176
Summary	199
Excursus I.	205
,, II.	207
,, III.	211
Some Books Cited	212
Index	215

LIST OF ILLUSTRATIONS

	PAGE
Charcoal Burner's Hut	5
Plan of House in British Village, Glastonbury	7
House at Scrivelsby	19
Section of House at Scrivelsby	20
Plan of House at Scrivelsby	21
"Oratory" of Gallerus (from a photograph by Mr. Lawrence, of Sackville Street, Dublin)	23
"Crucks" of Demolished House	30
"Crucks" in Barn at Treeton	31
Plan of Mud House, Great Hatfield	39
"Outshut" at North Meols	43
Plan of House at Westward, North Meols	45
House at Burscough	48
Plan of House at Burscough	49
Plan of House at North Meols	50
Roof and Mantel-piece at North Meols	51
Plan of House at Upper Midhope	53
"House-place" at Upper Midhope	55
Stair at Upper Midhope	57
Plan of "Coit" at Upper Midhope	71
Winnowing Door of Barn, Grindleford	73
Section of Barn at Bolsterstone	75
Saxon House	80
Plan of Saxon House	81
Plan and Section of House in Saterland	83
"Balk" or "Scaffold" at Fulwood	87
Chimney at Warrington	113

LIST OF ILLUSTRATIONS

	PAGE
Flues from Ground-floor Fire-places	118
Dots and Lines on Walls	123
Plan of Kensworth Manor House	130
Plan of Padley Hall	136
Outer View of Padley Hall	138
Inner View of Padley Hall	139
Plan of Chapel and Bower, Padley Hall	141
Plan of Ground Floor, Castleton Castle	156
Plan of Upper Floor	157
Section A. B., Castleton Castle	160
Plan of Gable Window and Watching-Place, Castleton Castle	161
Section C. D., Castleton Castle	166
Section of Crypt, Pompeii	189
Plan of Tribunal, Pompeii	192
Plan of Crypt at Repton	192
Plan of Crypt at Hornsea	193

THE
Evolution of the English House

CHAPTER I.

THE ROUND HOUSE—UNDERGROUND HOUSES

The round hut the earliest form of European house—The modern charcoal burner's hut a type of the earliest form—The marsh village near Glastonbury—Round or roundish houses there built of wood and mud-clay—Circular hearths—The village near Glastonbury fortified by palisades, and of pre-Roman date—The arts practised by its inhabitants—Resemblance of the village to prehistoric villages in North Italy—Roofs of these houses—Oval forms very difficult to build—Stone "bee-hive" houses—Tendency of such houses to assume a rectangular form—Underground houses—Late survivals from them—Traditions about underground passages—Underground dwellings of the ancient Germans.

IN Great Britain, as elsewhere in Europe, the evidence leads us to the conclusion that the earliest form of dwelling, fit to bear the name of house, was round. Round huts are still used in Africa, and such huts seem to have been common to many different races at an early stage of their development.[1] In Italy the type of the round form of house lasted down to historical times

[1] LANGE, *Haus und Halle*, p. 51; SMITH's *Dictionary of Greek and Roman Antiquities*, 3rd ed., i. 654.

in the temples of Vesta.[1] In England it may have been preserved in the round temple found at Silchester and one or two round churches, like that at Little Maplestead in Essex.

In Ireland, says Professor Sullivan, "round houses were made by making two basket-like cylinders, one within the other, and separated by an annular space of about a foot, by inserting upright posts in the ground and interweaving hazel wattles between, the annular space being filled with clay. Upon this cylinder was placed a conical cap, thatched with reeds or straw. The kreel houses of many Highland gentlemen in the last century were made in this way, except that they were not round.

The early Irish houses had no chimney. The fire was made in the centre of the house, and the smoke made its exit through the door or through a hole in the roof, as in the corresponding Gaulish and German houses."[2] The walls of this kind of round house did not slope inwardly, so as to meet in a point at the summit. But the sloping jambs of doors, so often found in the oldest examples of Scotch and Irish buildings, may afford evidence that in some forms of round houses the walls were not upright, but took the shape of a cone. The sloping jambs of Pelasgic buildings may also point to the same conclusion.

An account of the building of a round wicker house is given in the Gaedhelic Life of Saint Colman Ela. It was

---

[1] See the whole subject discussed in HELBIG, *Die Italiker in der Poebene*, p. 51 *et seq.*
[2] In *Encyclopaedia Britannica*, 9th ed., xiii. 256.

completed by the weaving in of a single rod at a time. The writer says:

> "Of drops a pond is filled;
> Of rods a round-house is built;
> The house which is favoured of God"[1]

In England charcoal burners, whose occupation is ancient, build round huts to this day. They are composed "of a number of thin poles laid together in the form of a cone. The feet are placed about nine inches apart, and they are interlaced with brushwood. A doorway is formed by laying a lintel from fork to fork, and the whole is covered with sods laid with the grass towards the inside, so that the soil may not fall from them into the hut. A lair of grass and bushwood is formed upon one side, and a fire, often of charcoal, is lighted upon the hearth in the threshold."[2] The hut shown in the illustration stood in Old Park Wood, near Sheffield. We have here a curious survival of the way in which some prehistoric dwellings seem to have been built. The sloping jambs of the door should be particularly noticed, and compared with those found in ancient Irish and Scotch stone buildings.

The Gaulish huts shown on the Antonine column have both a round and a rectangular shape, and the forms there given show a higher stage of development than that exhibited in the modern charcoal burner's hut, for the walls had already become straight and the roof domical. The

---

[1] O'Curry's *Manners and Customs of the Ancient Irish*, iii. 32. It is popularly said of a London minister of religion that he built his church round to keep the devil out of the corners.

[2] T. Winder in *The Builders' Journal*, vol. iii. p. 25.

charcoal burner's hut, shaped like a cone, and having neither window nor chimney, is a type of the very earliest forms of human dwellings, though it is better than were the miserable huts of the ancient Fenni. This savage German tribe, according to Tacitus, slept on the ground, and had no other protection for its children against wild beasts and the weather than a few boughs twisted together. These people lived a nomadic life, and thought that better than groaning over agriculture or toiling at building houses.[1]

In Great Britain the foundations of circular houses, with much else of great historical value, have been found of late years in marsh villages or lake villages. The most interesting of these is the village lately discovered near Glastonbury. Here between sixty and seventy huts or houses stood upon an artificial island raised above the surrounding marsh. The village covered nearly three and a half acres.[2] It was surrounded by a palisade formed of poles from five to ten feet in height, and so close together that more than fifty have been counted in a space of three yards. The palisading was "kept together by more or less coarse hurdle work." The mounds which cover the remains of the huts vary "from eighteen to thirty-five feet in diameter, and are about four feet high in the centre, where in most cases is a hearth either of stones or simply of clay."[3] The surface of the artificial island was formed

[1] TACITUS, *Germ.* 46.
[2] A. BULLEID in the *Somersetshire Arch. and Nat. Hist. Society's Proceedings*, 1894. (Reprint, 1895.)
[3] *Daily News*, 19th Feb., 1895.

CHARCOAL BURNER'S HUT

of "large pieces of timber placed side by side and reaching a foot in depth. Under these were six to nine inches of carefully layered brushwood, resting on more pieces of timber and on olive-brown peat containing logs—these together being three feet deep—and lastly, between the above layer and the yellow peat, eighteen inches or so of much decayed wood mixed with rushes and dark peat."[1] The upper layers of timber and brushwood were kept in position by hundreds of small piles.

Each of the mounds covers the remains of a house or hut. "The hut walls were constructed of upright posts placed about one foot apart, the spaces between them being filled with wattle and daub. This is shown not only by the quantity of baked clay bearing wattle and timber marks, but also by the stumps of the actual wall-posts *in situ*. A large number of fragments of baked clay show impressions of square-cut timber. The entrance to the huts has been clearly traced: a few rough slabs of lias stone forming the doorstep, with a piece of timber as the threshold. These are shown in the accompanying plan of a small dwelling, the diameter of which is about eighteen feet."[2]

The shape of the huts is said to have been for the most part circular or oval, but an important exception was discovered in 1896. "Amongst the wood and *débris* underlying the clay of a dwelling mound three hurdles were uncovered; the more complete one measured 6 ft. 3 in. high by 10 ft. 6 in. wide, with an average space between the upright posts of five inches. In close proximity to the hurdles was a beam of oak, having small mortise holes along one side parallel to the edge; the distance between the holes exactly tallied with the space between the hurdle posts. From the way the under surface of the beam was cut and notched it was evident that it had been placed at right angles to a similar piece of timber. We have here

[1] A. BULLEID, *ut supra*, p. 20.
[2] A. BULLEID, *ut supra*.

VILLAGE NEAR GLASTONBURY

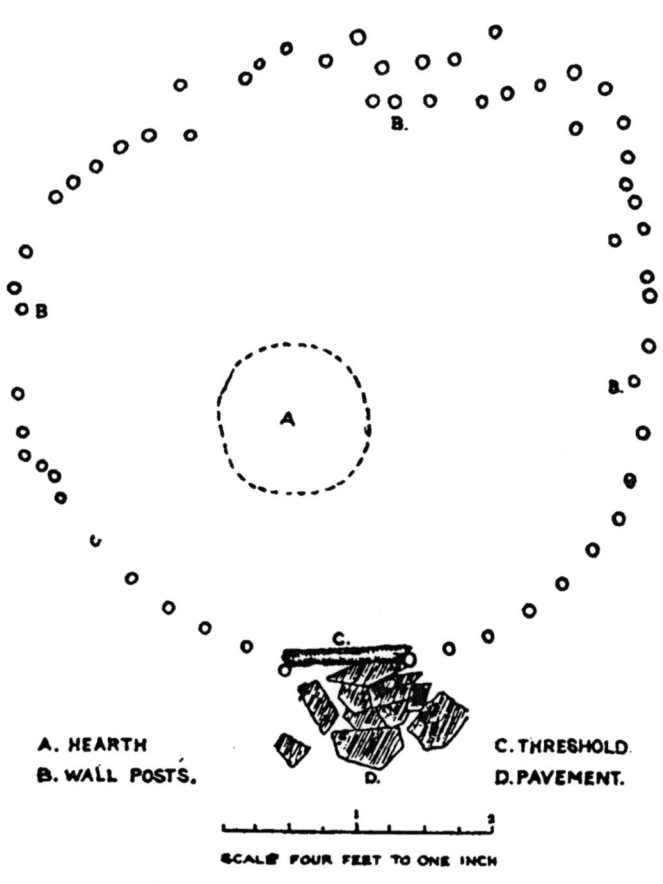

A. HEARTH
B. WALL POSTS.
C. THRESHOLD.
D. PAVEMENT.

SCALE FOUR FEET TO ONE INCH

PLAN OF HOUSE IN BRITISH VILLAGE, GLASTONBURY

distinct proof that some of the dwellings were rectangular, and that the walls were about six feet in height."[1] In a very large number of old English cottages which still exist, the height, measured from the ground to the eaves, is six feet, and such is still the usual height of the rooms in the smaller kinds of old houses. The timber walls of these existing houses, as we shall see further on, are constructed in the same way as the walls of this rectangular house at Glastonbury. It is not apparent how the roofs of the Glastonbury huts were supported, but we shall see hereafter in what way the sloping roofs of still-existing timbered houses are supported, viz. by pairs of "crucks." The "beam of oak" containing mortise holes, found at Glastonbury, corresponds to the beam which, as will be seen on a subsequent page, is called the "pan" or "pon." In modern English it is known as the wall-plate.

The position of the village near Glastonbury and its palisades seems to show that its inhabitants lived in constant danger of attack by foes. Nevertheless the village must have lasted for a long period, as the various hearths in the dwellings, superimposed one upon another, show. In one hut these superimposed hearths amounted to seven in number, the two uppermost being of stone. It appears from the shapes of the skulls discovered on the site that the inhabitants were of an Iberic type.[2] The skulls were long, like those

---

[1] Report of the Committee on the Lake Village at Glastonbury submitted to the British Association. (*Manchester Guardian*, 22nd Sept., 1896.)

[2] BOYD DAWKINS at British Association. (*Times*, 19th Sept., 1895.

found in the long barrows. No coin was discovered, nor a single fragment of Samian or other Roman pottery, "though there are numerous villas and extensive Roman potteries in the neighbourhood." The village is said to belong "to a period dating from somewhere between 200 and 300 B.C. down to the Roman occupation."[1] It is wonderful that a people living under such unfavourable conditions could have practised so many arts. The vast number of remains which have been unearthed show that they were spinners and weavers, their weaving combs being both abundant and perfect. They used iron instruments, including the knife, the awl, the spade, the bill-hook, and the gouge. They also used the lathe. They made pottery; they practised metal-working. "They used rings of jet, amber, and glass, and bracelets of bronze and Kimmeridge shale, and beads of glass, and fastened their clothes together with safety-pins and split-ring brooches of bronze."[2] They practised agriculture, and ground their corn in querns. They used decorated and highly-finished pottery, large quantities of which have been found. Amongst the remains are a well-preserved bowl of bronze, a complete ladder seven feet long, and a small door of solid oak[3] Their skill in the arts is perhaps best shown in the specimens of gracefully-carved woodwork which have come to light. If these men had not the civilization of their

---

[1] A. BULLEID, *ut supra*.

[2] BOYD DAWKINS, in *The British Lake Village*, Taunton, 1895. (*Somersetshire Arch. etc. Proceedings.*)

[3] MUNRO, at the meeting of British Association. (*Times*, 19th Sept., 1895.)

contemporaries in Greece and Italy, at least they were far removed from barbarism.

In many respects the village near Glastonbury resembles the prehistoric villages discovered in North Italy. These villages were for the most part "oriented oblongs," and usually had an area of from seven to ten acres, though some of the larger villages had an area of nearly twenty-five acres, whilst in others the area was less than three acres.[1] They were surrounded by a ditch and an earth-wall, the latter being in some cases strengthened by wooden palisades. As at Glastonbury, the huts within the area stood upon an elaborate framework of wooden balks, the walls being composed of brushwood, straw, and clay. These pile-dwellings were erected on dry land, as well as in the water, and there seems to be no doubt that the former kind of settlement was copied or evolved from the latter.[2] We do not know for certain how the huts in the marsh village at Glastonbury were thatched. But the thatched Gaulish huts shown on the Antonine column, and the thatch, held in place by branches or logs slung over it, which appears on Albanian hut urns, make it probable that the Glastonbury huts, so similar in other respects, were thatched in like manner. It appears from the Albanian hut urns that the doorway served both to admit light and to let smoke out, and we have seen that such is the case in the modern charcoal burner's hut. But

---

[1] HELBIG, *Die Italiker in der Poebene*, p. 11. Orientation is very distinct in the sites of some prehistoric villages in England popularly known as "camps."

[2] HELBIG, *ut supra*, p. 58.

besides the doorway the hut urns sometimes show a small triangular dormer window or louvre, either on the front or back slope of the roof.[1] It is most likely that the smoke in the Glastonbury huts escaped by holes in the roof.

Dr. Lange thinks that the round hut gradually assumed an oval form.[2] Although oval forms have been noticed amongst Etruscan and Albanian hut urns, we must bear in mind that a house in that form would be very difficult to build, and we shall see further on that in Great Britain the rectangular house arose in quite another way. Only in stone "beehive houses" can we find any trace of a gradual transition from a round to a rectangular form. On the island of Skellig Michael, in the county of Kerry, there are six "beehive houses" built entirely of dry rubble masonry. "The cells are rectangular in plan inside, and round or oval outside; except in one case where the outside is rectangular at the bottom. The roofs are domed, and formed with horizontal overlapping courses, as in the pagan 'Clochhauns.' The only openings are the door, which has inclined jambs and a flat head, and a small rectangular hole to allow the smoke to escape."[3] With this exception, there is nothing to show that the rectangular house was gradually evolved from the round house. And we must remember that whilst the "beehive house" was built of stone, nearly all other ancient houses, whether round or rectangular, were built of wood.

[1] HELBIG, *ut supra*, p. 50.   [2] *Haus und Halle*, p. 51.
[3] *Arch. Cambrensis*, 5th Ser., ix. p. 157. See also LORD DUNRAVEN'S *Notes on Irish Arch.*, ed. by Miss Stokes, vol. i. p. 31, and ANDERSON, *Scotland in Early Christian Times*, 1881, p. 80.

Each of these "beehive" cells was a separate house. There are, however, double cells of the beehive type, both in Ireland and Scotland. On Eilean na Naoimh, one of the Garveloch Islands, between Scarba and Mull, is a cell with a diameter of fourteen feet. Contiguous to it "is another of the same form, thirteen feet in diameter, and communicating with the first by a square-shaped opening through the point of contact."[1] These double cells seem to suggest the twofold arrangement of "hall and bower," which we shall have occasion to discuss further on.

Besides the round huts built on artificial platforms in marshes, the early inhabitants of Great Britain made use of round dwellings sunk below the ground. Pit-dwellings, as they have been called, have been found at Fisherton, near Salisbury, and elsewhere. They "are proved to be of neolithic age by the absence of metal, and by the spindle-whorls of baked clay and fragments of rude pottery. The pits are carried down through the chalk to a depth of from seven to ten feet, and the roofs are made of interlaced boughs coated with clay. They were entered by tunnels excavated through the chalk, sloping downwards to the floor."[2] The depth to which such dwellings were sunk in the ground grows less as we approach historical times. In the neighbourhood of Bologna a great number of round huts sunk in the ground to a depth of rather less than three feet have been found. The walls were made of a mixture of clay and brushwood, and were supported by a circle of

---

[1] ANDERSON, *ut supra*, p. 97, and the authorities cited by him.
[2] TAYLOR, *The Origin of the Aryans*, 174; TACITUS, *Germ* 16; CLODD, *The Story of " Primitive " Man*, p. 106.

wooden posts. The diameter of the huts was usually from three to four metres, but never exceeded six. In Bologna this kind of building extended down to the fifth century B.C., about which time fragments of Greek vases began to appear in the larger huts. Then, too, the walls of that part of a hut which was sunk below the ground began to be strengthened by a sort of "footing,"— the "basing" as we shall see that it was called in England—made of rough sun-dried bricks laid together without mortar.[1] To this day there is a great abundance of old English houses built a foot or more below the surface of the soil, and into which you descend by one or two steps.

On the subject of these underground houses we may get some help from tradition. The very numerous tales, current in every part of England, about passages communicating between one old house and another must have had some reasonable foundation in fact.[2] That fact is not far to seek. Many of the huts at Bologna, to which we have just referred, were united to each other by passages dug in the earth, and similar passages between houses have been noticed in other parts of Italy. According to a statement of Ephoros, reported by Strabo, the Kimmerians dwelling on the Lake of Averna inhabited underground houses, which they called *argillae*, and which communicated with each other by underground passages.[3] We read in the

---

[1] HELBIG, *ut supra*, p. 47 *et seq.*

[2] In castles, abbeys, and old cities, the traditions may relate to the large sewers often found.

[3] HELBIG, *ut supra*, p. 49; STRABO, v. 244; ADDY, *Household Tales*, etc., p. 57.

Landnáma that "Leif harried in Ireland and found there a great underground house. He went in, and it was dark till there shone out a light from a sword that a man was holding. Leif then killed the man, and took the sword, and much money besides."[1] In Ireland, according to Professor Sullivan, "every *Dun* and *Rath* had small chambers excavated under the *Airlis* or ground within the enclosing mound or rampart. These chambers vary in size, but are usually nine or ten feet long, three or four broad, and three or four feet high. The entrance is a very narrow passage, barely sufficient to allow a man to creep in on his belly; and similar narrow passages connect the several chambers with each other."[2] The huts built within the enclosing mounds were almost invariably round. Is not the English "worth," which occurs in so many place-names, and means an enclosure adjoining a house, identical with the Irish "rath"?

We learn from Tacitus that, in the first century of the Christian era, some of the wilder and remoter tribes of Germany occupied subterranean dwellings. "They are accustomed," he says, "to make artificial caves in the ground. They cover these with great heaps of dung, so as to form a shelter during the winter, and a storehouse for the produce of the fields. For in such dwellings they moderate excessive cold, and if at any time an enemy should come he ravages the parts that he can see, but either discovers not such places as are invisible and

---

[1] *Landnáma* in Vigfusson and Powell's *Icelandic Reader*, p. 5.
[2] Introduction to O'Curry's *Manners and Customs of the Ancient Irish*, p. ccxcvii. *et seq.*

subterraneous, or else the delay which search would cause is a protection to the inmates."[1]

Judging from extant remains, Professor Sullivan has expressed the opinion that "they had two stories, the upper for living in, the lower to serve as a store-room for corn and other food. This custom seems to have been common to the inhabitants of Switzerland, Gaul, and Britain, as well as to the Germans. The women especially lived in such earth holes, where they wove the fabrics used for clothing; for this purpose they continued in use after the knowledge of lime would have enabled them to build better houses. The German name for such holes appears to have been *tunc* or "dung"; among the Frisians and Franks the name was *screuna*. . . . In England such underground dwellings are called pennpits."[2] Modern architects say that the object of building old English houses somewhat below the ground was to obtain warmth. The old German *tunc* or *dung* had also the meaning of a winter house or winter-room, and was used either as a weaving-room or as a store-room for preserving the fruits of the earth. We may compare it with the Icelandic *dyngja*, a lady's bower.

[1] *Germ.* 16.
[2] Sullivan's Introduction to O'Curry, *ut supra*, p. ccxcvi. We are reminded of our own cellar kitchens, and of the "taverns," to be discussed on a subsequent page. The M. H. German *tunc* seems to be unknown in English unless it occurs in place-names like Dungworth. It seems more probable that the caves described by Tacitus were separate rooms, and resembled the chambers under the Irish "duns" and "raths."

CHAPTER II.

THE RECTANGULAR HOUSE IN ITS SIMPLEST FORM

Evolution from an oval form possible—But the evidence is strongly against such possibility—Building in "bays"—The house of one bay—Examples of this near Horncastle and Dingle in Ireland—The house of one bay known in the Welsh laws as a "summer house"—Description of it—Its resemblance to the Numidian *mapalia*—Resemblance of such a house to an inverted ship—The "nave"—The "hulk"—How straight walls were introduced—The roof reared before the walls were added—Materials used for walls—Gradual transition from "crucks" to "pairs of principals"—The "bay" was a standard of architectural measurement—Houses sold and let at so much a "bay"—The "bay" in the Middle Ages—Pastoral origin of houses built with "crucks"—Place-names compounded with "summer" and "set"—Two kinds of "summer houses"—The "summer house" in ancient Italy and elsewhere—"Grass-houses" and grassmen—A mud house at Great Hatfield described.

WE have already said that an oval house would be difficult to build. It is of course possible that an oval may have been occasionally evolved from a round shape, the sides of the building may have been flattened, and the ends left round as in the remains of some Romano-British houses, and in the chancels of old churches where apses exist. Although it must be granted that such a course of evolution is possible, and although oval forms are said to have been noticed in the Glastonbury marsh village, there is abundant evidence that in England the rectangular form of house had quite another origin.

In whatever part of England we look for examples of the smaller or humbler domestic house or cottage we shall find that an old method of construction prevails. These buildings were erected in "bays," the house of one "bay" being the simplest form. The principle of construction of the house of one bay was simple. Two pairs of bent trees, in form resembling the lancet-shaped arches of a Gothic church, were set up on the ground, and united at their apexes by a ridge-tree. The framework so set up was strengthened by two tie-beams and four wind-braces, and was fastened together by wooden pegs. The bent trees or arches were placed at a distance of about sixteen feet apart, and the space included between them was known as a "bay." Thus the "bay" formed a sort of architectural unit, for the building of one "bay" might be increased indefinitely in length by adding other "bays."

These couples or pairs of bent trees were anciently known as "forks," or, in Latin, *furcae*. They were also known as "gavels,"[1] or "gavelforks," but this term can only be strictly applied to the "forks" at the two ends of the building, which thus acquired the name of "the gable end."

The "forks" were also known by other names. They are now popularly called "croks," "crucks," and "crutches," and a building erected in this way is now said to be "built on crucks." In some old surveys these "crutches,"

---

[1] A. S. *gaflas*, forks.

which were intended to support the building, are described as "couples," or "couples of syles," or "siles." The distinction which in old documents is made between "couples of syles" and "gavelforks" arose from the fact that the "syles" were straight, and were two straight pillars inclined towards each other, whilst the "gavelforks" intersected each other at the top. Usually all the "forks" were curved, and this is the form usually met with at the present day. So when a building is described as containing "one couple of syles and two gavelforks," we know that it would have two "bays" and be thirty-two feet in length; if it contained "three couples of syles and two gavelforks" it would be four bays in length, and so on.[1]

The oldest of these buildings had no upper story, and the walls were made of wattle-work plastered over with clay or mud. Sometimes they were covered by planking resting on the "crucks" and laid parallel to the ridge. Bede tells us that Bishop Eadberht removed the wattles from a church built in this way, and covered the whole with lead, both the roof and the walls themselves. Again, according to Malmsbury, an old church at Glastonbury was covered with lead from the summit to the very ground (*usque deorsum in terram*).[2] In Iceland the shieling was

[1] "Precium hyemalis domus est viginti denarii de unaquaque furca que sustinet laquear."—*Leges Wallice*, ii. 802. In 1365: "Et edificabit unam domum sufficientem, infra duos annos, de ij copul de siles, quas cum firstis et ribis habebit de meremio Domini."—*Durham Halmote Rolls* (Surtees Soc.), i. 48. In 1371: "Unam grangiam de uno pare de siles, et duobus gauilforks."—*Ibid.*, p. 111.

[2] See the subject discussed and authorities quoted in GUEST's *Origines Celticae*, ii. 73.

built with one main beam as a ridge-pole, and this rested on the two gable ends.[1] The door of these buildings was in one of the gable ends. A house at Scrivelsby, near Horncastle, popularly known as "Teapot Hall," is an

HOUSE AT SCRIVELSBY

excellent example of a building of this kind. It is built of two pairs of straight "crucks," which extend from the four corners of the house to the ridge-tree, and which support the ridge-tree, the framework being further strength-

[1] *Laxdæla Saga* in VIGFUSSON and POWELL'S *Icelandic Reader*, p. 53.

Joist ab! 4x2

Thatch

19'-0"

Grey Slate

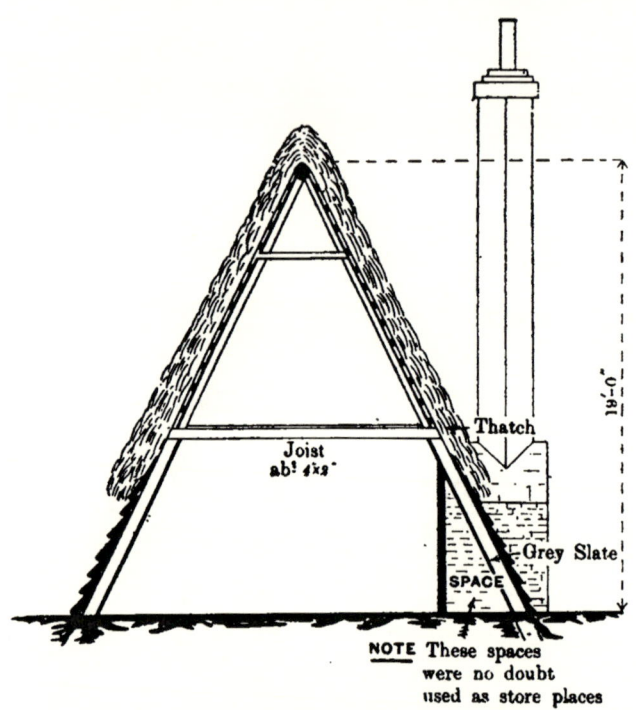

SPACE

NOTE These spaces were no doubt used as store places

SECTION OF HOUSE AT SCRIVELSBY

ened by the addition of wind-braces. The length, breadth, and height of the building is nineteen feet respectively. The doorway is in the south gable end, and a small "outshot" building, whose roof is considerably below that of the main building, projects from the opposite gable end. This "outshot," built of wood, and coeval with the house, contains the buttery and scullery, the buttery being, as is usually the case, in the north-west.

From the floor of the "outshot" a ladder goes up to the bedroom above.

The walls, which are about six inches thick, are composed of wooden studs, with twigs or branches of trees interwoven, the whole being overlaid with mud and plaster.

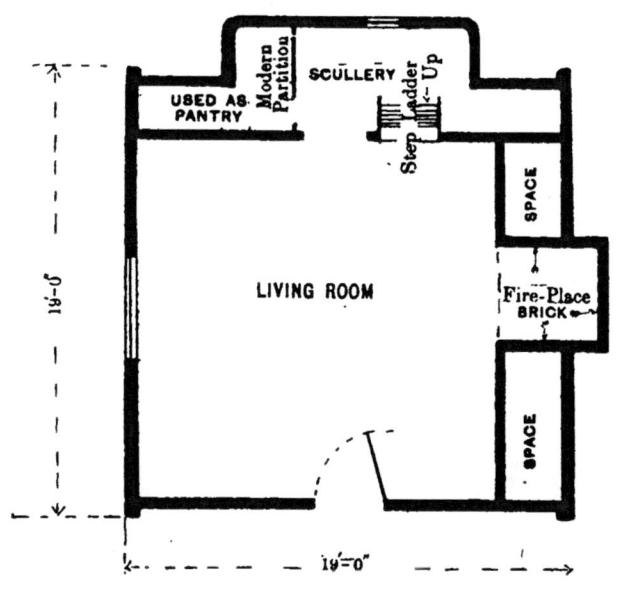

PLAN OF HOUSE AT SCRIVELSBY

The sides are thatched with straw down to a point a little below the bedroom floor. From this point grey slates extend to the ground. The roof of the "outshot" is rounded, and thatched with straw. The fireplace, which may be in its original position, is of brick, and it, as well as the chimney, is of more recent date than the rest of the house. An additional room on the ground floor has lately been annexed to the building, and for that purpose a doorway has been cut through into the old structure. The greatest care, however, of this interesting house is taken by its owner.[1] It will be seen that if the fireplace is in its original position, the chimney, if used at all, must have been of the simplest kind. A house of this kind was formerly known as a booth, and it is interesting to notice that the size of the booth in the fourteenth century was about the same as that of the house which we are now examining.[2] In the fifteenth century the gable of such a house was regarded as the "front view."[3]

Owing to the perishable nature of wood and plaster-work, as well as to the inconvenient form of these buildings, existing specimens are extremely rare. But if we compare the house near Horncastle with a similar building near Dingle in the west of Ireland, known as the "oratory" of Gallerus,[4] we shall see that this form of building is very ancient. For the "oratory" of Gallerus is merely a "booth" copied in stone. If wood had been plentiful in the neighbourhood it would have been built of that

[1] For a survey and photograph of this house the author is indebted to Mr. E. C. Skill of Sheffield.

[2] c. 1350. "Iohannes Flesshewer ten. j botham de novo edificatam super vastum, longitudinis xx pedum et latitudinis xviij pedum."—*Bishop Hatfield's Survey* (Surtees Soc.), p. 32. Another booth, as well as the village forge, is described as being of the same size.

[3] "A gavelle of a howse, *frontispicium*."—*Cath. Angl.*

[4] Galley house, ship house, from the shape (?) COTGRAVE, 1632, has "*gallere*, a galley."

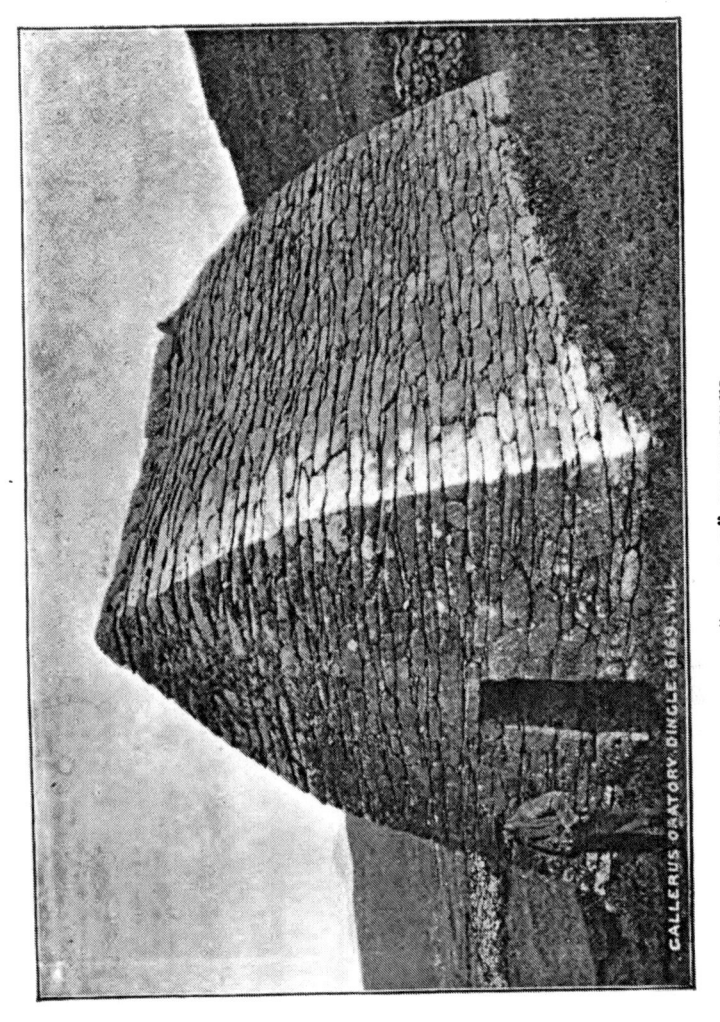

"ORATORY" OF GALLERUS

material. The "oratory" is composed of dry rubble masonry, and consists of a single rectangular chamber 15 ft. 3 in. long by 10 ft. wide inside.

"It has a flat-headed western doorway with inclining jambs, 5 ft. 10 in. high by 1 ft. 11 in. wide at the top, and 2 ft. 5 in. wide at the bottom inside. . . . The only other opening is a round-headed window in the east wall, deeply splayed on the inside. The outside aperture is 1 ft. 3 in. high by 9½ in. wide at the top, and 10 in. at the bottom. The window measures on the inside 3 ft. 3 in. high by 1 ft. 6 in. wide at the top, and 1 ft. 9 in. wide at the bottom. On the inside of the doorway, at a height of eight inches above the bottom of the lintel, is a projecting stone on each side, with a hole three inches square through it to receive the door-frame. Above the east window are three projecting stone pegs, at different levels near the roof. . . . The roof is constructed entirely of stone laid in flat courses, without cement. Up to the level of the lintel of the doorway the batter of the side walls is nearly straight, but above this it curves round gracefully, giving an outline like that of a pointed Gothic arch. The end walls have much less batter than the side walls, and are slightly curved outwards, so as to be convex at the middle of the height. . . . The present ridge-stones are restorations by the Board of Works. The flags below these are 1 ft. 4 in. wide."[1] The door faces the small window.

A few small stone buildings of exactly the same type remain in the west of Ireland and also in the west of Scot-

[1] *Arch. Cambr.*, vol. ix. (5th S.), 148.

land. Here it is unnecessary to consider the question whether they were intended for religious uses or not. In any case they are copies in stone of the boat-shaped type of house, which, in places where wood was abundant, were built of that material. A most interesting example of this type, built of stone, remains on Eilean Mor, the largest of the Flannan Isles, which lie to the west of Lewis. It is known as Teampull Beannachadh. It is "composed of rough stones joggled compactly together without mortar, built in the form of a squared oblong, but irregular on the ground-plan, the lengths of the side walls externally being respectively 11 ft. 11 in. and 12 ft. 2 in., and the lengths of the end walls 10 ft. 3 in. and 9 ft. 2 in. The walls vary in thickness from 2 ft. 5 in. to 2 ft. 11 in. The roof, which is formed internally by transverse slabs laid across from wall to wall, takes externally the form of the bottom of a boat. The chamber measures about 7 ft. long by 5 ft. wide, and 5 ft. 9 in. high. The doorway in the west end is but 3 ft. high, and there is no window or other opening of any kind in the building. Its exceptionally small size, irregular construction, and the want of the usual east window, are quite uncommon features, and wholly inconsistent with any attribution of an ecclesiastical purpose."[1] One cannot fail to be struck with its resemblance to the booth "built on crucks." It appears from the Brehon Laws that an Irish oratory (*duirtheach*) of 15 ft. in length and 10 ft. in breadth cost, when built of wood, ten cows, or a cow for every foot in breadth. We have just seen that the inside measure-

[1] ANDERSON, *Scotland in Early Christian Times*, 1882, p. 121, from MUIR'S *Characteristics*.

ment of the stone "oratory" of Gallerus is 15 ft. 3 in. by 10 ft.[1]

This simple form of house, built of wood, is mentioned in the old Welsh laws, and is there described as a "summer house." It consisted of two *nenfyrch* or "forks" supporting a *nenbren* or ridge tree, and *bangor* or wattles. These "forks" are identical with the "crucks" which we have just mentioned.[2] In other words, the form of the Welsh "summer house" was exactly like that of the one near Horncastle, and like that of the "oratory" of Gallerus. Thus we have seen how this simple form of house extended from the east coast of England to the west coast of Ireland. "Crucks" are mentioned, under the name of *sudes binales*, in Adamnan's *Life of St. Columba*.[3] They are still to be seen in Gloucestershire. They are common throughout Yorkshire and Lancashire, and are doubtless to be found in every English county.

This form of house can be traced into a higher antiquity and into distant lands. It was noticed by Sallust in the century preceding the Christian era. According to him the Numidian peasants had a kind of house which they called *mapale*. It was of oblong shape, with curved sides, and resembled the keel of a ship.[4] In other words, it was

---

[1] O'Curry's *Manners and Customs of the Ancient Irish*, iii. 49, 55.
[2] "Omnis camposus edificator a siluano herede tria edificii ligna debet habere, uelit, nolit; scilicet nenbren [tecti trabem] et dwe nenforch [duas tecti furcas]." *Welsh Laws*, ii. 777.
[3] Reeves' ed., p. 114.
[4] "Ceterum adhuc aedificia Numidarum agrestium, quae mapalia illi vocant, oblonga incurvis lateribus tecta quasi navium carinae sunt." *B.I.* 18. "Mapalia," with one exception, is only found in the plural.

like the house we have just been considering. That this form of house was unfamiliar to the Romans is evident from the surprise of Sallust, as well as of Procopius, that Roman civilization had not effaced these singularities. Sulpicius Severus speaks of such houses as being very liable to be blown over by the wind. From him it appears that they were small huts, contiguous to the ground, and covered by boards of sufficient strength.[1]

But although houses having an external resemblance to inverted boats or ships seem to have been unfamiliar to the Romans, they were not wholly unacquainted with the use of forks or "crucks." Ovid in his *Metamorphoses* relates how a small thatched cottage was magically changed into a temple. In the process of change, he says, "columns succeeded forks."[2] But it is evident from a remark of Vitruvius that building in this way was regarded as obsolete or barbarous in his time. He speaks of it as the oldest kind of building. "First," he says, "men erected forks, and, weaving bushes between them, covered the walls with mud."[3]

We have said that the house near Horncastle and the "oratory" of Gallerus, like the Numidian hut, resemble a boat or ship turned bottom upwards. It is

---

[1] See the passages cited in CAPES's *Sallust*, 1889, p. 252.
[2] " Dumque ea mirantur, dum deflent fata suorum;
 Illa vetus, dominis etiam casa parva duobus,
 Vertitur in templum; furcas subiere columnae;
 Stramina flavescunt; adopertaque marmore tellus,
 Caelataeque fores, aurataque tecta videntur."
    OVID, *M.*, viii. 700.
[3] "Primumque furcis erectis, et virgultis interpositis, luto parietes texerunt."—VITRUV. ii. 1.

from this source that we get our word "nave," which is the Latin *navis*, a ship, and probably also the pointed Gothic arch.[1] The German word, too, for the nave of a church is *schiff*, ship.[2] It is interesting to find that in England a house in the tenth century was sometimes called a "hulk,"[3] for that word also meant "ship." In old Norse poetry, too, the house was called the "hearth ship."[4] The resemblance of this kind of building to a ship was still more striking when the building consisted of several "bays."

The next evolutionary step was to make the walls of these buildings straight, whilst still retaining the original construction. For, obviously, when the walls were straight there was more space in the house, and it became a more convenient place to live in. The change was accomplished in the following way. The ends of the tie-beams which braced the "crucks" together were lengthened outwardly, so that the tie-beam became equal in length to the base of the arch formed by the "crucks." Upon the tops, or at the ends, of these extended tie-beams, long beams known as "pans" or "pons" were laid,[5] and then the rafters were laid

[1] The nave of a church is sometimes called the galilee, Low Lat. *galilea*. Is this connected with "galley," a long ship?

[2] *Schiff* is applied to the aisles as well as to the central division. On the other hand English writers sometimes speak of the central division as an "aisle."

[3] *Liburna*, hulc; *tugurium*, hulc—*Wright-Wülcker Vocab.*, 181, 28; 185, 12. The word is said to be derived from the Greek ὁλκάς a ship of burden, a merchantman.

[4] *Corpus Poeticum Boreale*, i. 245.

[5] They are "pans" in Yorkshire, "pons" in Lancashire. The modern name is wall-plate.

between the "pans" and the ridge-tree. Finally a side wall was built from the ground as far upwards as the "pan," so that the "pan" rested on the top of this wall.[1] The annexed illustration of a partly demolished house, in which a pair of "crucks" and their tie-beam are laid open to

"CRUCKS" OF DEMOLISHED HOUSE

view, shows how this was done. The walls were built in after the wooden framework had been set up. It is obvious that this must have been so when they were composed of upright posts and interlacing twigs. But we should hardly expect to find that such was the case when the walls were

[1] Compare the provincial verb *pan* = to unite, to fit.

of stone. Numerous extant examples, however, prove that it was so, and the annexed section of a barn at Treeton,[1] near Sheffield, will show one way in which stone walls were added to a building of this kind. In this case there was no complete tie-beam. Very often the feet of the "crucks," or

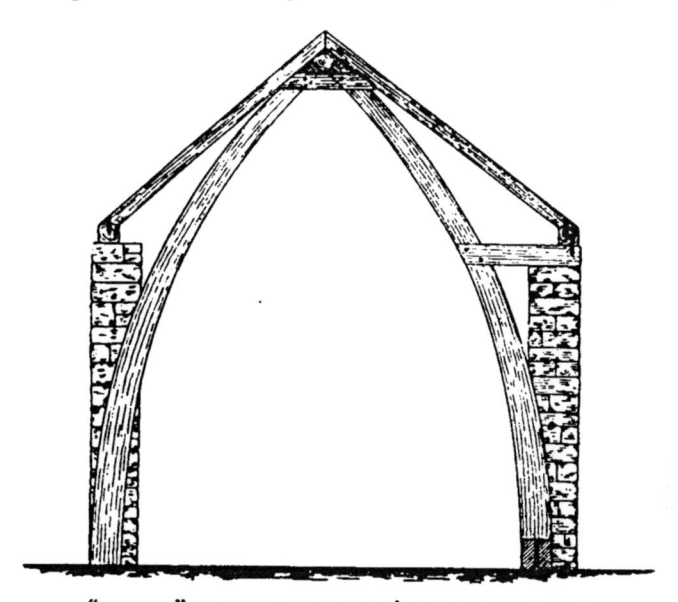

"CRUCKS" IN BARN AT JACKSON'S FARM AT TREETON

the large stones or pillars on which the "crucks" stand, project a little from the outsides of the walls, forming, as it were, the bases of buttresses. Sometimes they form small internal pillars, suggesting a Gothic arch in a church standing on pillars of stone. The walls were built of what-

[1] From a drawing by Mr. T. WINDER.

ever material could most conveniently be had. The material first in use was wood and clay, or, as it is variously called, "stud and mud," "clam staff and daub," or "wattle and daub." After this came stone and bricks. It often happened that after the wattle and daub had perished, new walls, either of stone or brick, were inserted. On the west coast of Lancashire, and in Gloucestershire, such substitutions are still made. Hence the wooden framework of a house is often far older than the outer walls, so that the plainest exterior may be accompanied by an ancient and picturesque interior.

The change from the ancient method of supporting the roof by pairs of arches springing from the ground to the modern way of supporting it by "pairs of principals" was made very slowly. To us, in these days, the modern roof resting on upright walls of stone or brick seems too plain and simple a thing to be regarded as a triumph of human skill. And yet it is of comparatively modern date in the English popular art of building. Nowhere is the spirit of conservatism more conspicuous than in architecture. As the Romans usually framed their roofs with tie-beam and king-post,[1] it is strange that the English people should have been so long in adopting this method of construction.

The old surveyors regarded the bay as a standard of measurement. Thus John Harrison, who about the year 1637 made a survey of the estates of the Earl of Arundel, in South Yorkshire, speaks of "a dwelling-house of 4 bayes, a stable being an out shut and other

[1] SMITH'S *Dictionary of Greek and Roman Antiquities*, i. 685.

out houses are 7 little bayes, besides a barne of 4 bayes."[1] Just as buildings were measured by the number of bays which they contained, so they were sold or let by the bay, as cloth is sold by the yard. In deeds and wills of the sixteenth and seventeenth centuries houses are very often estimated or described by the number of bays which they contain. Often too we meet with deeds of this period in which bays of houses or other buildings are separately conveyed.[2] In Derbyshire hay is somtimes sold by the "bay," and in the sixteenth century a "gulf of corn" was as much as would lie between any two pairs of "crucks."[3] Holinshed in 1577 speaks of "two and fortie baies of houses."[4] In *Measure for Measure* Pompey the servant says, "If this law hold in Vienna ten year, I'll rent the fairest house in it after three-pence a bay."[5]

As the length of the bay was sixteen feet, or a little more or less, measurement and valuation by this quantity was reasonable, and this length seems to have been everywhere maintained, except in the case of some cottages which consisted of a single bay. In 1352 we read that William de Strattone "appropriated to himself a piece of land sixteen feet in breadth on the property of the community without the gate of Ludgate, in London, and built thereon

[1] *Sheffield Glossary* (Dialect Soc.), 81.
[2] *e.g.* a conveyance dated 1679, "of one bay of a barne or lath abuting on the lath of Alexander Fenton in the possession of John Wood of Gleadless," county Derby.—Deed in the author's possession. Surrenders of "bays" are frequent in old Court Rolls.
[3] "Goulfe of corne, so moche as may lye bytwene two postes, otherwyse a baye."—PALSGRAVE. Compare the Icelandic *staf-gólf*, and *gólf*, an apartment. [4] *Chronicles*, iii. 1198. [5] Act ii. Scene i. 255.

a room (*camera*) 16 feet in length and 12¾ feet in breadth."[1] This was a single bay. The hall of Oakham Castle, Rutlandshire, of the twelfth century, consists of a nave and aisles, and is built of stone. It is in four bays of 16 feet each in length.[2] We shall see further on how this length of sixteen feet came to be fixed.

We have already seen that the Welsh "summer house" consisted of a pair of "crucks" and a ridge-tree, and was completed by wattles. Such a house was originally a sort of portable tent[3] which might be carried up to the elevated pastures where the cattle grazed in summer. It is well known that pastoral people "divide the year into two seasons—the one when the cattle are fed in the open, the other when they are housed in the stall."[4] Like many other nations, the inhabitants of Great Britain once divided the year between their winter houses and their summer houses, the winter house being larger and more substantial than the summer house. We shall deal with the winter house further on. In England many place-names speak plainly of the old summer house and temporary abode on the hills and moors. Thus we have Somerscales near Skipton, Summerlodge near Askrigg in Yorkshire, Somergraines, Somerguage, Somerby (summer dwellings), le Somergranges, Somerasse, Somersall, Somerset, Summerley. There are two parishes in Lincolnshire known as Somercoates. In Norway these temporary summer settlements

---

[1] RILEY, *Munimenta Gild. Lond.*, vol. ii. pt. ii. p. 454.
[2] See the plan in TURNER'S *Domestic Arch. of the Middle Ages*, p. 28.
[3] "Schepherdes house—*bourde portable*."—PALSGRAVE, 1530.
[4] CLODD, *Story of "Primitive" Man*, 1895, p. 161.

still exist, and are known as *sæters*. They lie "generally on a small piece of table-land some way up a mountain, whither the Norwegians bring their cattle during the summer months to feed upon the moist rich pastures of those high lands where they themselves live as in a sort of encampment."[1] In England these summer abodes or folds were known as "sets" or "seats," as in Somerset, Moorseats, Outseats, Woodseats, Thornsett, Runsett, Lord's Seat, and in hundreds of other examples. The pastures themselves were known as "summer gangs," and when sheep were brought into the valleys after the harvest they were called "winterers."

Besides the summer house and the winter house the Welsh laws mention the autumn house. Of this there were two kinds. The cheaper and inferior kind was "without augur holes." The better kind had augur holes; in other words the woodwork was more carefully put together.[2] The inferior kind of autumn house was even cheaper than the summer house, and was, of course, a step nearer to the primeval tent. In later times the "summer house" began to be occupied in winter as well as in summer.

A Roman writer on husbandry mentions summer houses as existing amongst his own countrymen in the century preceding the Christian era. When the flocks fed in woodland pastures in the summer time, and were far away from their winter homes, the shepherds took hurdles or nets with

---

[1] KEARY, *Norway and the Norwegians*, p. 41. The A. S. *set* usually means a fold or stall for cattle.

[2] *Leges Wallice* (*Ancient Laws, etc.*), ii. 803.

them (by means of which they made cattle-yards in desert places) as well as other utensils. For their custom was to feed their flocks up and down the country a long way from home, so that their winter pastures were often many miles distant from their summer pastures.[1]

This annual migration of the whole or part of the family to "desert places" in summer was due in part to nomadic habits. Even when the village had been formed down in the valley very little land was cultivated. Flocks of sheep could not be fed in summer in the town fields near the hamlet, for these for the most part were then covered by the "acres" of sown corn uninclosed or unbounded save by a turf balk, a few stones, or a temporary fence. By the old laws of Norway summer huts were to be built on the *almenning* or common pasture.[2] They were not to be built in the town fields, but on the uncultivated lands outside those fields. In later years the shepherds found out, as in Spain, that the annual visits of their sheep "to these upland pastures were essential to the beauty of their fleeces."[3] But in earlier times nomadic habits and a primitive form of agriculture can alone explain this annual migration to the hills. In Europe

---

[1] "Contra illae in saltibus quae pascuntur, et a tectis absunt longe, portant secum crates, aut retia, quibus cohortes in solitudine faciant, caeteraque utensilia. Longe enim et late in diversis locis pasci solent, et multa millia absint saepe hibernae pastiones ab aestivis."—VARRO, *De R. R.* ii. 2, 9.

[2] "Sel skal hverr göra sér í almenningi er vill ok sitja í sumar-setri ef hann vill."—*Norges Gamle Love*, i. 251. A man could build his shed where he liked on the common, and live in his summer abode the year round if it pleased him.

[3] *Quarterly Review*, vol. clxxxii. p. 488.

this custom of having both winter and summer houses is as widespread as it is ancient, and we find it in Israel: "I will smite the winter house with the summer house; and the houses of ivory shall perish, and the great houses shall have an end, saith the Lord."[1]

Besides the temporary summer houses built on the hills, there were in England certain houses known as "grasshouses."[2] These appear to have been occupied by a class of men called grassmen, to distinguish them from husbandmen,[3] or men engaged in sowing and tilling the land. The two classes are often referred to as husbandmen and cotmen,[4] though in one document we read of three classes—husbandmen, cotmen, and grassmen.[5] The grassman was engaged in tending cattle on the uninclosed lands or wastes,[6] and, unlike the husbandman, grew no corn and had no oxen for the plough. As affecting the old social life the distinction is an important one. The word "grasshouse" implies some corresponding term which would

---

[1] Amos iii. 15.

[2] 1504. "Quadraginta domibus pauperum, vocatis gresse-howses, in parochiis meis de Lowthorpe et Catton, singulis vj^d."—*Test. Ebor.* (Surtees Soc.) iv. 233. In 1557 a bequest was made of a bushel of rye "to every grisse house within the parish which hath no corne growing."—*Richmond Wills* (Surtees Soc.), p. 102.

[3] 1461. "Item lego cuilibet husbandman de Nid, xij^d. Item cuilibet gresman de eadem, vj^d."—Will in *Ripon Chapter Acts* (Surtees Soc), p. 100.

[4] Fourteenth century. *Durham Halmote Rolls* (Surtees Soc.), pp. 67, 83, 84, 81.

[5] *Circa* 1304. "Bondos, cottarios, gresmannos."—*Whitby Chartulary* (Surtees Soc.), i. p. 28.

[6] See the Grassmen's Accounts in *Memorials of St. Giles's, Durham* (Surtees Soc.). Compare the *bordarii* in Domesday.

describe the house of the man who grew corn. Such a term may perhaps be found in "berewick," meaning "barley-dwelling," or in "barton," meaning "barley-court."

The cot or booth was frequently built of mud, and without the support of "crucks." A good example of a mud house, not now occupied, may be seen at Great Hatfield, Mappleton, in East Yorkshire. The outside length is 28 ft., and the inside breadth 15 ft. 2 in. The height to the eaves, which project ten inches, is 6 ft. 2 in. The mud walls are 1 ft. 7 in. thick. The house has one door, 3 ft. 3 in. wide, facing south, and the original hearth is at the east end. The "speer," or screen, which stands opposite the door, is composed of mixed mud and straw. It forms one of the two sides of the open hearth, round which the family could sit, the other side being the north wall of the house. The length of the "speer" is four feet, so that it just covers the door. Its height is 6 ft. 2 in. Across the top of the wooden post at the west end of the "speer" one of the beams of the roof is laid, thus serving the twofold purpose of beam and mantel-tree. Above the mantel-tree, its three sides sloping upwards to the roof, is the chimney, built of studs and laths, plastered with mud. The fireplace next to the east wall, as well as that next to the west wall, is of modern brick; the original hearth in the east was open. Level with the beam which forms the mantel-tree the hearth is covered by a flat inner roof of lath and plaster, with a square hole left in it over the jambs of the modern brick fireplace for the smoke to escape. Thus the smoke found its way into a little smoke chamber with a hole in the top next the roof. There is also an opening in the western slope of the chimney, not in the centre, but in the southern half. This opening is 2 ft. 6 in. in height. At its base it is 1 ft. 9 in., and at its top 1 ft. 5 in. in breadth. The aperture is neatly formed, and may have been originally there. Its base is the beam which forms the mantel-tree, and its sides are two of the studs which

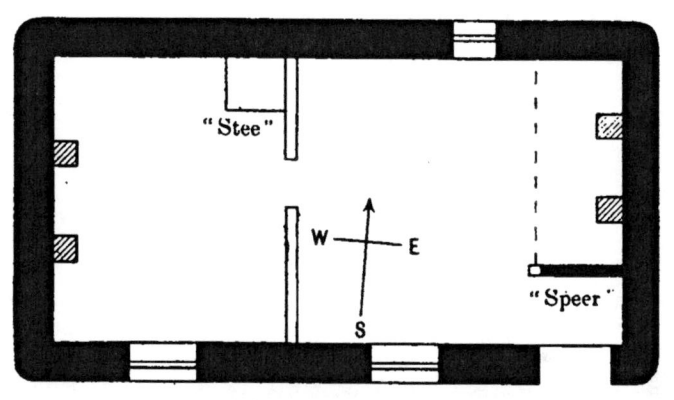

PLAN OF MUD HOUSE, GREAT HATFIELD

support the chimney. What it was used for can only be guessed. The roof is of tie-beam and king-post.

The house is divided into two lower rooms of unequal size by an old wooden partition which does not extend above the beams which support the chamber floor. In the ceiling of the inner room, next to the partition, was a "throp hetch," or "trap hetch," *i.e.*, a trap door which swung on hinges, and was lifted by an iron ring. Against the opening of the trap door a broad "stee" or ladder was placed to give access to the single room in the roof. The "stee" is still there, but the "throp hetch" has gone. The "chaamer" in the roof is not five feet high, and one wonders how human beings could have slept in such a place. The author was told by the tenant that the house was originally open to the roof, and that the "chaamer floor" was put in by her husband's father, who died a year or two ago, aged 93. If this was so, the lath and plaster roof in the chimney may have been put in at the same time.

The mud walls of this house are very interesting. They are perforated by countless holes made by a kind of bees, locally known as "mud bees" or "sink bees," which make a great noise when they are at work in hot weather. The walls are built of layers of mud and straw which vary from five to seven inches in thickness, no vertical joints being visible. On the top of each layer is a thin covering of straw, with the ends of the straws pointing outwards, as in a corn stack. The way in which mud walls were built is remembered in the neighbourhood. A quantity of mud was mixed with straw, and the foundation laid with this mixture. Straw was then laid across the top, whilst the mud was wet, and the whole was left to dry and harden in the sun. As soon as the first layer was dry another layer was put on, so that the process was rather a slow one. Finally the roof was thatched, and the projecting ends of straws trimmed off the walls. Such mud walls are very hard and durable, and their composition resembles that of sun-burnt bricks. This method of construction reminds us of the house-martin, which in making her nest of loam and bits of broken straws "gives it sufficient time to dry and harden. About half an inch seems to be a sufficient layer for a day. Thus careful workmen, when they build mud-walls (informed at first perhaps by this little bird), raise but a moderate layer at a time, and then desist."[1]

Close to the door of this mud house is a well, as is everywhere usual when the well is not in the house itself. The original windows, and also the door, were of "harden" —a kind of coarse sack-cloth. The door could be lifted up like a curtain, and there was no inner door.[2] Robbers were not feared.

[1] WHITE'S *Selborne*, letter lv.
[2] Information by Mrs. W. DUNN, derived from her father-in-law, who lived all his life in this house, and died there aged 93. The house was said to have been "in the family over 300 years." No date can be given. Compare an article on "Cob Walls" in *Quarterly Review*, lviii. 529.

CHAPTER III.

THE RECTANGULAR HOUSE WITH "OUTSHUTS"

A house of one "bay" inconvenient—Such a house increased in size either by adding fresh "bays" or by "outshuts"—"Outshuts" are additional buildings outside the "nave" or main structure—Examples of this kind of house—The "house part" or "house"—The "speer"—The "aitch"—The "chamber"—Clay floors—"Clam staff and daub"—The "house-place" is the *megaron* of the Greeks and the *atrium* of the Romans—A house near Penistone described—Long table made in, and forming part of, this house—Evolution of the staircase—How the long table was used—The "house" or "fire-house"—Combined dwelling-houses and barns—Position of the various rooms—The "entry" or "floor"—The "threshold."—The typical old Norse house—Sizes of Irish dwellings.

IT is obvious that a house consisting of one "bay" would be a poor place for a family to live in. It could, however, be increased in size by adding other "bays" to the ends, or by building additional rooms at the ends or the sides. When the latter course was adopted, the additional rooms were known as "outshots"[1] or "outshuts," the name being still preserved in the "outshot" kitchens often built at the back of workmen's dwelling-

[1] Compare O. E. *gescot*, O. N. *skot*, part of a building shut off from the rest; the chancel or apse of a church.

houses. Though "outshuts" adjoined and formed part of the house itself, they were not "built on crucks," and could not strictly be described as "bays." They were outside the "bays" or nave, as we may call the central or ship-like part of the building.

"OUTSHUT" AT NORTH MEOLS

The illustration shows a small "outshut,"[1] measuring 10 ft. by 4 ft., from an old house at North Meols in Lancashire. The boards which in this case covered the

[1] Compare the Norwegian *skut* or *utskut*, and the illustration in MEITZEN's *Das nordische un l das altgriechische Haus.* p. 480.

outer walls of the "outshut" have been removed, so as to show the posts of which the walls were framed. The posts or studs stand close together, and the walls are plastered by clay mixed with straw to the depth of an inch, the plaster being covered by several coats of white lime. This kind of building is known in Lancashire as "clam staff and daub."

In the larger buildings the "aisles" at the sides usually extended along the whole length of the structure, like the aisles of a church. We shall deal with these larger buildings further on, and shall now examine the cottage built of one bay only, with upright walls and with additions at the ends as well as the sides, in the nature of "outshuts." Our first example is a thatched cottage at a place called Westward, near North Meols. The cottage is plain, square, and whitewashed, with eaves 5 ft. 8 in. from the ground. There are no upper rooms, and there is no ceiling beneath the roof. In other words, it is not "underdrawn." The room in which the family live is here known as the "house-part." In Derbyshire it is called the "house-place" or "house." In London such a room was called "the house" (*domus*) early in the thirteenth century to distinguish it from the bower or chamber (*thalamus*).[1] The "house-part" contains the only fire-place, and consists of a single bay of sixteen feet long and about thirteen feet broad, the "crucks" being in the usual positions.[2] Within the doorway is a covered inner porch, with a screen which

[1] TURNER, *Domestic Architecture of the Middle Ages*, pp. 23, 282.
[2] In the plans given in this chapter, the bases of the "crucks" are shown by the letter *C*.

THE "SPEER" 45

keeps the wind out, and protects the "house-part" from the gaze of the stranger and from the wind when the outer door is opened. This screen is known as "the speer."[1] In Scotland and in the north of England, it was known as a "hallan" or "halland." The screen across the lower end of large halls, such as those in the colleges of Oxford and Cambridge, was known as the "speer," and was intended

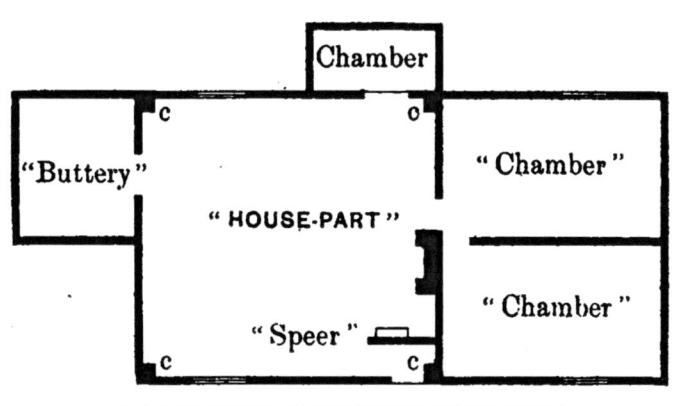

PLAN OF HOUSE AT WESTWARD, NORTH MEOLS

as a protection against the wind. In the smaller houses of Cumberland the screen was known as a "sconce." In 1530 Palsgrave gives *buffet* as the French for "speere in a hall." In the house we are describing a wooden bench is fixed against the inner side of the "speer," so as to form a

---

[1] "Spere or scuw. *Scrineum, ventifuga.*" *Prompt. Parv.* "In vj bordis empt. pro j spure pro camera Domini." Bailiff's Roll, dated 1337, in *Bishop Hatfield's Survey* (Surtees Soc.), p. 203. In the same roll, "In factura j spere infra hostium coquine, 3*d*."

seat. The top of the "speer" forms a large shelf for holding dishes, pots, and other things. These "speers" and benches are found in nearly all the oldest cottages on the west coast of Lancashire. Sometimes the door of a house is protected by wooden posts in front of it.[1] The mantel-piece, known in the West Riding of Yorkshire as "the aitch," extends across the whole width of the room. Upon it are displayed the pair of pot dogs so common in houses of this kind, and a number of small earthenware figures and statues. The chimney in such houses is rarely straight; it usually leans considerably to one side, and this is often the case when the chimney-stack is outside the wall. From the "house-part" a door opens into a small "outshut" room known as the "buttery," where food and pots are kept, this room having originally had no windows. Another door opens into two small bedrooms on the ground floor, known as "chambers,"[2] the inner "chamber" being divided from the outer "chamber" by a brattice or wooden screen—anciently known as a parclose or enterclose—which extends about half-way up to the roof, and is not unlike the partition which divides cow-stalls from each other. Opposite the "speer" is another small "chamber." The floor of these "chambers" is made of clay, as that of the "house-part" formerly was. The whole cottage was originally built of "clam staff and daub," there being no stone in the neighbourhood. Brick has, however, of late years been inserted in the place of the woodwork and clay,

[1] "Stoulpe before a doore—*souche.*"—PALSGRAVE, 1530.
[2] 1538, "One copborde next the chamber dore in the halle."—*Bury Wills* (Camden Soc.) p. 136.

so that only a part of the original outer walls can now be seen. The present occupant can remember when this was done, and she also informed the author that she had seen men tread the clay used for similar walls with their feet,[1] and mix it with the star grass which grows upon the sand hills in the neighbourhood. The cottage is thatched with rye straw, as is usual in the neighbourhood. It is whitewashed within as well as without, and is exquisitely neat and clean.

Our next example is at Burscough in Lancashire, about eight miles from North Meols. The illustration shows a very quaint cottage resembling in plan the cottage just described. But it is rather larger at one end, and has one little upper room, with a tiny window which may be seen peeping through the boards at the gable end. The way in which the roof slopes downwards at the gable ends will be noticed. Roofs like the one in the illustration are still common in Lancashire, and they are usually rounded off at the gables. This cottage at Burscough, with its fencing of stakes, may remind us of the cottage of the poor widow in Chaucer's tale:

"A yerd sche had, enclosed al aboute
With stikkes."[2]

The "house-part" consists of a single bay of the usual size "built on crucks," and without an upper story. Instead of a "speer" there is a rude outer porch. On

---

[1] Mud for building (*lateum*) was usually carried by women or girls. —*Durham Household Book* (Surtees Soc.), p. 181.

[2] *The Nonne Prestes Tale*, l. 27.

one side of the fire-place is a large brick oven, with a flue leading into the chimney of the fire-place. The oven projects about two feet into the "chamber" behind the "house-part," and would make that room warm. The chimney is of lath and plaster. On the side opposite

HOUSE AT BURSCOUGH

the fire-place are the "buttery" and a small "chamber," about seven feet square and not quite six feet high. The buttery, as usual, is in the north-west corner. Over the "chamber" and the "buttery" is a small low "chamber."[1]

[1] Compare "the ij chambrys with the soler above in the ende of the halle towarde my gardeyn."—Will, dated 1463, in *Bury Wills* (Camden Soc.), p. 32.

The stairs are modern, and probably access to the upper room was formerly gained by a ladder, as is still the case in some small cottages. The wooden lintels of the inner doors are arched. Adjoining the buttery, and under the roof which covers the cottage, is the *latrina*. The cottage was built of "clam staff and daub," which still remains in a perfect state on the north side, but the walls have been strengthened by the addition or insertion of brick-work.

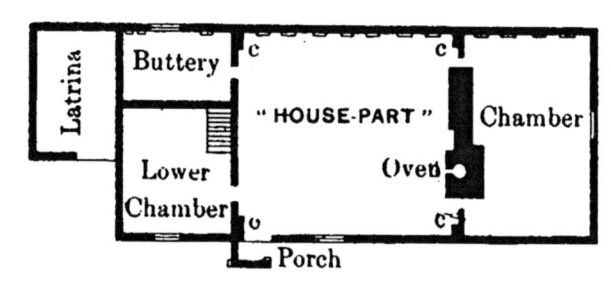

PLAN OF HOUSE AT BURSCOUGH

Our third example is a larger cottage or farm house at North Meols, now disused. It contains the usual central "house-part," which is "built on crucks," and the length of the bay, measured from the centre of one "cruck" to another, is fifteen feet six inches. The "house-part" has no upper story, and is open to the roof. It contains the usual "speer." The top of the "speer" is in the same plane with the top of the mantel-piece, and the shelf of the mantel-piece is continued across the room on both sides. Annexed to the "speer" on the inner side is the usual wooden bench. A crooked beam is fixed to the side-trees in the roof, just over the fire-place. Such a beam seems to have been formerly known as a "perch," and was used to hang clothes on, as in the line:

"Pertica diversos pannos retinere solebat."[1]

These beams are found in many of the old cottages of West Lancashire. But often the fixed beam has been replaced by a clothes rail which can be moved up and down by a rope. The fire-place at the east end of the house is modern. This cottage differs chiefly from that at Burs-

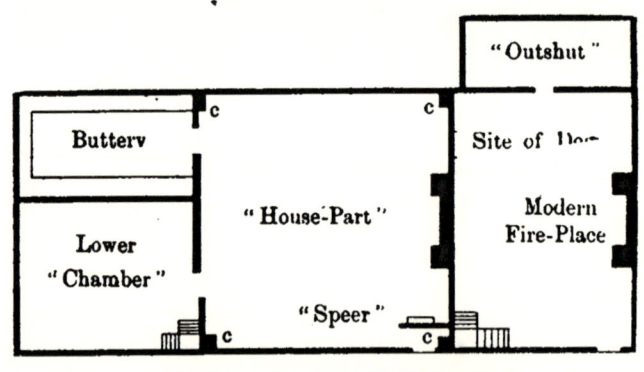

PLAN OF HOUSE AT NORTH MEOLS

cough in having an upper chamber over both the end rooms, and two staircases. Two staircases were necessary because, as the "house-part" is open to the roof,[2] there could be no communication on the upper floor between the

[1] In WRIGHT'S *Vocabularies*, p. 133. The author has never heard people call this beam the "perch."
[2] Of the vicarage of Selborne, WHITE says, "According to the manner of old times, the hall was open to the roof."—*Antiquities of Selborne*, letter iv.

two upper chambers. The stairs are of later date than the rest of the building, and originally ladders may have been used instead. The oak shelves or benches of the buttery are of great thickness, as also are the posts on which they rest.

ROOF AND MANTEL-PIECE AT NORTH MEOLS

The floor is of clay. Only the "house-part" is "built on crucks." Brick-work has taken the place of the original "clam staff and daub," but a good specimen of the latter material is preserved in the small "outshut" on the north side, a view of which is given at the beginning of this chapter. The house faces south, and the buttery is in the north-west corner.

The oak used in the construction of these Lancashire houses is very roughly hewn. For the most part the wood displays all its natural crookedness, and is merely trimmed by the adze, or split by wedges.[1] In some houses the "lats" or laths are laced to the ribs or rafters by star grass. There is no stone in the neighbourhood of North Meols, the subsoil being sand, which is of a great depth. The walls which surround the fields are made of mud or sods, and timber must have been brought from a considerable distance in early times. In such a place one might expect to find many interesting examples of old houses, but they are rapidly passing away.

The "house-part" of these cottages corresponds to the *megaron* of a primitive Greek house, the *megaron* being the kitchen and men's room of the family. It also corresponds to the *atrium*, or "house-place" of the Romans, that word being derived by some authorities from *ater*, black, on account of the blackened roof.[2] In Chaucer's time the "house-part," with its open hearth, must have been black enough, as in the tale told by the "Nonne Prest"—

"Full sooty was hir bour, and eek hir halle."

Although in most cases the "house-part" is in the centre of the old English cottage, it is sometimes found at one

---

[1] For *asseres* or spars of wood obtained by splitting (*laceratio*) see the glossary to the *Durham Household Book* (Surtees Soc.).

[2] SMITH'S *Dict. of Greek and Roman Antiq.*, i. 668. The suggested etymology is very doubtful. Compare the "inseat" of a Scotch farmhouse.

end of the building. Such is the case in a well-preserved house at Upper Midhope, near Penistone, which bears over its doorway the date 1671, though that is not necessarily the date when the wooden framework of the house was reared. This house is "built on crucks," in two bays, the fire-place at the end being outside the "crucks." The

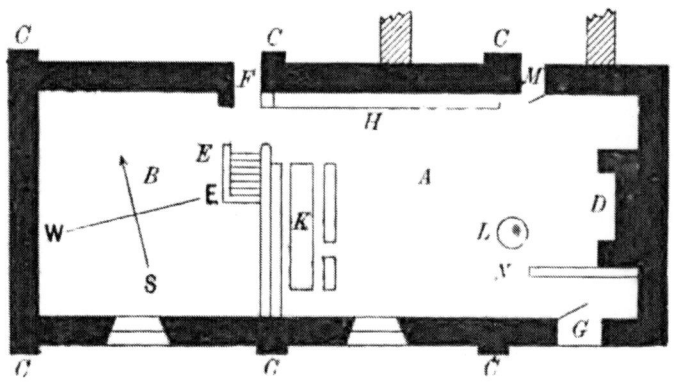

GROUND PLAN OF HOUSE AT UPPER MIDHOPE

A House-place.
B Store-room.
C Bases of "crucks."
D Fire-place.
E Stair.
F Back door.
G Front door.
H Delf rack.
K Table.
L Round table.
M Modern door.
N "Speer" or screen.

"crucks" are massive beams of oak whose bases rest on stone slabs, or stylobats. These slabs project about three inches from the outside walls. The original building consists of four rooms, two on the ground floor and two on the upper, and is unequally divided by a massive oak framework or wooden partition wall which extends from the floor to the roof. The "house-place," 7 ft. 2 in. high, is entered by a door adjoining the road. Here a portion of the oak framework is seen. It is highly polished, and against it is placed a heavy carved oak table, with heavy carved benches to form seats. The largest bench is fastened to the oak framework which divides the building. The other two benches are movable, and the smaller of them can be put at the head of the table so as to form, when required, a seat in that position. This table and its benches are an original part of the building, for the table could not have been brought in either through the door or the windows. An identical arrangement of bench and table may still be seen in Norway.[1] At one end of the table is a doorway leading into the adjoining room, which is used as a pantry or buttery, and on the north wall next to this doorway is a delf-rack filled with bright pewter plates and dishes, and blue-and-white pottery. A pair of white wooden trenchers, which the family once used as dinner plates, will be noticed on the table shown in the illustration. They are made hollow on both sides, so that meat could be eaten on one side and pudding on the other. The trenchers are very neatly turned, and show no signs of the use of knife or fork, as though people had used their fingers only, as the custom once was.

The "house-place" contains a wide fire-place screened from the street door by a "speer." In one corner of the

---

[1] See a plan in KEARY's *Norway and the Norwegians*, p. 43. Anciently it was known as a "table dormant," as in the Prologue to the *Canterbury Tales*:—

"His table dormant in his halle alway
Stood redy covered al the longe day."

buttery is the wooden box or case which contains the stair leading into the two upper rooms, the stair being supported by a massive inclining beam. Opening the staircase door we see an almost perpendicular series of steps, arranged like the rungs of a ladder. The lowest step is of stone;

"HOUSE-PLACE" AT UPPER MIDHOPE

the rest are thick triangular blocks of oak, not fastened together in any way, but with open spaces between them. The first five steps are perpendicular, and the remaining steps incline slightly towards the top. A round oak hand-rail, as old as the stair itself, is fastened to the wooden wall, and by its help we can get into the two bedrooms above. The stair leads straight to the bedroom floor, there being no lobby or outer passage.[1] On one side the opening in the floor is protected by the framework which divides the house, and on the other side it is protected by an immense "ark," or meal chest. Otherwise the landing or stair head is unprotected, and there is nothing which would prevent a somnambulist sleeping in the outer bedroom from falling down to the bottom. In East Yorkshire the opening in the floor was protected by a trap door known as a "trap hetch," or "throp hetch." In some old cottages the bedroom is still approached by a "stee" or ladder fastened by hooks to a hole in the chamber floor. This stair at Midhope is of no little interest, for it shows us the intermediate stage between the ladder and our modern stair with its "case." In Yorkshire the staircase is often called the "stair hole." In a house at Treeton in South Yorkshire the upper chamber was reached by a ladder which was set in a round well or hole cut in the thickness of the wall.[2]

The walls of this house at Midhope are two feet thick; they are plastered, but are apparently built of stone. The floor is of stone.

Adjoining the west end is another room of later date, not shown in the plan, with a chamber above it. This does not communicate with the store-room, but is entered by an

---

[1] 1556. "The lytyll chamber at the greisshedde. . . . The utter chamber at the gresse hed."—*Richmond Wills* (Surtees Soc.), p. 91. Old wills often mention the outer and inner chambers at the stair head.

[2] Information by Mr. T. WINDER.

EVOLUTION OF THE STAIRCASE 57

STAIR AT UPPER MIDHOPE

outside door. Now it is a workshop, but formerly it was the weaving room. Here spinning and weaving were done for the use of the inmates, the surplus of the woven material being sold.[1] Such a room was formerly known

[1] Tradition among the present occupants.

as a "spinning house."[1] A range of buildings of later date is connected with the "house-place" by a door opening into it on the north side. In this neighbourhood houses "built on crucks" which had no upper rooms, but were open to the roof, are still remembered.

In the plan of the house at Midhope it will be noticed that there is a round table near the fire. The use to which the tables in this house were put may be explained by a communication made to the author by an old Derbyshire farmer from the memories of his youth.

"The master of the house and his servants had dinner in one and the same room—the kitchen—a large apartment. The master and his family sat at a table near the fire, and the servants at a long table on the opposite side of the room. First the master carved for his family and himself, and then the joint was passed on to the servants' table. The head man presided over the servants' table, and always sat at the end of it, and at the opposite end sat a woman. The men sat next to the chair in order of seniority, and were very particular about keeping their proper places."[2]

At Midhope the farm servants still have their meals at the long table, the place of honour being the small round table near the fire.[3] It is remarkable that the

---

[1] 1463. "The dore that is out of the parlour into the spynning hous."—*Bury Wills* (Camden Soc.), p. 20.

[2] In Iceland the seat at table marked a man's degree.—VIGFUSSON and POWELL's *Icelandic Reader*, p. 358.

[3] "In a corner or recess stood a round table, with its attendant carpet or cover of plain or raised work."—*Richmond Wills* (Surtees Soc.), p. xi.

Roman *villicus* dined with his farm labourers in the same way.[1]

We have just seen that the common living room, corresponding to the Roman *atrium* or the Greek *megaron*, is called "the house-place," "the house-part," and "the house." It was also called "the hall," "the hall-house," and "the fire-house." The best and possibly the oldest of these names was "fire-house"—the *eld-hús* of the Norsemen. The room which usually contained the only fire in the building, and which gave warmth to its inmates by day and night, may well have been called "the house," as an abbreviation of "fire-house." In 1392 the Prioress of Nun Monkton took a lease of property at Nun Stainton and in it covenanted to repair the buildings of the messuage, viz., "a house called the fire-house, containing five couples of syles and two gavelforks, a storehouse for grain containing three couples of syles and two gavelforks, and another storehouse for grain containing one couple of syles and two gavelforks, a little house to the west of the said fire-house containing three couples of syles and two gavelforks."[2]

It is probable that the fire-house and the "little house" were contiguous, so that the fire-house was the

---

[1] "Consuescatque rusticos circa larem domini, focumque familiarem semper epulari, atque ipse in conspectu eorum similiter epuletur." COLUMELLA, xi. i. 19.

[2] "Omnia ædificia dicti messuagii, videlicet, unam domum, vocatam le Fire-house, continentem quinque coples de syles et duo gavelforkes, unam grangeam continentem tres coples de syles et duo gavelforkes, et unam aliam grangeam, (continentem) unum copille de syles et duo gavelforkes, unam parvam domum ex parte occidentali dicti Fyrehouse, continentem tres coples de syles et duo gavelforkes."—*Feodarium Prioratus Dunelm.* (Surtees Soc.), p. 167.

hall, and the "little house" the bower or women's side of the house, a division to which we shall have occasion to refer again. The identity of hall and fire-house can be proved from a document of the seventeenth century.[1] In the sixteenth century the word fire-house was also used as a synonym for the better kind of dwelling-house.[2] In the eleventh century an apartment with a chimney was known as *caminata* or *caminatum*, and an English vocabulary of that period explains the word as "fyrhus," *i.e.* a room containing a fire. In old German the room was known as *kemenate*. In larger country houses the fire-house or hall was often in the centre of the building, with the women's apartments consisting of the "chamber" and buttery at one end and a barn or combined barn and ox-house at the other.[3] The main entrance to the building was a passage which divided the "fire-house" from the ox-house or barn, and which was the threshing floor. This passage was known by various names. Anciently it was called the "floor"[4] or the "threshold," a word which means

[1] 1632. "The Hall or Fier-house of the nowe mansion house of the said John Parker, etc., with the entry leading into the same."—*Derb. Arch. Journal*, v. p. 45.

[2] 1532. "I witto every hows within the parisheing of Acclome whar os fyer is dailly used, xiij*d*."—*Test. Ebor.* (Surtees Soc.) v. p. 291. 1542. "The fyer-howse that Foxe wyffe off Ulverston dwellithe in."—*Richmond Wills* (Surtees Soc.), p. 32.

[3] WRIGHT in his *Homes of Other Days*, 1871, p. 141, says that in the twelfth century the chamber was at one end, the hall, open to the roof, in the middle, and a *croiche* or stable at the other end. There was a doorway between the hall and *croiche*. His opinion was founded on statements in old French romance writers.

[4] "*Excussorium*, flor on huse."—WRIGHT-WÜLCKER, *Vocabularies*, 126, 5.

"threshing-floor," because in ancient times the floor at the entrance was for threshing.[1] It was sometimes called the "entry." Doors opened out of this passage both into the "fire-house" and into the barn or ox-house. Where there was no barn or ox-house the "fire-house" sometimes formed one end of the building; and where there was no barn or ox-house there was no "entry" or threshold, but the door opened straight into the "fire-house," and, as we have seen, was screened by a "speer."[2]

There were usually separate doors at the free end of the ox-house for the admission of the oxen. A very large number of English farmhouses still exist in which the dwelling-house, barn, and stables are combined under one and the same roof. But it is now a rare thing to find a communication between the threshing-floor and the dwelling-house. What is generally seen in these days is a long row of old buildings divided transversely by a barn floor, or entry, at one end of which is a small "winnowing door," and at the other a large barn door, or a pair of folding doors. In these buildings the barn floor forms a dividing line between the dwelling-house and the barn, or the combined barn and cowhouse.

[1] VIGFUSSON'S *Icelandic Dictionary*, s.v. preskjöldr. In South Yorkshire the threshold is called the "threskeld." In Derbyshire it is the "threshel" and the "threskut."

[2] At Fulham in 1428 the widow of a customary tenant was to have for the rest of her life "mansionem suam in una camera ima ad finem orientem domus vocate le Ferehows cum Feer et Flet in eadem."— Court Rolls in Public Record Office, 188/70. It is interesting to compare this "camera ima" or chamber on the ground floor in the east with similar "chambers" *ante*, pp. 45, 49.

The arrangement of these houses corresponds to the arrangement of an old Norse house. There are, says an old Norse law book, three apartments in every man's dwelling. The first is the women's apartment or "chamber" (*stofa*), the second is the fire-house, *i.e.*, the house-place or hall, the third is the pantry or buttery (*búr*), where women make the food ready.[1] At a later period the *stofa*, which is the German *stube*, lost its distinctive character as a women's apartment, and became the "parlour." The fire-house, the chamber or women's apartment, and the buttery are well illustrated in the Lancashire houses described in this chapter. A good example of the entry or "threshold," paved with stone, and dividing the fire-house, chamber, and buttery from a small barn, may be seen in a long, ruined farmhouse at Fulwood near Sheffield. Here the barn floor was the "threshold" in the true sense of the word, for it was at once the threshing-floor and the main entrance to the building. At one end of the "threshold" is the large barn door, and at the other the "winnowing door." From the "threshold" a doorway leads into the house-place or "fire-house." The hearth of the "fire-house" adjoins the "threshold" wall.

Some years ago there was a combined house and barn at Hornsea, in East Yorkshire. The barn was built of mud, and had the usual "winnowing door," and a pair of barn doors on the other side. The two doorways

---

[1] Eitt er stofa, annat eldhus, et iii. bur þat er konor hafa matreipo i."—*Grágás*, ed. SCHLEGEL, i. 459. In the *Sturlunga Saga* the *stofa* is distinguished from the *skáli*, or men's hall.

had round arches. The only way into the house was across the barn floor. The house consisted of two lower rooms, with two chambers over them. The room next to the barn floor was the "house-place," and the hearth, as in the house at Fulwood, stood against the wall which divided the barn from the house. The barn floor was a little below the level of the house floor, and one or two steps led up into the "house-place." The fire-place was open, and the fire burnt on a square brandreth, supported by four legs, the embers lying on flat pieces of iron about as wide as the "strakes" of a cart-wheel.[1]

According to Valtýr Gudmundsson the typical old Norse house was a long building with the *búr*, or store-room, at one end, and the *stofa*, or women's room, at the other, the *skáli*, or fire-house, being in the middle.[2] This, as we have seen, is the form taken by the houses at Westward and Burscough already described. It will, however, be readily understood that when the ox-house in an English dwelling was placed at one end of the fire-house, and the women's apartments and store-room were placed at the other, these last-mentioned rooms would be readily included under one name.

In Ireland the length of the houses occupied by the different ranks of *aires*, or landowners, was fixed by the

---

[1] Information by JAMES RUSSELL of Hornsea, aged 84. Compare "plate, of a fyyr herthe. *Lamina, repocilium.*"—*Prompt. Parv.* p. 403.
[2] *Privatboligen paa Island i sagatiden, samt delvis i dat övrige, Norden*, Köbenhavn, 1889, p. 76; MEITZEN, *Wanderungen, Anbau, und Agrarrecht, etc.*, Berlin, 1895, iii. 491.

ancient laws. The following are the lengths of the "houses" and of the store-rooms of the eight respective classes of these landowners[1]:—

No.	Length of "House."	Length of Store-room.
1	19 feet	13 feet
2	20 ,,	14 ,,
3	27 ,,	15 ,,
4	(Not given)	(Not given)
5	27 feet	12 feet
6	27 ,,	"A proper store-house"
7	29 ,,	19 feet
8	30 ,,	20 ,,

The first two sizes of "house" correspond to the size of the booth near Horncastle already described. It is possible that each of the remaining six "houses" was divided into two "bays," one for men and the other for women. If so, these last-named dwellings were composed, like the houses of the ancient Norsemen, of three parts, viz. (1) a room for men, (2) a room for women, and (3) a store-room.

[1] Tabulated from O'Curry's *Manners and Customs of the Ancient Irish*, iii. 26 *et seq.*

CHAPTER IV.

THE LARGER RECTANGULAR HOUSE WITH AISLES

The "winter house"—The length of the bay fixed by the space required for four oxen—The modern English cow-stall corresponds to the Roman ox-stall—Statements of Vitruvius and Palladius about ox-stalls—The "perch" was an architectural as well as a land measure—The combined house and "shippon"—Great width of farm buildings which contain aisles—The *camera*, or *kell* annexed to the Welsh *bostar* or "shippon"—Farm building at Bolsterstone built on "crucks," with an aisle—Combined houses and "shippons" in the sixteenth century—Harrison's statement in 1577—Pigs and cows in London houses in the fourteenth century—Oblong houses with aisles in Ireland and Wales—Sleeping in the hall.

WE have already seen that the Welsh "summer house" consisted of a single bay. But the "winter house," as it was called, or permanent abode in the valley, consisted of several bays joined together in a line. It was more substantially built than the "summer house," for whilst the "summer house" was only regarded as worth twelve pence, the "winter house" was estimated at the rate of twenty pence for every "fork" that it contained.[1] Sometimes the "winter house" had upright columns (*columnae*),[2] and it then appears to have been

---

[1] *Leges Wallice* (*Ancient Laws*, etc.), ii. 802. And see also p. 864 for the value of the roof.   [2] *Ibid.*, ii. p. 863.

built in the basilical form, or with a central nave and aisles.

We have also seen that sixteen feet, or a little more or less, measured in the direction of the long axis of the building, was the length of the bay. So widespread and uniform was the practice of building in bays of a fixed length that it cannot have had an arbitrary origin. There must have been a reason for it, and before we can understand the construction of our larger and older dwellings it will be necessary to ascertain what that reason was.

We shall find that the length of the bay was determined by the space required for the accommodation of two pairs of oxen. And inasmuch as the "shippon" or ox-house frequently was, together with the barn, under the same roof as, and in a line with, the dwelling-house, the practice arose of making all the bays, whether of the "shippon," the barn, or the dwelling-house, of uniform length. Let us examine the evidence on which this statement rests.

To begin our proofs with modern times, it is well known that English farmers regard a width of 7 ft. as the minimum amount of standing space necessary for a pair of cows. "When stalls are put up," says a writer on farming, "they seldom exceed 4 ft. in width; more frequently two oxen are put into a double stall of 7 ft."[1] Taking 7 ft. as the space required for a pair of oxen we get the width of the stall, exclusive of partitions, as 14 ft. Taking 8 ft. as the full space required we get the width, exclusive of partitions, as 16 ft. In either case we have to add something for the width of partitions. Vitruvius, who is said to have

[1] STEPHENS, *Book of the Farm*, 1855, vol. i. p. 254.

written about B.C. 10, says that "the breadth of ox-stalls should be not less than 10 ft.[1] or more than 15 ft. As regards length, the standing room for each pair of oxen should not be less than 7 ft."[2]

Palladius, whose work is ascribed to about A.D. 210, says "8 ft. are more than sufficient standing room for each pair of oxen, and 15 ft. for the breadth [of the ox-house.]"[3]

Now we have seen from these two writers that whilst the breadth of the Roman ox-house varied from 10 ft. to 15 ft., its length was determined by the space required for each pair of oxen, viz., from 7 ft. to 8 ft. This is exactly analogous to the English practice; for whilst the length of the English bay is rigidly fixed in farm buildings by the standing room required for two pairs of oxen, considerable variation occurs in the breadth.

In the twelfth century English buildings were measured by the linear perch of 16 ft. Thus "the great barn of Walton was 10½ perches in length (a perch being 16 ft.) and 3 perches and 5 ft. in breadth."[4] Another barn was

---

[1] The breadth of a cow-house at Bolsterstone, described hereafter, is 10 ft. 8 in.

[2] "Bubilium autem debent esse latitudines nec minores pedum denum, nec majores quindenum. Longitudo, uti singula iuga, ne minus occupent pedes septenos."—*De Architectura*, 6. 9. See also COLUMELLA, 1. 6. 6. This author fixes the breadth at 10, or at least 9, feet.

[3] "Octo pedes ad spatium standi singulis boum paribus abundant, et in porrectione xv."—*De R. R.*, 1. 21. *Porrectio*, "extension," must mean "breadth" here.

[4] "Magnum orreum Walentonie habet x. perticas et dimid' in longitudine (et pertica est de xvi. pedibus) et in latitudine iii. perticas et v. pedes."—*Domesday of St. Paul's* (Camden Soc.), p. 130.

64 ft., or exactly 4 perches in length.[1] Now if we turn to land measures we find that the linear rod or perch is now 16½ ft., as it was in the year 1222,[2] a rod of this length being still used for measuring purposes by builders.

It appears from an old German book on surveying that the linear perch or rood was the unit of measurement. The way in which this length was determined is very curious. "To find the length of a rood in the right and lawful way, and according to scientific usage, you shall do as follows:—Stand at the door of a church on a Sunday and bid sixteen men to stop, tall ones and small ones, as they happen to pass out when the service is finished; then make them put their left feet one behind the other, and the length thus obtained shall be a right and lawful rood to measure and survey the land with, and the sixteenth part of it shall be a right and lawful foot."[3] In the measurement of English land the perch was also the unit. For, says an old writer on surveying, "when ye measure any parcell of land, ye should painfullye multiply the breadth of the perches therof with the length of the perches of the same."[4]

If we ask ourselves how it was that the perch became the unit we shall see that it was so because sixteen feet was the standing-room required for four oxen in the stall, and

---

[1] "Apud Torpeiam est orreum, habens lxiv. pedes in longitud'."—*Domesday of St. Paul's* (Camden Soc.), p. 131.
[2] *Ibid.*, p. 92.
[3] Jacob Koebel's *Geometrei*, Frankfurt, 1556. *Notes and Queries*, 9th S. i. 306.
[4] Valentin Ligh's *Surveying*, 1592. (Table at the end.)

also the standing-room for four oxen in the field, inasmuch as they ploughed four abreast. Accordingly the length of the bay, viz. sixteen feet, corresponds to the breadth of a rod or rood of land, the acre being composed of four roods, each 16 feet broad and 640 feet long, lying side by side. This was the origin of the bay, as well as of the normal width of a rood of land.[1]

To what extent the normal length of bay was carried into great buildings, such as churches, remains to be determined. An inquiry on this point would be curious and interesting, but no opinion on it can be given here. The author has measured the bays of the great Roman building lately found in Bailgate, on the west side of Lincoln Cathedral, and found them, when measured from the centre of each pillar, 14 ft. 6 in. apart. He has also measured the bays of a few churches and found them about fifteen feet apart. In cathedrals they are much wider.

We are now in a position to describe a "coit," or combined dwelling-house and "shippon," which may be taken as a type of the kind of dwelling described in the Welsh laws as a "winter house." The example chosen is in the basilical form, and is built in bays of approximately fifteen feet in length. It is plain enough to look at, but it forms a striking illustration of our subject.

At Rushy Lee, about a mile from the house at Midhope described in the last chapter, is one of those rather

---

[1] The Romans measured their land by the *decempeda* or ten-foot rod. The *actus*, however, was four feet wide, and this, on the English system, was the full standing-room of a single ox. Strictly the English *land* measure is 16½, and not 16, feet.

numerous buildings known in Yorkshire as "coits."[1] In the plan will be seen a building with a small dwelling-house at one end of it. The main part of the building on the north side, with the larger door, is the "shippon." This contains the cow-stalls and a large "fodderum," or storehouse for hay or other food, from which the cows were fed. The larger door, 6 ft. high and 4 ft. 8 in. wide, is the main entrance to the building, and the "shippon" can be entered from an inner door in the house. The plan will show the arrangement of the building and the relative size of its divisions. Its length is forty-four, and its breadth thirty-seven feet. Four cows stood between each pair of wooden pillars, two in a stall. The stalls are separated from each other by wooden partitions called "skell-boosts." The cows entered by a separate door at the end, and stood with their heads to the east or towards the centre of the building, and they were fed from the "hecks" inside. Thus, during the snows of winter, the occupier of the "coit" had only to open the inner door of his house, go into the "shippon," and throw hay from the floor into the "hecks." His house, which is not occupied now, can hardly have been a cheerful place to live in. It contains a single bedroom approached by a ladder in the inner and smaller room, with a window looking out at the end of the building. The interior

---

[1] Combined houses and barns of small size, and forming dependencies of a larger farmhouse or "capital messuage," are known on the Yorkshire wolds as "barns." Each of these buildings is, or was, occupied by a "hind." The house is divided from the barn by a wooden screen.

walls of the house are coloured throughout by "archil," as is usual in the neighbourhood — a cold, bright blue. Many of these "coits" have only one aisle. A house in Bradfield called Half Hall seems to have derived its name from the fact that it had only one aisle.

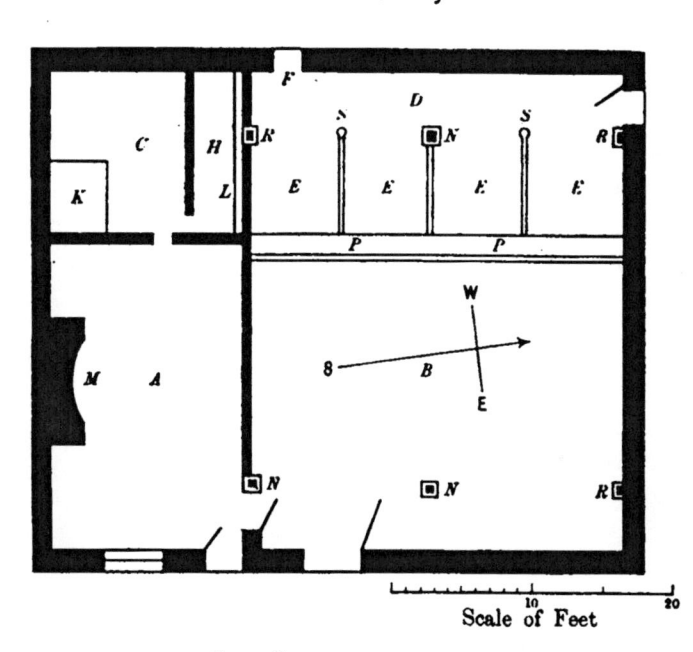

PLAN OF "COIT" AT UPPER MIDHOPE, PENISTONE

A House-place.
C Store-room.
K Hole in floor for ladder giving access to bedroom.
H Pantry.
L Shelves.
F Manure hole.
D Cow-house.
N Pillars with stone stylobats.
E Standings for cows.
R Responds.
P Hecks.
B Main floor.
S Skell-boosts or boskins.
M Fire-place.

The building consists, like a church, of a nave and two aisles,[1] the house at the end corresponding, as it were, to the chancel. The plan shows the position of the pillars which support the roof, and which divide the nave from the aisles. Each pillar rests on a stone stylobat or block of stone. There are three bays, the one in the south forming the house. There are no wooden pillars or responds in the wall next to the fire-place. Altogether there are four wooden pillars, with two wooden responds in the north wall. The space between pillar and pillar, measured in the direction of the length of the building, or in other words the length of each bay, is 14 ft. 9 in., which is exactly the distance between the "crucks" in the house at Midhope already described. The building is about twenty yards from a brook, and there are no other buildings near.

"Coits" of a similar kind may still be found in the wilder parts of Yorkshire. Usually they have an aisle on one or both sides, and therefore present a great extent of sloping roof, so that their breadth is often nearly as great as their length. The side walls are always about a man's height, and the doors in such walls go up to the eaves. There is always a door in one of the side walls which forms the chief entrance to the building, and there may be one or two other smaller doors. This combination of house and "shippon" is not always built in the form of nave and aisles; sometimes there is a nave without

[1] 1519. "Unum magnum orrium. Lez hiles standis stayd w^t proppes haldyng up ye pannes."—*York Fabric Rolls* (Surtees Soc.), p. 271. Here the barn was out of repair.

aisles, and the building is then usually "built on crucks." The shell of a stone building of this latter kind exists at Grindleford in Derbyshire. Here there was a "shippon" with a house at one end of it. The inside

WINNOWING DOOR OF BARN, GRINDLEFORD

partitions have been removed, but the windows of the house, now built up, still remain *in situ*. The main entrance is by a doorway containing an old semicircular wooden arch, shown in the illustration, opposite a pair of folding barn doors.

The house at the end of the "coit," which corresponds,

as it were, to the chancel of the building, seems to be identical with that part of the dwelling mentioned in the Welsh laws as the *camera* or *kell*, the value of which was the same as that of the *bostar* or "shippon."[1] *Kell* is "cell," and this word is said to be a doublet from the same root as "hall."[2]

We know from forms which have survived to this day that the nave which was supported by "forks" or "crucks," instead of by upright pillars, had sometimes one or more aisles. Examples of this sort of construction are rare, but they are still to be found in old farm buildings. The nave of a barn at Bolsterstone in South Yorkshire, consisting of four "bays," is supported by "crucks" of the usual kind, extending down to the ground, and resting on stone bases. The inside width of the nave is 19 ft., and the length of each "bay," measured from the centres of the "crucks," is exactly 15 ft. The span of the "crucks" is from 16 to 18 ft. On the south side of the building two contiguous bays are extended outwardly[3] by means of an elaborate and massive framework shown in the section.[4] This extension or aisle forms an ox-house 30 ft. in length, and, measured from the feet of the "crucks," 10 ft. 8 in. in

---

[1] "[Pretium] camere ante frontem domus xxx^a denarii."—*Leges Wallice* (*Ancient Laws, etc.*), ii. 803. "Kell [camera] ante frontem domus, xxx denarii."—*Ibid.*, p. 864. "Bostar uel bouiale, scipen."—WRIGHT-WÜLCKER, *Vocab.*, 185, 5.

[2] SKEAT, *Etym. Dict.*

[3] The author has a deed, dated 1617, which relates to a cottage (*cotagium*) at Crookes, near Sheffield, containing " duas baias structure ex se." Compare the "little bays" *ante*, p. 33.

[4] From a drawing by Mr. THOMAS WINDER.

width. In the ox-house there is room for eight oxen and no more. Four oxen stood in a bay, a length of nearly 15 ft., two in each stall. Now in this case it is obvious that each bay was intended to give the exact accommodation required for two pairs of oxen. As usual, the oxen faced inwards, and were fed from the main floor. Rather more than 6 ft.

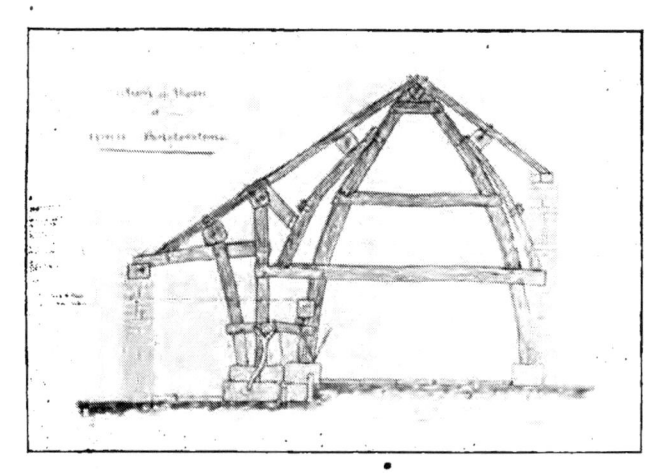

SECTION OF BARN AT BOLSTERSTONE

above the ground floor of the ox-house are the remains of an upper floor, showing that there was a loft or gallery above.[1] The oxen entered by a door in the east end of the "aisle." To the west of the four "bays" which formed the original building is some newer work which bears the date 1688 in two places. At the west end is the

[1] Compare the Saterlander's building, *postea*.

inscription, "William Couedell: Sarah his wife," and over one of the dates the letters $\tfrac{C}{WS}$. At right angles to the ox-house are some ox-stalls in the newer part of the building. These face the old main floor, and the oxen in them were fed from that floor. The barn doors are, as usual, on opposite sides of the nave, and the threshing-floor between them, paved with stone, occupies the whole of the second bay from the east. It is impossible to fix the date of the older part of the building. The walls are of stone, which is plentiful in the neighbourhood, and they are built without mortar. The building here described should be carefully compared with the description of the Saterlander's house on page 82.

Buildings like this were not always slated with stone, though farm buildings were so slated at an early period. The great wooden framework was often completed by an interlacing of twigs, and then roofed with turf or moss.[1] Vertical holes near the feet of the "crucks" will be noticed in the drawing. Such holes are usually found in these timbers. What they were for is unknown, but builders think that they were used for lifting or carrying the wooden framework. If so they would hold the ends of "levers" or lifters. Cow-houses in barns were frequent,[2] and they usually formed aisles.

We have historical evidence that in 1577 there were

[1] 1586. "Item payd to Nicholas Atkinson and Wm [Turner] for mossing ij bayes and bygging j baye with wrastlers at Sheffeld mannor let to them by great, iijs. iiijd."—*MS. Steward's Accounts of Sheffield Manor.* "Wreston', *plecto.*"—*Prompt. Parv.*

[2] 1605. "The payver, iij days payvinge both the cowhouses in the new barne, xijd."—*Shuttleworth Accounts* (Chetham Soc.), p. 170.

in the north parts of England buildings which enclosed the house and other offices under a common roof. According to William Harrison "the mansion houses of our countrie townes and villages (which in champaine ground stand altogither by streets, and ioining one to an other, but in woodland soiles dispersed here and there, each one vpon the seuerall grounds of their owners) are builded in such sort generallie, as that they haue neither dairie, stable, nor bruehouse annexed vnto them vnder the same roofe (as in manie places beyond the sea and some of the north parts of our countrie), but all separate from the first, and one of them from an other. And yet for all this, they are not so farre distant in sunder, but that the goodman lieng in his bed may lightlie heare what is doone in each of them with ease, and call quickly unto his meinie[1] if any danger should attach him."[2] Notice should be taken of the last sentence of this quotation, for we shall see further on how the "goodman" or *hausherr* in Frisian and Saxon houses "from the hearth and from his bedstead can superintend the whole management of the household, and hear every sound." In these still-existing Frisian and Saxon houses the master and his family sleep under the same roof as the cattle in one common building. We should take particular notice that Harrison speaks of houses "beyond the sea," as well as in "some of the north parts of our country," in which men and cattle occupied the same building.

Before the year 1419 there were people in London

[1] Household or family.
[2] HARRISON's *England*, ed. Furnivall, pp. 233, 237.

who kept pigs and cows in their houses, for the practice was forbidden by an order of the civic authority made in that year.[1] One still occasionally hears of pigs being kept in English houses.

In Ireland the oblong house was divided, "in the direction of its length, into three parts by two rows of pillars, which supported the roof," the fire being placed in the central division.[2] The large Welsh house was built in the same way, with beds of rushes along the aisles and the fire-place in the nave.[3] Aubrey, writing in 1678, says that in English houses "the beds of the men-servants and retainers were in the hall, as now in the grand or privy chamber."[4] Aubrey's recollections only apply to men-servants and retainers. But there was a time when the entire family lived and slept in one room, though the men and women were separated. This custom was common not only to the English, Welsh, and Irish, but also to the Germans and Scandinavians. "When night came, straw, dried rushes, heath, or dried ferns were spread upon the floor; and those unprovided with beds or couches laid themselves down, each under the bench or table upon or at which he or she sat."[5] It is probable that in many houses the men slept over the cattle stalls in one aisle, and the women over the cattle stalls in the other.

[1] RILEY, *Munimenta Gild. Lond.*, i. p. 335.
[2] SULLIVAN's Introduction to O'CURRY's *Manners and Customs of the Ancient Irish*, p. cccxlvi.
[3] SEEBOHM's *Village Community*, p. 239.
[4] In HONE's *Table Book*, i. 391.
[5] SULLIVAN, *ut supra*, p. cccliii.

CHAPTER V.

FOREIGN PROTOTYPES: STATEMENTS OF ANCIENT WRITERS

Frisian and Saxon houses—Beds in English ox-houses—The "balk"—Main difference between the German and the English farmhouse—The Roman country house compared to the Germanic—Horses not to face the fire in Roman farm buildings—The typical farmhouse in Schleswig, Hanover, and Westphalia—Galen's description of the Greek peasant's house—The *aedificia* which Caesar saw in England—German houses in the time of Tacitus.

AS we are closely akin both in blood and language to the Frisians and Saxons, it is fair to suppose that the early forms of our houses resembled theirs. The combination of house and "shippon" which we have just described is found to this day in Friesland and Saxony in an older and more elaborate form than with us. A German writer shall describe one of such combinations :—

"Its chief characteristic is that it unites in one body the space necessary for a very considerable establishment under one and the same roof, and therefore represents an extremely large building. Its ground plan is that of a basilica with nave and aisles. The middle always forms the so-called 'floor' (*diele*) (*a*), which is entered at the gable end through a large gate, and which goes through the whole house as far as the dwelling rooms at the end. Owing to the want of an exit this floor is used for backing wagons out. . . . In the forms of the Frisian and Saxon house generally in use the horses (*b*) and cows (*c*) are always so placed on both sides of the 'floor' that they are foddered from it. Over the 'floor,' over the cattle stalls, and over all the other rooms up to the ridge of the roof the corn harvest and hay harvest are stored on boards and poles laid between the joists. In the

SAXON HOUSE (FIG. 1)

Saxon house (Figs. 1 and 2) the back ground of the 'floor' ends in a low hearth (*d*), on both sides of which are the bedsteads of the family arranged in a kind of narrow and rather high cupboards, whilst over against them, and near them, the men-servants sleep over the horses, and the maids over the cows. To the right and left of the hearth extends the space used for the household (*e*), which is uninterrupted as far as the two opposite side walls of the house. This part of the house is lighted by high and broad windows, and on either side a glass door forms an exit into the open air. Usually, too, the well is inside the house at the side of the hearth.[1]

Thus the master of the house can superintend the whole management of the household from the hearth and his bedstead, and hear every sound. So he exercises the fullest supervision, and so long as the smoke of the great hearth fire, which had no chimney, permeated the whole building, insects and the bad stench of the cattle were driven away, so that not till the most recent times was the need felt for building additional rooms behind the hearth-wall

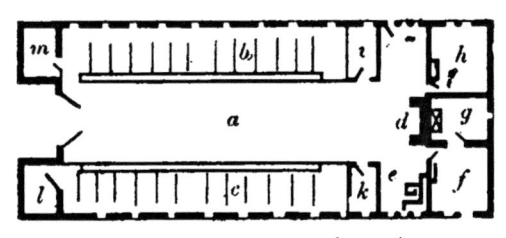

PLAN OF SAXON HOUSE (FIG. 2)

(*heerdwand*). Of these rooms, shown in Fig. 2, *f* is usually the best room, *h* a living-room, and *g* a store-room, kept dry by the fire on the hearth."[2]

People are still living who remember how farmers' menservants in England used to sleep on the hay in a gallery or hay-loft over the cows. Some of them have been known to sleep there for a year together. It is said that they often

---

[1] There are wells in some English houses and castles. Usually the well is 4 or 5 feet from the threshold or entrance.

[2] MEITZEN, *Das deutsche Haus*, p. 10. In the plan *i* and *k* are "chambers"; *m* and *l* the pigsty and calf-house.

did so to save money to be spent in drink! When Irish labourers came over in the autumn to assist in getting the harvest in they usually slept on the hay or straw in the barn or in the "balk." In the sixteenth century ox-houses in Yorkshire still contained beds, blankets, sheets, mattresses, pillows, bolsters, and happings, or coarse coverlets.[1] As no bedsteads are mentioned, we may presume that the mattresses were laid on the floor of the loft over the ox-stalls.

It appears from a passage in Ovid that Roman husbandmen sometimes lived in stables or ox-houses.[2]

In Saterland, in Oldenburg, are buildings, said to be of the sixteenth century or a little earlier, which have the dwelling-house, cattle stalls, and store-rooms under the same roof. The side walls are so low that the thatch reaches nearly to the ground. The walls are made of timber framework filled in with bricks, or, in the smaller houses, with wattles and mud. They are thatched with straw and heather. There are upright pillars (Fig. 2, *a*) with beams (Fig. 2, *b*) stretched across them. Both rows of pillars are overlaid by horizontal beams extending the whole length of the building, which is about sixty-five feet

---

[1] 1556. "In the oxen housse viij coverletts, iij blanketts, xiij*s*. iiij*d*."—*Richmond Wills* (Surtees Soc.), p. 92.

1567. "Servannts bedes in the oxhousse, iiij*s*. iiij*d*."—*Ibid.*, p. 203.

1567. "The oxe howse. One mattres with a happin, ij*s*., ij codds with a window clothe, xij*d*. One pare of shetes, xij*d*. Summa iiij*s*."—*Ibid.*, p. 209.

1569. "In the cowe house, iij olde coverlets, a paire blanckets, a paire sheits, a matteras, and a bolstar, x*s*."—*Ibid.*, p. 218.

[2] "In stabulis habitasse, boves pavisse, nocebat,
  Iugeraque inculti pauca tenere soli."—*Fasti*, iii. 191.

long by forty-nine broad. Upon the oblong so made (*A*), which forms the inner room of the building, rafters (Fig. 2, *d*) are fixed. The garret or loft (Fig. 2, *B*) is called *bölke*. Now the low side walls are erected, and long rafters (Fig. 2, *e*) laid from them to the ridge of the roof. By this means a sort of outer room going round the building is obtained, divided by a floor. Under the floor are cattle

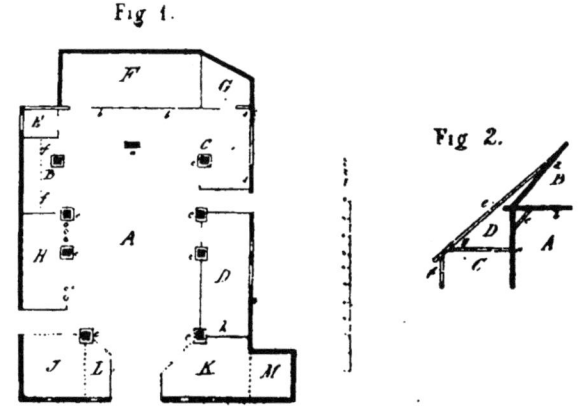

PLAN AND SECTION OF HOUSE IN SATERLAND

stalls and rooms (Fig. 2, *C*). The upper portion (Fig. 2, *D*), lying immediately under the long rafters, is used as a place to store fodder for the cattle, and for a gallery.

Entering the great door we find ourselves on a spacious main "floor" (Fig. 1, *A*). The smaller partitioned rooms on both sides usually serve for cattle stalls. On the left of the entrance lies the turf nook (*L*) where turf for the fire is stored, and by the side of it the calf-house (*J*). Then crossing over a little passage which leads to a side door in the building, we come to the cow-house (*H*). There, separated from the "floor" by the great pillars (*c*) and by small posts, stand the cattle, their heads facing inwards. On the right of the entrance, divided from the "floor" by a narrow partition wall, is the stable (*K*), and next to it the pigstyes (*M*). Adjoining the pigstyes is the weaving-room (*D*), made light by a large window and containing a loom (*h*) and weaving apparatus. A smaller apartment, used as a washing room, lies near, with an exit to the yard.

The whole domestic life of the Saterlander is spent on the spacious "floor." In the background, about $6\frac{1}{2}$ feet from the back wall (Fig. 1, *b*), burns the open fire (Fig. 1, *a*), the centre of domestic intercourse. It is continually kept burning, for there is no lack of turf. In many houses it even serves for giving light, and by its dark red glow people work and amuse themselves. The older dwellings have no chimneys. The smoke of the turf fire spreads through the whole building. That has its advantages, for it scares vermin away and makes a very big smoke chamber. Meat and bacon are well preserved on the beams of the roof over the hearth. The space on both sides of the fire serves for kitchen, dining-room, living-room, and bedroom alike. On the right of the fire, in a room (*C*) made light by a broad window, stand a table and a chair (*e*), which at meal times are sometimes brought up to the fire. There are also two large clothes chests (*d*) by the walls near the windows, which are commonly used as settles. On the opposite side of the "floor" are four alcove beds (*f*) one over another. They are concealed by a curtain, and sometimes by a sliding partition. Near the sleeping-place a room (*E*) is screened off, to which fresh air is conveyed by a separate window. The corn harvest lies in the cock-loft or *balk* (Fig. 2, *B*).[1] For the hay an additional room (Fig. 1, *F*) is made, which in many houses has a separate entrance. Under the hay-room the potatoes are laid in a cellar; a little side room (*G*) is used as a sleeping room.[2] It will be noticed that the aisles of this German building resemble the aisle of the farm building at Bolsterstone already described.

The main difference between the combined house and "shippon," as still found in England, and the German dwelling just described lies in the position of the "floor" or barn floor. In the German dwelling the great doors are at the gable end of the building, and the "floor" extends longitudinally from the great doors through the building as far as the hearth-wall. But in the English buildings the great doors, otherwise the great barn doors, are at one of the sides, and the threshing-floor intersects the building transversely so as to separate the dwelling-house from the "shippon." In the English, as well as in the German, building, the corn harvest appears to have been stored in the "balk" above the cattle, and to have been thence thrown down upon the "floor" to be threshed. On one side of the "floor" of the typical old English farm building

[1] In Yorkshire a hay-loft, and also a ceiling of a room, is known as "the balk."

[2] From a paper by Prof. THEODOR SIEBS entitled "Das Saterland," in the *Zeitschrift des Vereins für Volkskunde*, iii. p. 257.

is a wall reaching up to the joists of the "balk," and dividing the "floor" from the "shippon." On the other side of the "floor" the wall goes up to the ridge-tree, and behind this last-named wall the chimney-stack of the "house-place" or fire-house is often found. In one case which the author has seen,[1] the corn harvest was said to have been stored over the house-place, open spaces being left on each side of the chimney-stack for loading or unloading the sheaves. The open spaces are still there, and the outer side of the wall which divides the "house-place" from the "floor" has been plastered and white-washed, as though it had been the "entrance hall" as well as the threshing-floor of the building. In Lancashire the "balk" has a complete partition wall, and is called the "scaffo'd," hay being thrown through a hole in such wall called the "scaffo'd hole."

In advising upon the plan of a Roman country house Vitruvius says:—"The great hall (*culina*)[2] is to be placed in the warmest part of the court; united to this are the ox-stalls, with the cribs towards the fire and the east, for oxen with their faces to the light and the fire do not become rough-coated. Husbandmen, who do not understand aspects, think that oxen should look towards no other quarter but the sunrise. Stables, especially in the villa, should be placed in the warmest places, so long as their aspect is not towards the fire. For if horses are stalled near the fire they become rough-coated. Hence

---

[1] At Fulwood, near Sheffield.
[2] LANGE renders the word as "hauptraum."—*Haus und Halle*, 33. The basilica, too, was to be placed on the warmest side of the forum.—VITRUVIUS, v. I.

stables are not without advantages when they are placed in the open space outside the great hall and towards the east."[1] A reminiscence of the notion that horses

"BALK" OR "SCAFFOLD" AT FULWOOD

should not face a fire seems to be preserved in England in the proverb :—

"A lantern on the table
Is death in the stable."

In a Yorkshire farmhouse the lantern was hung over the

[1] VITRUVIUS, vi. 9.

kitchen door. In the west of Ireland it is kept in a hole in the wall. Columella advises that "a big and lofty hall be built, of such size that the domestics may conveniently inhabit it during every season of the year."[1]

Of houses still existing in Schleswig, Hanover, and Westphalia, Lange says, "The great 'floor' (*Deele*), with the hearth at the back end (*auf der Fleet*),[2] on the right and left the cattle stalls, behind the hearth three dwelling-rooms, the middlemost of which is the state-room, laterally in a line with the fire-place doors, through which the smoke also escapes—these are the chief characteristics." "The great covered middle room," he continues, "with smaller rooms round it, and with the dwelling-rooms at the back divided into three parts, seems to have been a common type of all the dwelling-houses of Aryan peoples at a certain stage of their evolution."[3]

Again Lange, following Galen, describes the old Greek peasant's house as it existed in Asia Minor in the second century of our era. "It was divided by Galen into two kinds, the poorer and the richer. The former consists of a single big room with the hearth in the middle, and the cattle stalls on the right and left, or on only one of the two sides. Before the hearth, towards the door, stand

---

[1] "Magna et alta culina ponetur . . . ut in ea commode familiares omni tempore anni morari queant."—COL. i. 6.
[2] For "fire and flet," with the meaning "fire and house-room," see *Hist. Eng. Dict.*, s.v. "Flet." Ducange (s.v. "Flet") cites a passage from "Leges Burgorum Scotic.," which mentions "interiorem partem domus capitalis quæ dicitur *Flet*."
[3] *Haus und Halle*, pp. 32, 33.

stove-benches. The chief room serves at the same time for kitchen and living room. And as no separate rooms are mentioned besides the chief room, one may suppose that it served at the same time as a sleeping apartment for the inmates, who prepared in it their simple bed by the side of the fire.

On the other hand the better kind of peasant's house has an *exedra* at its back end, and always a sleeping-room at the side of it. Over these in an upper story are likewise three rooms, which are used for household purposes, and especially for storing wine. At the sides, however, over the cattle stalls there are rooms which, following the arrangement of the cattle stalls, probably also extend to the entrance side. What their use was we are not directly told, but it is plain that they served partly for the purposes of husbandry and partly for sleeping rooms for the servants. . . . If the smoke of the hearth could be made of use for the store of wines in the chambers over the *exedra*, it may be argued that in the better kind of farm-houses the hearth stood more towards the back end than towards the middle of the hall." [1]

We have thus seen that the basilical form of house is widespread, and that it was a common type of dwelling-house in Asia Minor as far back as the second century.

When Caesar came into England he found both an extremely large population and a great abundance of

---

[1] LANGE, *ut supra*, p. 32. GALEN, *De Antidotis*, i. 3, vol. xiv. p. 17 (ed. Kuhn).

houses (*aedificia*) almost exactly resembling those of the Gauls.[1]

The Belgic or Germanic people who emigrated to England before Caesar's time would naturally continue their own method of building, and Tacitus has left some account of what that method was. "It is sufficiently well known," he says, "that none of the Germanic peoples dwell in cities, and that they do not even tolerate houses which are built in rows. They dwell apart, and at a distance from one another, according to the preference which they may have for the stream, the plain, or the grove. They do not lay out their villages after our fashion, with the buildings contiguous to each other and in close contact. Every man surrounds his house with a space, either for protection against the accident of fire, or from ignorance of the art of building. They do not make use of stone cut from the quarry, or of tiles; for every kind of building they make use of unshapely wood, which falls short of beauty or attractiveness. They carefully colour some parts of their buildings with earth which is so clear and bright as to resemble painting and coloured designs."[2] When Tacitus says that no cities were occupied by the Germans, he means that they had no cities to be compared with those of Italy and Greece. He can hardly mean that they had no towns. We should

---

[1] "Hominum est infinita multitudo creberrimaque aedificia, fere Gallicis consimilia."—*B. G.* v. 12. MEITZEN, *Das deutsche Haus*, pp. 24, 28, thinks that Caesar would have used such a word as *tuguria* or *casae* had he meant "huts."

[2] *Germ.* xvi. (ed. CHURCH and BRODRIBB).

notice that he speaks of houses (*domus*), not of mere huts or cabins. The words which he uses would have served to describe an English, as well as a German, village. "He finds," says Meitzen, "the difference between German and Italian villages in that wherein it consists to this day, viz., that the houses in Italian villages, as also in the towns, are built wall to wall, so that for every one of them a wall-thickness can be spared. In Germany, however, they were built in the country not in contiguous buildings, but the houses stood alone."[1] We shall not, perhaps, be far wrong in supposing that the "space" by which the German village house was surrounded was the "toft"—the ground or place on which the house stood—of the old English village. Nothing is more frequent among old English deeds than grants or conveyances of a messuage *cum tofto et crofto*. In the English village street each house stood in its own "toft" adjoining the street, with a croft behind it, the "toft and croft" forming together a long and rather narrow strip. We learn from Tacitus that the German houses were built of rudely-shaped wood, and it has already been shown that English houses built of wood which was split by wedges, or which retains the bark, still exist. We have also seen that English farm-houses were often coloured throughout by the bright hues of "archil." When, in addition to these resemblances, we consider the close parallel which is known to have existed between the ancient German and the English methods of agriculture, it can hardly be doubted that the arrangement of the houses and their construction were very much alike in

[1] *Das deutsche Haus*, p. 24.

both countries. It is improbable that either the German or the English village house of the first century was round. It is far more likely that it resembled the still-existing German houses which have been described, as well as the smaller existing wooden houses of which examples have already been given.

CHAPTER VI.

THE TOWN HOUSE

Foreign influence—The "rows" of Chester—"Taverns" or shops below the street—Carriage traffic not permitted in narrow streets, as in Roman times—"Wints" or "wynds" and "turnpikes"—Different trades in different streets or quarters—Appentices, booths, and shops or sheds—The height of appentices fixed by law—The projecting upper story of Roman origin—Its use—"Solars"—In the twelfth century town houses had only one upper floor—The "garret"—Height of rooms—Stone party walls in wooden houses—Size of rooms—Probable early use of decorated woodwork in fronts of houses—A goldsmith's house in York in 1490.

AS regards the great country houses, and many of the houses built in cities, we have no reasons for believing that the chain which still links us with the old Roman civilization was ever broken. The forms of such houses were largely modified by foreign influence.

At Chester, for example, the two main streets intersect each other at right angles, as though the city had sprung from a Roman stationary camp.[1] "The streets, being cut out of the rock, are several feet below the general surface, which circumstance has led to a singular construction of

[1] The streets of Lincoln are nearly on the old Roman lines; even the Roman sewers are there. York, Gloucester, and Exeter are also good examples of Roman quadrangular towns.

the houses; level with the streets are low shops or warehouses, over which is an open balustraded gallery with steps at convenient distances into the streets. Along the galleries, or, as they are called by the inhabitants, 'rows,' are houses with shops; the upper stories are erected over the row, which consequently appears to be formed through the first-floor of each house, and at the intersection of the streets are additional flights of steps."[1] Here we have a distinctly Roman method of building. For the "open balustraded gallery" is the *pergula* or covered balcony which in some Roman towns rested on the top of the *tabernae* or shops.[2]

On the other hand, in Pompeii and other Roman towns, "the street front on the ground-floor, even of large and handsome houses, was usually occupied by a row of shops. In some cases these shops have no doorway or passage communicating with the main house, and were probably rented by the owner to independent tradesmen; in others the shops could be entered from the house."[3] This Pompeian arrangement of shops resembles that of mediaeval and modern Italy, and is like our modern arrangements.

In England shops in front of town houses were some-

---

[1] LEWIS, *Topographical Dictionary of England*, 1831, vol. i. p. 429.

[2] SMITH'S *Dictionary of Greek and Roman Antiquities*, ii. 368. *The Corpus of Latin Inscriptions*, iv. 138, mentions "tabernae cum pergulis suis." Halliwell gives "tavern" as a Yorkshire word for cellar. In Chester the *tabernae* must have been below the "rows." There are cellars or store-rooms beneath the "rows" yet.

[3] SMITH' *Dictionary of Greek and Roman Antiquities*, i p. 679.

times known as "taverns," from the Latin *taberna*, and were below the surface of the street, like cellars. They were even known as "cellars." Thus by a statute passed in the reign of Henry VIII., merchant gilds were heavily fined if they bound an apprentice by oath or bond not to "set up, nor kepe any shop, house, or *seller*."[1] Cellars were used as places of business in London as early as the first half of the reign of Henry III.[2] We learn from a very full account[3] of the building of a house in Sheffield in 1575 that down to a late time "taverns" or underground shops were dug out in front of town houses. The following entries show this:

"Payd to ij dykers for casting earth furth of the taverne
iiij daies . . . . . . ijs. viijd.
Item paid to Roades and Batley for workeinge and
castinge earth ij daies in my taverne . . xxijd.

Then follow some payments for walling the "tavern," which seems to have been built of stone and covered with boards. Assuming that the accounts are in chronological order, the "tavern" was dug out and finished after the house was "reared."

These "taverns" were entered by stairs, which sometimes encroached on the public street, and the old accounts of the Burgery or municipal corporation of Sheffield show that the burgesses exacted a small rent or acknowledgment for such encroachments.

---

[1] Rastell's *Statutes*, 1557, f. 77b.
[2] Riley, *Munimenta Gild. Lond.*, vol. i. p. xxxii.
[3] MS. in the author's possession.

Thus in the year 1566 this entry occurs: "William Tomson for his taverne stare iiij*d*."[1]

In London during the thirteenth century steps led into such shops from the street; "they seem to have seriously encroached upon the footway at times, for at later periods they are the subject of frequent enactments."[2] It is interesting to find the same practice on the other side of the English Channel. "In some towns of Flanders," says Viollet-le-Duc,[3] "the shops were sometimes below the ground; to get into them you had to go down a number of steps, and these steps even encroached on the public street. By the sides of the balustrade were benches, on which samples of merchandise were displayed; an awning protected these as well as the benches from the rain. It is well to observe that in trading towns the shopkeepers did all they could to block the public way, to stop the wayfarer by putting obstacles to traffic. This custom, or rather this abuse, lasted for a long period; it became absolutely necessary to establish footpaths and rules for the inspection of the highways, which were rigorously enforced under a heavy penalty for disobedience. During the Middle Ages, trading streets, with their open shops and their display of goods in the public street, were like bazaars. The street, then, became the merchants' property, and foot passengers could hardly make their way through it during business hours; as for horses and carriages, they had to abandon all attempts to pass through narrow streets impeded by dis-

---

[1] LEADER, *Records of the Burgery of Sheffield*, p. 14.
[2] RILEY, *ut supra*, vol. i. p. xxxii.
[3] *Dict. de l'Architecture*, ii. p. 239.

plays of merchandise and buyers. During meal times business was suspended, a considerable number of shops were shut up. When curfew sounded, and on holidays, these streets became silent and almost deserted."

When many "tavern stairs" were made in a narrow street it is obvious that vehicles drawn by horses could not pass through. To remedy such an inconvenience two courses were possible. One was to remove the stairs and fill up the holes in the streets, leaving mere cellars beneath the *pergula*, to be entered by steps inside the houses instead of outside. The other was to excavate the whole street down to the floors of the "taverns," and this seems to have been the plan adopted at Chester.[1] The numerous cellars still found under the footpaths of streets in old towns which contained shops show that the expedient of filling up the holes was also adopted.

To this day English shopkeepers prefer narrow streets, as, for instance, New Bond Street in London. Experience has shown them that more business can be done in such streets. The practice of touting at the shop door for custom was of long duration. An English poet[2] of the fourteenth century laughed at the noises they made in the streets, as when cooks and their servants cried "hot pies, hot!"

Such was the narrowness of the streets, and such the importunity of the shopkeepers, that if a man got into a

---

[1] The floors of the cellars in some of the old houses in Bailgate, Lincoln, are on a level with the Roman road, the modern road being on a level with the first-floor.

[2] LANGLAND, *Piers the Plowman*, Prologus, 225.

street at one end he could hardly get out at the other without buying something. It was the old way of advertising.

In English towns there were streets closed to all but foot passengers. The hundred and fifty-six "rows" of Yarmouth, each about eight feet wide, are an example of this, and it is said that in later years vehicles called "trollies" or "harry-carries"[1] were specially built to traverse them. Such names as Waingate and Fargate in Sheffield imply that in ancient times there were streets in that town which could only be traversed by foot passengers. For Waingate is "wagon street," and is the road which leads to the old bridge crossing the river. The name implies that there were other streets through which wagons could not pass. Fargate means[2] "public street" or "driving street," and implies the same thing. It is obvious that in old cities the larger streets would lead to the bars or gates, as they do, for instance, to the four gates of York and Chester. Here the plan of the Roman camp, with its *via principalis* and its four gates, is followed.

In the Roman provincial towns there were also streets which could only be traversed by foot passengers. At Pompeii "the narrow streets are practically blocked by single large stones in their centres; the broader streets are crossed by rows, containing from two to five stones." Some twenty-five years before the destruction of Pompeii

---

[1] THORNBURY, *A Tour Round England*, 1870, ii. 36.
[2] From O. N. *far*, means of passage, and *gata*, a road. Compare O. N. *far-vegr*, a track, road, Swedish *farwag*, via publica; O. E. *fær*, passing, transit. The author here desires to correct a former opinion on this point. Compare the German *fahren*, to drive.

Claudius forbade travellers to drive in carriages through provincial towns. "Heavy burdens were carried on the backs of horses, mules, or cattle. . . . In the case of Pompeii horses and carriages were, beyond a doubt, confined to certain streets." Occasionally these streets were closed by iron gratings.[1] The smaller streets of English towns were, as we have seen, mere alleys leading into the wider or public streets. In Warrington they are known as "wints"; over the portal of one of the alleys in that town is inscribed the name "Little Weint." In Edinburgh they are called "wynds," in Yarmouth "rows." "Row" is also found in London, as in Paternoster Row. "Wint," or "went,"[2] is equivalent to the Latin *angiportus*, and was a vent or exit leading to the public street, to the gates, or the walls. In some northern towns such a passage is known as a "jennel." At Market Weighton it is called a "galing" or "goaling." In other parts of East Yorkshire it is called a "rent." At Scarborough the streets in the old part of the town are on the slope which leads up to the castle, and are extremely narrow. Some of these streets, like those at Clovelly in Devonshire, contain steps by which the slope can be ascended, and have a very un-English appearance. It was easy to close such streets if necessary by barriers at either end, and the spiked contrivances known as "turnpikes" were everywhere used for this purpose.[3]

[1] SMITH's *Dict. of Greek and Roman Antiq.*, ii. 952.
[2] HALLIWELL'S *Dict. of Archaic Words.*
[3] "Torne pyke, suche as lyeth over away—*roulis.*"—PALSGRAVE, 1530. Compare Cheyne Row, lane barred by a chain.

A striking feature of the old English town was that each craft had its own quarters or street. Everybody has heard of the Jewry or Jews' quarter of the larger towns, where the business of money-lending was carried on. In London a great number of old street-names are associated with particular trades — Goldsmiths' Row, Needlers' Lane, where needles were made or sold, Carriers' Row, Stockfishmongers' Row, Paternoster Row, where the "paternoster makers" lived—these may suffice for examples. The same divisions are found in the smaller towns. Baxtergate in Pontefract, Whitby, and Doncaster was the bakers' street. Fishergate in Doncaster and Ripon was the street where the fish dealers carried on their trade. There is a Butcher Row with interesting old shops in Shrewsbury.

Other examples are: Ropergate in Pontefract, where ropes were made; Salter Row in the same town, and Saltergate in Chesterfield, which were occupied by the salt dealers or the meat-salters; and Packers' Row, Irongate, Knifesmithgate, and Glumangate in Chesterfield. The last-named street was the abode of gleemen or minstrels. Such minstrels were employed by old municipal corporations, and the part of the town which they inhabited was generally known as St. Julian's quarter.[1] The same arrangement of trades in various quarters was the rule in German towns.[2] It also prevailed in

---

[1] ROWBOTHAM, *The Troubadours*, p. 189 *et seq.* Compare Gillygate in Pontefract, Durham, York, and other towns.

[2] A long list is given by FOERSTEMANN, *Die deutschen Ortsnamen*, p. 167.

England during the Roman occupation, as we may see by the *insulae* at Silchester, occupied by dyers.[1]

It was long before the practice of making the shop within the house itself began to be usual. The booth, open shed, or shop in front of the dwelling-house, like the Lucken Booths of Edinburgh, began at first to take the place of the underground "tavern." In the year 1258 there were 120 booths (*selde*) in Pontefract, and of these 42 were occupied by cobblers and persons who sold salt. Beside these there were 60 stalls.[2] In London the stalls on which goods were offered for sale were fixed to the walls in the streets by means of hinges, so that they could be taken up and let down. They were ordered to be 2½ feet in breadth.[3]

In A.D. 1419 it was declared that if a man fixed "appentices" to a house either by iron or wooden nails, such "appentices" were to be regarded as landlords' fixtures, even if the lease were for a considerable period.[4]

It was also ordered that "appentices" should be so high that a man could easily ride or walk beneath them.[5] Again, it was declared that "appentices," rain gutters, and "jetties" (*i.e.* projecting stories) should not be less

[1] *The Builder*, vol. lxx. p. 378.
[2] *Yorkshire Inq.* (Yorkshire Arch. Record Series), i. 50.
[3] STOW's *Survey of London*, ed. 1633, p. 678.
[4] RILEY, *Munimenta Gild. Lond.*, vol. i. p 432. Compare COTGRAVE, 1632: "*Soupendué.* A penthouse; iuttie, or, part of a building that iuttieth beyond, or leaneth ouer the rest." The appentice seems to have been fixed at the *end* of a house. "Pentyce, of an howse ende."—*Prompt. Parv.*
[5] "Item, qe lez appentices soient si hautz qe home puisse aisement alere et chivalere southe ycelles "—*Ibid*, vol i. p. 336.

than nine feet high, so that people could ride under them.[1]

The projecting stories which, with their quaint and decorated fronts and their many gables, make some old English towns so beautiful, were not born of a mere freak or of an artist's fancy. They were intended for use, namely, to give shelter from the sun or rain to stalls and booths, and to goods displayed in the streets. The evolution of the projecting "solar" or upper room can be traced by reference to Roman practices. In Rome the tops or roofs of the colonnades in front of the houses, or of the *insulae*, were known as *solaria*, meaning literally "places for basking in the sun."[2] Hence when rooms began to be built over these colonnades such rooms were known as "solars," so that the sense of "basking place," or "sunning place," originally applied to the tops of the colonnades, was afterwards transferred to the rooms built over them. Projecting stories may still be seen in some of the houses at Pompeii, and the Roman Emperors forbade their erection in narrow streets.[3] In England they belong to town houses, though occasionally they may be found in the country. In such cases the country house is a copy of the town house, as there could be no actual need in the country for such projections.

In the twelfth century it appears that the houses in

---

[1] "Qe Pentis, Goters, et Getez soyent sy hautz, qe gens puissent chivacher dessouz, et a meyns ix pees haut."—RILEY, *Munimenta Gild. Lond.*, vol. i. p. 584.

[2] SMITH'S *Dictionary of Greek and Roman Antiquities*, i. p. 672.

[3] *Ibid.*, i. p. 666, where see the engraving.

London had only one story above the ground floor.[1] In the original sense of the word a garret was a watch-tower or look-out. When it was first added to the "solar" does not appear, but in the early part of the fourteenth century we find houses in London of two or three stories mentioned, and each of these stories, as also the cellar beneath, occasionally formed the freehold of different persons.[2] As the "solar" projected beyond the room beneath, so the garret projected, though only to a slight degree, beyond the "solar." This projection of the garret would afford some little additional shelter to the stalls below. The "solar" was the chief dwelling-room of the family, the garret being often used as a store-room for corn and other provisions.[3] "From a deed bearing date 1217 or 1218, it appears that the corbels or joists for supporting the upper floor were inserted at a height of eight feet from the ground."[4] It is a common thing nowadays to find in houses of the sixteenth and seventeenth centuries rooms not more than 6 feet high, and this is especially the case in the smaller houses. So long as a man of average height could walk in without knocking his head against the ceiling everybody was satisfied.

The document known as "Fitz-Alwyne's Assize," dated A.D. 1189, shows that the party-walls of London houses "were of freestone, 3 feet thick and 16 feet high, from which the roof (whether covered with tiles or thatch)

---

[1] RILEY, *Munimenta Gild. Lond.*, vol. i. p. xxxi.
[2] *Munimenta, etc., ut supra.*
[3] TURNER and PARKER'S *Domestic Arch. of England* (fifteenth century), part i. p. 34.   [4] *Munimenta, ut supra*, p. xxxi.

ran up to a point, with the gable towards the street."[1] These stone walls were built as a protection against fire, the rest of the building being of wood and plaster. From the height of this wall we may conclude that both the upper and lower rooms were less than 8 feet high. The length and breadth of the rooms we do not know, but we have already referred to a room without Ludgate which in 1352 measured 16 feet in length by 12¾ feet in breadth,[2] this being the "bay" to which we have so often referred.

The earliest timber buildings of our old towns have perished, but they must have been as well carved and as picturesque as any of the later examples which yet remain. A gable over the north doorway of Cormac's chapel in Ireland,[3] which is said to date from the year 1120, is an imitation in stone of the fine carving which decorated the gable of a wooden house. The transition from wood to stone was gradual. Just as the early printers copied the manuscripts, so, we may be sure, the first builders of stone houses and churches copied the wooden ones.

In 1490 a goldsmith's house in York consisted of a hall, parlour, bolting house for sifting bran, kitchen, buttery, great chamber, another chamber, and a shop. The hall was hung with tapestry embroidered with flowers. The parlour contained a bed, with its tester ornamented by a figure of the Blessed Mary. The walls were hung with tapestry, embroidered with figures of St. George and the

---

[1] *Munimenta, etc., ut supra*, p. xxx.
[2] *Ante*, p. 33.
[3] STOKES, *Early Christian Architecture in Ireland*, 1878, Plate xli. LORD DUNRAVEN, *Notes on Irish Architecture*, ii. p. 75.

Blessed Mary. Amongst other things, the great chamber contained two feather beds and a "sprosse" chest, this being apparently identical with what was afterwards known as a Flanders chest. The other chamber contained a parclose,[1] or wooden partition, which probably separated it from the great chamber. This smaller chamber contained, amongst other things, a bed, a basket, and a bushel of coals. We may infer from this that the great chamber with the small separated chamber were in the upper floor, these rooms being approached by a ladder passing through a hole in the floor of the smaller chamber, as in the house at Upper Midhope already described.[2] The contents of the great chamber show that it was used for a bedroom only. The shop contained stithies, a forging hammer, and the usual tools of a goldsmith's trade.[3]

It frequently happened that all the wood-and-plaster houses in a street fell into decay. Such a street was then called Rotten Row, or "ruinous street."[4]

[1] "Parclos to parte two roumes, *separation.*"—PALSGRAVE.
[2] *Ante*, p. 57.
[3] *Test. Ebor.* (Surtees Soc.), iv. 56 *et seq.*
[4] See the Author's account in *N. & Q.*, 9th S., i. 470.

CHAPTER VII.

BUILDING MATERIALS—CHIMNEYS—WINDOWS— MURAL DECORATIONS—ROOFS

Wood the commonest building material for ordinary houses—The "reared" house—The rich man's house sometimes built of stone—The wattled house—"Parging"—Sod houses—Use of bricks—The evolution of the chimney—Remarkable chimney at Warrington—Flues and louvres—The "reredos"—The "room in the chimney"—Chimneys of wood or wicker work—Comparison of the chimney in the megaron at Tiryns—The window or "wind-hole"—Small size of the oldest windows—Window frames covered by linen dipped in oil—Early glass windows—Dearness of glass—Decoration of walls—The usual colours were blue and yellow—Wattled posts imitated in the mural decorations of the peasantry—The painting of leaves on walls—Squares drawn on the floor—The serpentine mark at the entrance—Decorated hearth in lake village near Glastonbury—Whitewash a protection against fire—Universal use of plaster and whitewash in churches—Roofs of turf, rushes, and heather—Houses without fires.

IN historic times the houses of the English peasantry were mostly built of wood, stone being only used where wood could not be obtained. We have seen that the houses in the Glastonbury marsh village were built of wood and clay, and also that these materials were used for building houses which still exist. The old English word for build was *timbran*, to "timber," and the man who built the house was called the *treowwyrhta* or carpenter.[1] Houses were built of wood even in places where stone was most abundant, and this kind of building continued to the close of the sixteenth century. A very full account of the building of a house in Sheffield in the year 1575 has been preserved.[2] The builder begins to enter up his payments thus :—

"First paied to Johne Ronksley for gayting me xxx c
slate stones . . . . . xxx*s*.
Item paied to my Lord for the delph yre of the said
stone . . . . . . x*s*. *s*.
Item paied to my Lord for viij trees after x*s*. the tree . iiij*l*.
Item paied to Mr. West for vij trees and he gave my
wiffe one tree besydes . . . . xvj*s*."

So the builder paid thirty shillings for 3000 "slate stones," and £4 16*s*. for fifteen trees, another tree being given to his wife for luck. He tells us further on that he paid £2 6*s*. 8*d*. "for meat and drink that day the house was reared."[3]—a large sum considering the rate of wages at that period. The "rearing" of the house was the setting up of the timber framework of which it was composed, a wooden house, or house built of wood and plaster, being still known in Yorkshire as a "reared

[1] ALFRIC'S Colloquy in WRIGHT - WÜLCKER, *Vocab.*, p. 100. In mediaeval Latin timber for building was known as *meremium*. In the fourteenth century a good deal of timber for building purposes was brought from Norway.—*Priory of Coldingham* (Surtees Soc.), Appendix, p. lvii.

[2] MS. in the Author's possession.

[3] 1349. "In iiij lagenis cervisiæ empt. et expenditis circa levacionem meremii, 4*d*."—Appendix to *Bishop Hatfield's Survey* (Surtees Soc.), p. 234.

house" to distinguish it from a stone house. The rearing of a house, described in mediaeval Latin as *levatio*, was the lifting or setting up of the timber-work or skeleton structure which supported the whole building. The timber-work was prepared and made ready before it was set up. That such was the case is shown by the statute 37 Hen. VIII., which recites that certain novel outrages had of late been practised, such as "the secret burnynge of frames of tymber prepared and made, by the owners thereof, redy to be sett up, and edified for houses." This misdemeanour was made felony.[1] We have already alluded to the mortise holes at the feet of old "crucks," which seem to have held levers, and the considerable sums of money spent in ale when the timber-work was reared show that the assistance of many men was required.

The builder of the house in Sheffield paid two shillings "for gayttinge basinge stone," *i.e.*, foundation stone. The house was "mossed" and slated.[2] It was completed by the plasterers and "dobers" (colour-washers), these two classes of workmen being separately paid. Sixteen stones of lead were used for the gutter, the cost being 13*s.* 2*d*. The builder paid :—

"to Dewk the glasyer for
xvi foots of glasse for my windows viij*s.*"

[1] See the note in *Prompt. Parv.*, p. 176. In the seventeenth century the framework or skeleton of a house was known as "the carcass." *Hist. Eng. Dict.*

[2] "Payd in parte of a recconing for mossing of and slating my howse, xx*s.*"—Were the slates laid over the moss or the moss over the slates? Probably the former, lead being used for the gutter.

No other payment for glass is mentioned, so that the windows must have been few or very small. The house seems to have adjoined the street, for it was "next unto Mrs. Braye's," and the yard was paved at the back. As gable ends faced the street in town houses, the mention of the leaded gutter shows that there were two gable ends facing the street in this house. Below the ground, in front of the house, was a "tavern" or shop.

In the houses of the wealthy stone was used at an early period; we do not know how early.[1] In such houses it may have been used continuously, though by no means frequently, since the Roman occupation. Where in existing houses the lower part of the wooden framework is filled in by stone or bricks, such houses are said, in common phraseology, to be "half-timbered." But they are really "whole-timbered"; they are essentially wooden houses, built of wood from the foundation, the interstitial spaces having been filled in by the material nearest at hand, whether that material were clay, mud, stone, or brick. The oldest way was to weave twigs or brushwood in and out of the posts. After that came laths, which were fitted into "slots" in the posts by a process known as "shooting." In a house at Warrington examined by the author, wattle and daub, stone and brick are filled into the woodwork of different parts. Here the wattles are rods of hazel,[2] with the bark on, laid close together in an oblique direction,

---

[1] Under the name of *estland* boards, or *estrich* boards, much wood for building purposes was brought from Norway and Sweden.

[2] "A hartheled wall, or ratheled with hasill rods, wands or such other. *Paries craticius*."—WITHALS' *Dictionarie*, 1616, p. 191.

and covered by a thick coating of clay mixed with cow-dung. The act of throwing this material on is still known in South Yorkshire as "parging," and in Derbyshire as "sparging," from the Latin *spargere*, to sprinkle; the term is now only applied to the rough plastering of the inside of a chimney. Many of the poorer houses were built of mud or sods. Thus when Grimm the fisherman, as the old tale goes, founded Grimsby:—

"Biȝan he þere for to erþe,
A litel hus to maken of erþe."

"Began he there for to dwell,
A little house to make of earth."[1]

There was a place called "Sodhowses"[2] in Yorkshire which seems to mean "turf houses." Some of the Scotch "summer huts" were built of sods, or of turf upon a foundation of stones, and roofed with turf and straw. Sometimes a dry stone wall "was lined with turf and wattled with twigs, which kept the earth from falling."[3] Many houses in Cambridgeshire are built entirely of "clunch," a kind of hard chalk marl.

The word "brick" does not occur in English literature before the middle of the fifteenth century, and "perhaps the earliest true brick-building existing is that of Little Wenham Hall,"[4] believed to date from the end of the thirteenth century. But we are not to suppose that the

---

[1] *Havelock*, l. 739.
[2] *Yorkshire Fines*, part ii. p. 127.
[3] JOHNSON, *A Journey to the Western Highlands of Scotland*, ed. 1886, p. 44.
[4] PARKER, *Concise Glossary of Arch.*, 4th ed., p. 45.

art of brick-making, so commonly used by the Romans, was ever lost in England. Such a loss would have been exceedingly improbable. The old name for a brick was *tigel*, or "tile,"[1] and the tiler was the brickmaker. Formerly bricks were much thinner than they are at present, and there was little to distinguish them from tiles. Though they were not much used in the Middle Ages, the art of making them was not lost. It is a curious fact that the walls known in Yorkshire as "parpoint" walls, consisting of thin and rather small stones, resemble walls faced with Roman bricks.

The evolution of the chimney is one of the most interesting questions which concern domestic architecture. We have seen that in the English prehistoric hut the open hearth stood in the middle of the floor, and that in a German house already described it stood at a distance of several feet from the nearest wall. Having regard to the central position of the prehistoric hearth, it is on that ground likely that the fireplace of the Middle Ages did not adjoin an outer wall, as the custom now is, but stood at some distance from the outer wall.

Till very lately a central chimney existed at a house known as Oughtibridge Hall near Sheffield, "where a large stone chimney-stack from the kitchen passed through the middle of a bedroom, rendering the room useless. A length had been cut out of the heavy ridge-tree to make room for this stack, and the ends were left with-

---

[1] "*Luteres*, tigelan."—WRIGHT-WÜLCKER, *Vocab.*, 434, 5. (For *luteres* read *lateres*.)

out support, excepting such as they derived from the pins of the spars."[1] A remarkable chimney in an ancient timber house at Warrington in Lancashire, shown in the illustration, is nearly in the centre of the building. The jambs and lintel, as well as the whole framework of the deep fire-place, are of wood, and "that part of the framework of the flue, if framework it were originally, which is on a level with the sleeping shelf or chamber is of wood to the height of about a foot, but above that the curving structure is of brick. Whether or not this was the original condition it is difficult to say."[2] The present stove, with its modern surroundings, fills up the cavity of the ancient hearth and wide fire-place, whose sides were hung with hams and flitches.

In 1538 Leland expressed his wonder that the chimneys, otherwise the flues, in Bolton Castle were carried up the sides of the walls. "One thinge," he says, "I muche notyd in the haulle of Bolton, how chimneys were conveyed by tunnells made on the syds of the wauls, betwyxt the lights in the haull; and by this means, and by no covers, is the smoke of the harthe wonder strangly convayed."[3] He means that, in his time, the practice was to erect a sort of "cover," to use his own word, over a fire,

---

[1] T. WINDER, in *The Builders' Journal*, vol. iii. p. 41. Often there were seats or shelves within the chimney. 1575. "j burde within the chymney, jd."—*Richmond Wills* (Surtees Soc.), p. 255.

[2] From a note by Dr. CHARLES WHITE, of Warrington, who has kindly supplied the photograph done by Mr. BIRTLES of that town. The "sleeping chamber" is problematical.

[3] *Itin.* (1710-2), viii. ii. 66b.

CHIMNEY AT WARRINGTON

such a cover being a canopy made usually of wood and plaster. Carew, in his *Survey of Cornwall*, published in 1602, says that "the ancient maner of Cornish building was ... to set hearths in the midst of the roome for chimneyes which vented the smoake at a louer in the toppe."[1] Unless "chimney" in this passage is to be taken as meaning a portable fire-grate, Carew's statement confirms that of Leland, who, as we have just seen, uses "chimney" in the sense of "flue." A later writer, who was born in 1626, speaks to the same effect. "Antiently before the Reformation, ordinary men's houses, as copyholders and the like, had no chimneys, but fleus like louver holes: some of them were in being when I was a boy."[2] Aubrey is here using the word "chimney" in the sense of a stone passage in the side of a wall. He is recalling a time when no such passages existed in ordinary houses, and when flues like that at Warrington were used instead. William Harrison, writing in 1577, uses "chimney" in the same sense. After telling us that in the "young days" of old men who lived in his own village in Essex there were not above two or three chimneys "in most uplandish towns," he says that "each one made his fire against a reredosse in the hall where he dined and dressed his meat."[3] The "reredosse" seems to have been the canopy made of wood and plaster, which so often stood over the open fire-hearth and received the smoke. In an old bailiff's roll, dated 1337, and relating to Auckland in Durham, we read of a tree

---

[1] *Survey of Cornwall*, ed. 1723, f. 53.
[2] In *Antiq. Report*, i. 69.
[3] HARRISON's *England*, ed. Furnivall, pp. 239, 240.

being sawn to support the chimney in the lord's chamber.[1] This record is rendered more interesting by the fact that Richard de Bury, Bishop of Durham, author of *Philobiblon*, then resided at Auckland. One wonders how a book-lover and collector could preserve his treasures unless they were protected from soot and smoke.

The structure which Leland calls a "cover," and which Aubrey calls a "flue," seems to have been known in mediaeval Latin as *mantellum camini* and also as *fumarium* or *epicaustorium*,[2] and in English as a "fomerel"[3] or "tuel."[4] In *Gawayn and the Grene Knight*, written about A.D. 1360, "chalk whyt chymnees" are described as appearing on the roof of a castle. These may have been the summits of whitewashed flues made of wood and plaster. Bequests of chimneys are not uncommon in old wills, but it is doubtful whether or not the term refers to wood or metal flues which could be removed, or to portable fire-grates. The summits of the oldest stone chimneys resemble louvres, and the smoke did not escape from the top, but from one or more holes in the sides.

---

[1] "In j arbore sarranda. pro camino in camera Domini supportando, 2d."—*Bishop Hatfield's Survey*, ed. Greenwell (Surtees Soc.) p. 204. Probably it was the mantel-tree.

[2] "Papias the grammarian, who wrote about 1051, explains the word *fumarium* by *caminus per quem exit fumus*; and Johannes de Janua, a monk, who about 1268 wrote his *Catholicon*, printed at Venice, says, 'Epicaustorium, instrumentum quod fit super ignem caussa emittendi fumum.'"—BECKMANN, *History of Inventions* (English ed.), 1846, i. p. 311.

[3] "Fomerel of an halle, *fumarium*."—*Prompt. Parv.*

[4] "*Epicausterium*, a thuelle."—WRIGHT-WÜLCKER, *Vocabularies*, 777, 13.

When, therefore, we read in old authors of the absence of chimneys in England, we are not to suppose that the open hearth, except in the hovels of the poorest inhabitants, was without a funnel of some kind to convey the smoke. It is true that stone or brick flues which formed tubes "in the sides of the walls" were only to be found in castles or large buildings, but wood-and-plaster canopies or "covers" to convey the smoke were commonly used from a very early period.

Where there was an original upper story, or where an upper story was made in a room which was originally open to the roof, the floor of that upper story was often level with the mantel-tree of the canopy which covered the fire. Such, as we have seen, was the case in the mud house at Great Hatfield, already described. As the canopy itself was large, covering stove-benches, and even cupboards beneath, the effect was that there was a large chimney-breast, receding like a cone from three sides, in the room above. This chimney-breast often projected four or five feet into the interior of the upper room. It was in this way that the so-called "room in the chimney," about which so many tales have been told, grew up. This "room" was not "a priest's hiding-hole," but a survival of the old way of building a chimney. As there was a great open hearth below, the canopy which covered that hearth was necessarily very large, and protruded a long way into the upper room.

"At Derwent Hall, Kimberworth Hill Top, and Worksop, flues from ground-floor fire-places were found corbelled out at the first-floor so as to form a small room 6 ft. or 8 ft.

long by about 4 ft."[1] That at Worksop is shown here in elevation and section. Here the canopy of the chimney—a wood-and-plaster framework—rested upon the chamber floor, the actual opening for the smoke being a comparatively small hole adjoining the wall. As there was no door leading into the so-called "room in the chimney," and no

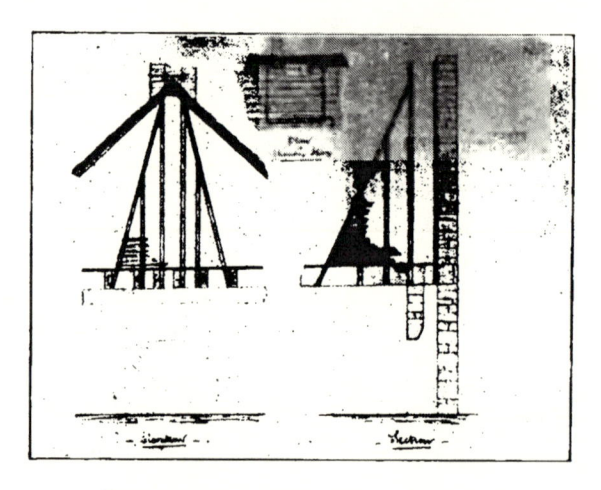

FLUES FROM GROUND-FLOOR FIRE-PLACES

opening into it except the small hole, that "room" was of course useless. It was so much wasted space. It has been remarked that "many of the earliest flues were of wicker, which is said to account for the disappearance of them

[1] T. WINDER, in the *Builders' Journal*, vol. iii. p. 41. Compare the description of the chimney in the mud house at Great Hatfield, *ante*, p. 38.

from many of our castles. The writer removed one of stud and mud from a farm-house at Hill Top, Grenoside, last year."[1] We have express evidence that at the beginning of the fifteenth century chimneys were built of wood, for it was declared by the ordinances of the city of London, compiled A.D. 1419, that no chimney should thenceforth be made unless it were of stone, tiles (*i.e.* bricks), or plaster, and not of wood, under pain of being pulled down.[2] It is obvious that chimneys built of timber and mud[3] would be easily destroyed, or would fall down and leave no trace of their existence.

Some writers have maintained that Greek and Roman houses had no chimneys except in the kitchens. We are also told that in Greek houses the chimney "seems only to have been used in the kitchen."[4] And as to the Romans it has been a subject of much dispute whether they "had chimneys for carrying off the smoke, except in the baths and kitchens."[5] If the Roman, like the early English, chimney were made of wood or wicker-work, one could not be surprised at the absence of all traces of its existence. It is probable, as we shall see, that chimneys made of wood existed in large Greek houses in very early times. In the centre of the megaron or men's hall at Tiryns

[1] T. WINDER, *ut supra*, p. 41.
[2] " Item, qe nulle chimenee soit desore en avaunt fait, sinoun de pier, tielles, ou plastre, et nemy de merisme, sur peyn destre abatuz."— RILEY, *Munimenta Gild. Lond.*, vol. i. p. 333.
[3] "Dalbura camini lutei ac murorum."—Account, dated 1482, of the Prior of Finchale in *Priory of Finchale* (Surtees Soc.), p. ccclv.
[4] SMITH'S *Dict. of Greek and Roman Antiq.*, i. p. 664.
[5] *Ibid.*, i. 686.

Schliemann found round hearths, about 3·30 m. in diameter, within a space enclosed by four pillars, which were shown to have been of wood. The hearth at Tiryns "was surrounded by an upright rim of plaster. . . The hearth, being in the middle of the hall, could be approached from all sides to obtain warmth in the winter. The four pillars surrounding the hearth are so far apart as to allow a convenient passage between them and the hearth, and even room to sit there. The smoke, too, did not fill the room, but found a convenient outlet through the openings of the central dome."[1] It is very interesting to compare this account of the hearth at Tiryns with the hearths which we have described, and especially with the central hearth and wooden chimney posts of the old house at Warrington.

It may be taken almost as an axiom that the smaller the window the older the house. It is true that there are many houses belonging to the sixteenth and seventeenth centuries in which very small windows may be found. But these are never the chief windows in the house, though they may represent survivals from older types. The smallness of the oldest windows may be inferred not only from extant examples, but also from the dearness of glass. Another proof is to be found in the fact that the word window means "wind eye"[2] or "wind hole," as though its main use was to admit air rather than light. Another old English word for window was *egþyrl*, meaning "eye hole."

---

[1] *Tiryns*, ed. 1886, pp. 222, 223.

[2] O. N. *vind-auga*. "In Egyptian houses, when it was decided to open windows on the street, they were mere air-holes near the ceiling." —MASPERO, *Manual of Egyptian Archaeology*, 1895, p. 11.

What the oldest forms of English mural windows were like may still be seen in the various "lowp-holes," loop-holes or apertures found in the walls of old barns. Here we have narrow, vertical slits, triangular, and sometimes round holes. It is probable that the original loop-hole or "lowp-hole" was a "leap-hole" or aperture, through which light or air could enter, or through which smoke could escape.[1] In a much more ornate condition all these forms of "lowp-holes" are to be found in churches. With the Romans, as with us, holes in barns were for ventilation.[2] Amongst the Norsemen "the ancient halls and dwellings had no windows in the walls, but were lighted by louvres and by round openings (*gluggr*) in the roof, covered with the caul of a new-born calf."[3]

In David Loggan's time (1675), college rooms in Oxford had often extremely small windows, these having remained unaltered in the seventeenth century. "Glass windows," says Aubrey, "except in churches and gentlemen's houses, were rare before the time of Henry VIII. In my own remembrance, before the Civil Wars, copyholders and poor people had none in Herefordshire, Monmouthshire, and Salop: it is so still."[4] There seems to be no evidence that the small windows of English houses were ever covered with the cauls of new-born calves, as in Iceland. But a good substitute for these was supplied by

---

[1] See *Academy*, May 30, 1896.
[2] "Fenestras habere oportet ex ea parti unde commodissime perflari possit."—VARRO, *De Re Rustica*, i. xiii. 5.
[3] CLEASBY and VIGFUSSON's *Icelandic Dict.*, s.v. *gler*.
[4] In *Antiq. Repert.*, i. 72.

framed blinds of cloth or canvas, called "fenestralls."[1] In the time of Henry VIII. they used linen dipped in oil, as well as glass.[2] Glass, however, was used in great houses from the days of the Romans. At the recently-discovered Roman villa at South Darenth, in Kent, there were found "broken sheets of window glass, having on one surface the iridescence characteristic of all Roman glass, and on the other traces of staining in brilliant colours."[3] It was the comparative dearness of glass which prevented its more frequent use in early times. When it became cheaper in the sixteenth century a fashion arose of making the windows in great houses as numerous and big as possible. A good example of this was Hardwick Hall in Derbyshire, of which the people said:—

"Hardwick Hall,
More glass than wall."

It is a curious fact that, as late as the sixteenth century, glass windows did not pass to the heir as part of the freehold estate, but to the personal representatives. They consisted of a series of moveable casements, which could be easily taken out.[4]

In the north of England it is the custom to decorate the inner walls of houses, and occasionally the outside stonework, by means of a colour obtained from the plant liver-

---

[1] *Prompt. Parv.*, p. 155. Compare the "harden" windows in the house at Great Hatfield, *ante*, p. 41.

[2] *Antiq. Repert*, i. 273.

[3] *Daily News*, December 13, 1894.

[4] "Notices of Past Times from Law Books," by W. TWOPENNY, in *British Magazine*, iii. 650; *Northumberland Household Book*.

wort. This substance, known as "archil," or "orchil," is mixed with limewash to give it a deep blue colour. Phillips, the author of a dictionary printed in 1678, describes it as "archal, otherwise liverwort, because it groweth upon the freestones of the mountain Peak."[1] Unpleasing as this colour is to the eye of good taste, the practice has been very common till late years. In the north of Yorkshire it is usual to wash bedroom walls with a drab colour, and where they join the slanting roof to put waving lines of dark blue, with spots of the same colour in the folds. The pattern itself

is a reminiscence of the old wicker house,[2] with twigs or pliant boughs woven between the posts. Sometimes dots only are used. If we may believe an illuminated manuscript, the Anglo-Saxons painted their houses in various hues. "The colours most frequent are yellow and blue."[3] These two colours continued, as we have seen, in use to a comparatively late period. In stripping the plaster off an old house it will usually be found to consist

[1] Compare Latin *glastum*, Irish *glaisin*, woad. Prof. Sullivan thinks there must have been an Irish word *glas*, meaning "blue." Does the place-name Glassby mean "blue dwellings," in allusion to the colour of the houses? *Cf.* Whitby, or "white dwellings."

[2] O. N. *vanda-hús*, Edda, 52.

[3] WRIGHT's *Essays on Arch. Subjects*, vol. i. p. 193. The buildings of the Anglo-Saxons "in many cases, if not always, have been plastered on the outside."—PARKER's *Glossary of Arch.*, 1850, p. 405. Compare what TACITUS says about the German houses in *Germ.* xvi.

of various layers of blue and yellow colour-wash. In the north of Yorkshire yellow-ochre sometimes competes with archil, and it is interesting to notice that the latter substance was also used by the Romans for decorating walls.[1] Clay wash and umber are also used. The floors of houses are commonly flagged with sandstone or blue slate, and after they have been washed on Saturday the edges next the wall, and also the hearth, are decorated by waving lines and dots about a thumb in width, the pattern resembling the upper mural decoration just mentioned. This is done by means of a sharpened piece of whitening.[2] About Wakefield floors are occasionally washed with milk "to fetch a gloss on."

In Derbyshire the ceiling and the walls were sometimes decorated by a light green colour. This was done by putting copperas into the limewash. Before the introduction of wall papers it was usual to decorate the walls with patterns, such as green leaves with rather indistinct stems.[3] This was done by means of a contrivance resembling a large stencil plate. The practice is ancient, whether the stencil plate was used anciently or not. The regulations of the *Feste de Pui* in London provided that the room for the feast was not to be hung with cloth of gold, or silk, or tapestry, but decorated with leaves and strewed with rushes.[4] In Derbyshire "pot moul"

---

[1] VITRUVIUS, vii. 7.
[2] Information by the Rev. W. Slater Sykes.
[3] The canons of Beauchief had a room called "grenlyf chawmbur" (greenleaf chamber).—ADDY's *Beauchief Abbey*, pp. 58, 141. The room may, however, have been hung with tapestry, decorated with green leaves.
[4] RILEY, *Munimenta Gild. Lond.*, vol. ii. pt. i. p. 226.

and "rubbing stones" are used for the decoration of floors. Some women make spots on the hearth. This is done by dipping a piece of rag into a basin of "pot moul," or pipe-clay, moistened with water. Either the whole or part of the stone floor is covered by squares drawn by means of a sharpened piece of pipe-clay used like a crayon, and sometimes a small flower is drawn in the middle of each square. So the *megaron*, or men's apartment, at Tiryns had squares produced by scratched lines on its concrete floor.[1] The threshold is usually sanded, and a serpentine line or letter S made in the sand.[2] This decoration is done by a brush, and women rarely omit it. They are very particular about keeping these patterns clean from one Saturday to another, on which day they are renewed.

It is interesting to compare these still-existing customs of decorating floors and hearths with a discovery recently made in the Glastonbury lake village. In one of the houses there a hearth made of clay was found beneath four other hearths which had been superimposed. "Its shape was, roughly speaking, a square of 5 ft. 3 in., with the corners rounded; it was raised four inches above the surrounding floor level, and its edges bevelled off; the surface was smooth and flat, and covered with an impressed decoration of circles measuring $5\frac{1}{2}$ inches in diameter, arranged in rows parallel to the edges."[3]

[1] See the illustration in SCHLIEMANN'S *Tiryns*, 1886, p. 209.
[2] Is this a reminiscence of the "widespread rite of welcome, by which a stranger is received with the outpouring of blood at the threshold?" See TRUMBULL'S *The Threshold Covenant*, 1896.
[3] Report of meeting of the British Association in the *Manchester Guardian*, 2 Sept. 1896.

English houses were plastered and whitewashed from the earliest times of which we have any record. The Romans too had their *dealbatores*, whitewashers, or "dawbers." After the great fire of London in the year 1212 the civic authorities ordered that the cookshops on the Thames, as well as all bakeries and breweries, were to be whitewashed and plastered inside and out, as a protection against fire. They also ordered that all houses covered with reeds or rushes which could be plastered should be plastered.[1] Whitewash and fresco-painting were universally applied to the stone walls of ancient churches,[2] though modern "restorers" always strip them off as a late innovation. Limewash was used by the Germans,[3] and probably by us, in the days of Tacitus. The fresco-painter could exercise his art on the moist plaster, and the "dauber" could cover it with various colours. The whitewashed house which here and there adds a charm to the English landscape was anciently a very common object. In wooden buildings whitewash was intended, as we have seen, as a protection against fire, and not as an ornament. In the Kentish villages there are "noggin houses" with white flowers worked into a red or black foreground of plaster.

When the roof of a whitewashed house was covered, as it often was, with green moss or turf, its appearance must have been very striking. Although stone, slates,

[1] RILEY, *Munimenta Gild. Lond.*, vol. ii. pt. i. pp. 86, 87.
[2] LANGLAND, *P. P.*, Passus III. l. 61. TURNER, *Domestic Arch.*, p. xxvi.
[3] *Germ.* xvi.

straw, reeds, rushes,[1] and other materials were used for roofing, yet moss or turf, on account of its cheapness, was much used for farm-buildings and the cheaper kinds of houses. In the fifteenth century the turf used for this purpose was known in the north of England as "dovet," and it seems to have been laid on a foundation of ling or heather.[2] Turf roofs were common amongst the Romans. In Iceland the roofs of farm-buildings are still covered with "green fresh grass-covered turves," as they were long ago.[3] Old accounts often mention the heather and the moss which were used for covering or thatching buildings.[4] The practice continued in England to the middle of the last century, if not later. It is obvious that in such cases some contrivance was necessary to prevent the turf from falling down, especially before it had grown together. Such a contrivance was known amongst the Norsemen as a *torf-völr*, a thin plank which ran along the eaves. Moss and stonecrop still continue to grow on the thatched roofs of old cottages.

[1] 1614. "For one thrave of spartes [rushes] to the bull house and for lainge on of them, vij*d*."—*Memorials of St. Giles's, Durham* (Surtees Soc.), p. 44.

[2] 1478. "In reparacione murorum, tecturæ de le cothous et le yowhous, cum le watlyng et factura murorum ejusdem, et adquisicione de le lynge et dovet pro eisdem domibus, etc."—*Inventories of Jarrow and Monk-Wearmouth* (Surtees Soc.), p. 120.

[3] *Laxdæla Saga* in VIGF. and POWELL'S *Icel. Reader*, pp. 53, 354.

[4] 1370. "In c travis de hathir emptis pro coopertura domorum x*s*."—*Inventories, ut supra*, p. 56. 1605. "A laborer, for gettinge mosse for the great barne and the newe stable, vppon his owen chardges x*s*. viij*d*. (and he must have ij*s*. viij*d*. more when the stable ys covered)."—*Shuttleworth Accounts* (Chetham Soc.), pt. i. p. 169.

"Many churches in Norfolk are still covered with thatch, and some of the high-pitched, ornamental roofs would hardly bear a heavier covering."[1] It appears from the writings of an Ulster poet, who flourished between the years 1220 and 1250, that the walls of Armagh Church, in Ireland, were of polished stone, covered with whitewash:—

> "Well hath its polished sides been warmed
> With lime as white as plume of swans."[2]

We have seen that there were cottages in Yorkshire in which fire was not used daily, or perhaps not used at all.[3] The occupants of such cottages must often have sought warmth at some place of common resort, like the village smithy or like the *lesche* or public inn of the ancient Greeks. The place-name Cold Harbour, which occurs so often in England, and is found in Germany as Kalteherberge, seems to refer to an inn of this kind.

[1] PARKER, *Glossary of Architecture*, 1850, p. 461.
[2] O'CURRY'S *Manners and Customs of the Ancient Irish*, iii. 58.
[3] *Ante*, p. 60, note 2.

CHAPTER VIII.

THE MANOR HOUSE

Rooms of manor houses in the twelfth century, and their dimensions—The "house"—The "woman house"—The "bower" and "hall" correspond to the *gynaeconitis* and *andronitis* of a Greek house—Quadrangular arrangement of the manor house and its outbuildings—Great size of the barns, which contained whole stacks—"Hall and bower" the two essential parts of a manor house—Continuance of this form to recent times—The British manor house as described in the Eddic Songs—Description of Padley Hall—The hall and buttery—The "trance" or entry—Outside stairs—Chapel containing fire-place—Its use—The bower over the buttery—The pigeon-cote over the chapel window—The curtilage—Manor houses at Charney Basset and Beaurepaire—The inner chamber—Furniture—The windows faced inwards to the court—Apparent absence of upper rooms in the oldest manor houses.

IN the twelfth century the manor house of Sandon, in Essex, consisted of a hall, a bower, and a latrina. Adjoining it were ample storehouses for grain, an ox-house, a washhouse in which clothes were trodden in vats by the feet, a brewery, a pig-cote, and a hen-house.[1] In the same century the manor house of Kensworth, in Hertfordshire,

---

[1] "Numerus domorum Sanduṇe . Aula . Camera . privata . Grangiæ due magnæ . Grangiæ ii. minores . Bovaria . Bateressa . Bracinum . Porcaria . Gallinaria." Appendix to *Domesday of St. Paul's* (Camden Soc.), p. 134. The editor explains *bateressa* as a "washhouse."

consisted of a hall 35 feet long, 30 feet broad, and 22 feet high, viz., 11 feet to the tie-beams, and 11 feet from the tie-beams to the ridge-tree. There were two other rooms, viz., the "house" (*domus*)[1] and the bower, or women's apartment (*thalamus*), the "house" standing between the hall and the bower. The "house" was 12 feet long and 17 feet broad; it was 17 feet high, viz, 10 feet to the tie-beams, and 7 feet from the tie-beams

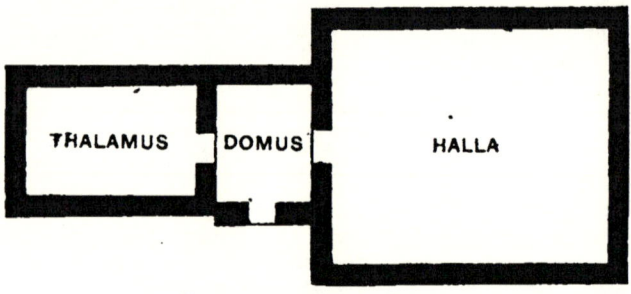

KENSWORTH MANOR HOUSE
(Conjectural plan)

to the ridge-tree. The bower was 22 feet long and 16 broad; it was 18 feet high, viz., 9 feet to the tie-beams, and 9 feet from the tie-beams to the ridge-tree. The annexed plan, drawn to scale, shows the relative size and position of the three rooms, the three doorways being conjectural. Besides these rooms there was an ox-house 33 feet long, 12 feet broad, and 13 feet high. There was

[1] Here *domus* is equivalent to "entrance hall" or "entry." Compare BARET's *Alvearie*, 1580: "an entrie, a porch, or portall before an house, wherein sometimes men use to dine, and therefore is taken for a hall .... *Atrium*."

THE BOWER, OR WOMEN'S ROOM

also a sheep-cote, 39 feet long, 12 feet broad, and 22 feet high, with a lamb-cote, 24 feet long, 12 feet broad, and 12 feet high.[1] From the above measurements we learn that the "hall" at Kensworth was nearly twice as big as the "house" and bower put together. At a later period the bower was known in the north of England as "the woman house."[2] The bower and hall of this manor house correspond, both as regards relative size and position, to the *gynaeconitis* and *andronitis* of a Greek house as described by Vitruvius.[3] According to him the principal entrance led at once into the woman's room, the men's room being by its side. The dwelling of the Irish *aire*, the man who possessed twenty cows, had also its hall or "living house," and its bower or "woman house." The aire, says Prof. Sullivan, "had the living house, in which he slept as well as took his meals; the women's house, in which spinning and other domestic work was carried on; the kitchen, the barn, the calf-house, the pigsty, and the sheep-house. In the residence of chiefs and flatha a sun-chamber or *grianan* was also pro-

---

[1] "Halla hujus manerii habet xxxv. pedes in longitud', xxx. ped' in latitud', et xxii. in altit', xi. sub trabibus. et xi. desuper. Domus, que est inter hallam et talamum, habet xii. pedes in longitud', xvii. in latit' et xvii. in altitudine, x. sub trabibus et vii. desuper. Thalamus habet xxii. pedes in longit', xvi. in latitud', xviii. in altitud', ix. sub trabibus et ix. desuper."—*Domesday of St. Paul's, ut supra,* p. 129.

[2] 1569. "In the woman house." *Richmond Wills* (Surtees Soc.), p. 219. The same wills also mention, in 1579, "the maydens house" and "the woman's house" (p. 285). Compare *kvenna-hús*, women's apartment, in *Fornaldar Sogür,* ii. 162.

[3] "Conjunguntur autem his (*i.e.*, the Gynaeconitis) domus ampliores," *i.e.*, the andronitis, vi. 7 (10).

vided for the mistress of the house, which in the large dúine appears to have been put on the rampart, so as to escape the shadow of the latter."[1] The sun-chamber corresponds to the English solar.

The buildings of these manor houses were so arranged as to form a quadrangle or courtyard, and often their barns, which contained the whole crop, were of great size. Thus, in the twelfth century, the great barn of the manor house at Walton was 168 feet long, 53 feet wide, and 33½ feet high, viz., 21½ feet to the tie-beams, and 12 feet from them to the ridge-tree.[2] A large barn with a nave and two aisles adjoining Gunthwaite Hall, near Penistone, still remains. It is 165 feet long, 43 feet broad, and 30 feet high, viz., 15 feet to the tie-beams, and 15 feet from them to the ridge-tree. It consists of 11 bays of 15 feet each in length. It has two rows of wooden pillars, each measuring 14 inches by 9, and standing on stone pedestals. The length of the tie-beams from one pillar to another is 23 feet. The roof is in a single span extending across the whole breadth. The building is of timber framework filled up with stonework to the height of 8 ft. 9 in. There are six barn doors. Vast and church-like as this building seems, as we watch the barn-swallows flitting across its

[1] In *Encyclop. Brit.*, 9th ed., xiii. 256.
[2] "Magnum orreum Walentonie habet x. perticas et dimid' in longitudine (et pertica est de xvi. pedibus) et in latitudine iii. perticas et v. pedes, et in altitudine sub trabe xxi. ped' et dimid', et desursum trabe xii. ped'."—*Domesday of St. Paul's, ut supra*, p. 130.
There was formerly a barn at Cholsey, in Berkshire, 303 feet long and 51 feet high. The pillars were four yards in circumference.—PARKER'S *Glossary of Arch.*, 1850, p. 241.

ancient timbers, it is smaller than that at Walton. In different parts of these large barns stacks of wheat, barley, beans, peas, and other farm produce were stored, up to the ridge-tree if necessary.[1] Such buildings resembled the *nubilaria* of the Romans.

In the twelfth century the manor house of Ardleigh consisted, like that at Sandon, of a hall with a bower annexed. In this hall there were two moveable or reversible benches, a fixed table, and a "buffeth." There were also a kitchen, a stable, a bakehouse, two storehouses for grain, one at the manor house itself, and the other at the "berewick," and a servants' house.[2] The "chamber" and "hall" of such houses are the "bower and hall" of Chaucer,[3] and other old writers.

If we may take the buildings of Kensworth as our guide, the manor house of the twelfth century consisted of a central "house," with a *thalamus* or bower on one side, and a "hall" on the other. That such was the usual arrangement may be inferred from the typical manor house of later times. We know from many extant examples of the sixteenth and seventeenth centuries that the typical country house of the larger and better kind

[1] See *Domesday of St. Paul's, ut supra*, where full details are given.

[2] "Quando autem recepit manerium hæc fuerunt ibi edificia, quæ cum manerio reddet. Scilicet una aula, et una camera appendicia, et una coquina, et unum stabulum, et i pistrinum, et due grangie, una ad curiam, altera ad berwicam, et una domus servientium. In aula fuerunt duo bancha tornatilia, et una mensa dormiens, et unum buffeth."—*Domesday of St Paul's, ut supra*, p. 136.

[3] 1386. "Ful sooty was hir bour and eek hir halle."—*Nonne Prestes T.*, 12.

consisted of a "house-place," or central room, with a large room on either side of it; entrance to the building being obtained by a central door opening into the "house-place." This threefold arrangement was not, however, followed in the smaller houses. In these there was nothing more than a hall and a bower, so that the "house" and the "hall" became synonymous terms, and, as we have seen, this room was sometimes called the "hall house."

The Eddic Songs, which range between the ninth and the twelfth centuries, exhibit a striking picture of family life in the British Isles, and much may be learnt from them about the houses occupied during that period. They tell us of the "salr," or great hall, and of the "búr," bower, or women's room. In the bower "the lady sits with her maids, working the tapestry with figures of swans and beasts, and ships and heroes, fighting and sailing, precisely like the toilette of Bayeux." The hall and bower stand in a court, and "there is a 'ta' or forecourt, a broad platform probably on which the great hall stands, or the space just before it." In the court "games go on and ceremonies take place."[1] In describing the "salr" the author of *The Lay of Righ* says that it had "doors turned to the south; the door was down, there was a ring on the lintel." The meaning is that the door moved up and down in a groove like a portcullis, the ring being used as a knocker. The floor was strewn. The poet gives us a glimpse of the life led within. "Then *mother* took a broidered cloth of bleached flax and covered the table. Then she took thin

[1] VIGFUSSON and POWELL, *Corpus Poet. Boreale*, i., p. lviii.

loaves of white wheat and covered the cloth. She set forth silver-mounted dishes full of . . . . . . old [well-cured] ham, and roasted birds. There was wine in a can, and mounted beakers. They drank and talked whilst the day passed by."[1]

Let us now turn to the ruins of an ancient manor house. The remains of Padley Hall, near Hathersage, in Derbyshire, will supply us with as good an example as can now be obtained. In their original state the buildings formed a quadrangle Judging from the remains of a buttress, there seems to have been an entrance gateway in the south-east side. On this side, as well as on the opposite side, pieces of walls, dressed stones, and hillocks indicate the site of destroyed buildings. The north-east side appears to have contained no buildings, and to have been bounded on that side by a massive wall, built of large blocks of stone, which is now standing, and is of the height of about 12 feet. On the top of this wall was a terrace or walk, originally approached by a flight of stone steps. On the remaining or south-west side the main walls and roof of the buildings are complete.

The buildings on the south west side comprise on the ground floor a hall and a buttery, divided from each other by an entry or passage, which goes through into the quadrangle. This entry, which appears to take the place of the *domus* at Sandon, is a little more than 6 feet wide, and the arches at each end of it are 8 ft. 4 in. high.[2] The buttery

---

[1] *Ibid.*, i. p. 239.
[2] "At Appleton in Berkshire there remains the entrance doorway to the hall of a Norman house of this period, opening at one end of the

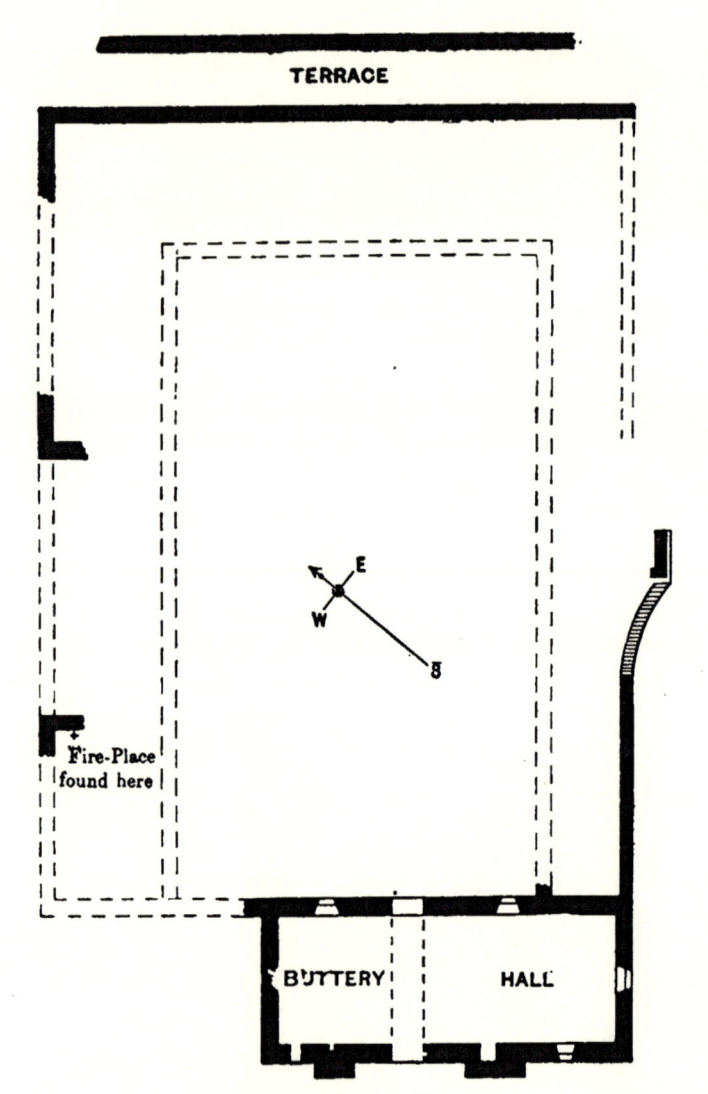

PLAN OF PADLEY HALL.

measures 15 by 17 feet, and, measured up to the original beams of the floor, is 12 feet high. It contains one window, 2 ft. 7 in. by 2 ft. 5 in , looking into the quadrangle. Like the hall, it was separated from the entry by a wooden screen, of which no traces remain, and this screen probably contained a hatch for serving provisions, like the buttery hatches in the colleges of Oxford and Cambridge, and in some old houses. Against the south-west wall of the buttery is a buttress, which dies into the wall, and which seems to have been intended to give strength and support to the building. Within the buttress, about two feet from the ground, is an opening 2 ft. 4 in. square, finished by dressed stones, which may have served for an ambry. It cannot have been a fire-place, for there is no flue leading upwards. The north-east wall of the buttery is fractured at its north-west end, as though it had continued further in that direction. The buttery is now occupied as a cow-house, and one of the doorways in the south-west wall, shown in the photograph but not on the plan, is modern. The other doorway in the same wall is ancient, so that there was an original doorway leading into the buttery from the outside of the quadrangle. As the buttery had only one rather small window, and was surrounded on its outer sides by walls nearly three feet thick, it was very suitable as a store-room for bread, ale, and wine. We have already seen that in old farmhouses the buttery was placed in the north-west corner of the building. It was so here.

vestibule or 'screen,' as it was often called; the two small doorways opening into the kitchen and buttery also remain."—TURNER, *Domestic Arch.*, p. 5.

A fire-place, much blackened by smoke, has been found in the north-west side of the quadrangle, at the place marked on the plan. As this was not far from the buttery, the kitchen may have been there

PADLEY HALL (OUTER VIEW)

The arches at the two ends of the entry are partly built up, but there seems to have been no door at either end. On the outer side, however, in the wall next to the hall, is a hole about three feet from the ground and 10 inches square and 1 ft. 2 in. deep, as though a wooden pole had been inserted there to bar the entrance. Such a pole would have served to keep cattle out. An entry or entrance of this kind was known in Scotland as a "trance," and in England as a "traunce,"[1] "tresawnce,"[2] or "tresaunte." These words are derived from the Latin *transitus*, a

PADLEY HALL (INNER VIEW)

passage. In the twelfth century such a passage leading to the hall, and dividing the hall from the buttery, was known in the Latin of that period as *trisantia*.[3]

[1] 1599. "*Tránsito*, a passage ouer from one place to an other, a traunce."—MINSHEU'S *Spanish Dict.*
[2] 1440. "Tresawnce, in a house.—*Transitus, transcencia.*"—*Prompt. Parv.*
[3] *Domesday of St. Paul's* (Camden Soc.), pp. xcix. 136.

The way into the hall was through a doorway in the screen, which once divided the hall from the entry. This room is 32 feet in length and 17 feet in breadth. Like the buttery it was 12 feet high. It has a square-headed window in each of its three outer walls. The largest window, which faces inwards, is 2 ft. 7 in. by 2 ft. 4 in. The two other windows are only 2 ft. 6 in. by 1 ft. With such small windows the room must have been badly lighted. The hall is now occupied as a stable, and there is a modern doorway in the south-east wall not shown in the plan. There is a fire-place immediately under the fire-place in the chapel above. The buttress or outside chimney-stack of the hall and chapel has lately fallen and been rebuilt with the old stones almost from the foundation. Its summit is a conjectural "restoration." Before this alteration, the top of the chimney-stack was slated like the roof of the building by old slates, and the chimney-stack did not rise above the eaves.

Over the hall is a chapel,[1] and over the buttery is a chamber or bower. These upper rooms were divided from each other by a massive wooden partition which extended from the floor to the ridge-tree, and the part above the tie-beams, with its lath-and-plaster work, still remains. Access to the chamber, as well as to the chapel, was gained by outside steps,[2] probably of wood, in the quadrangle.

[1] The popular, but erroneous, name for the whole of the remains is now "Padley Chapel." Old people speak of it as "the hall."
[2] The upper rooms of an ancient Egyptian house were reached by an outside staircase.—MASPERO, *Manual of Egyptian Archaeology* (English ed.), 1895, p. 11.

These have been removed, but the separate doorways still remain. The old floor of the chapel and bower has also been removed, and replaced by a floor three feet below the original floor. On removing the old floor some of the beams or joists were found to be so firmly fixed into the walls that they had to be sawn asunder, and a few of the ends, of hard oak, yet remain *in situ*. The original beams, which were thick and very numerous, were laid in and then

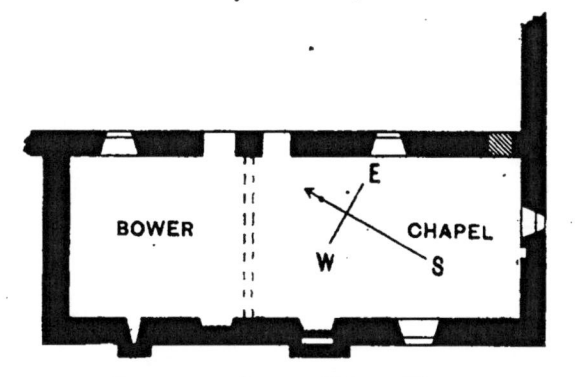

CHAPEL AND BOWER, PADLEY HALL

built over, so that they served to hold the building firmly together. This lowering of the original floor was done in recent times to give greater height to the two upper rooms, which are now used for storing hay. No traces of inner stairs can be found. Existing remains under the blocked-up doorway in the chapel show that the original floor was of thick oak boards.

The bower was lighted by a square-headed window of considerable size looking into the quadrangle. It had formerly also a square-headed window of about the same size on the south-west side, near the wooden partition. The stonework of that window remains in the wall, but there is no trace of it outside, and it must have been built up at an early time. It would appear that some early alterations were made in this wall, and possibly the builder changed his plan whilst the building was being erected. On the summit of the buttress which dies into the wall is a narrow window or pair of small loop-holes. These loop-holes have lancet-shaped heads, and are high up, near the junction of the wall and roof. They are contained within a recess, splayed inwardly, whose top is surmounted by a covering of wooden beams. Both the loop-holes have shallow rebates, as if to hold shutters or the framework of small glass windows. In the wall between the blocked-up window and the loop-holes are two large stones which seem to have been inserted to fill up a recess. Near to these stones the corbel on which one of the pendant posts supporting the roof rests is merely roughly "boasted" or blocked out, as if it was not intended to be exposed to view; the other corbels, which support pendant posts, are carefully moulded and finished. Accordingly the two loop-holes may have been intended to give light to a small inner apartment or closet.[1] There is no fire-place in the walls of the bower. Although the bower was, properly speaking, the women's apartment, it was "very accessible to the other sex."[2]

[1] "One doore taken from the priuie in the said parlor."—MS. of WM. DICKINSON, 1572, in the Author's possession.
[2] WRIGHT'S *Homes of Other Days*, p. 272.

It is not known whether any inner communication existed between the chapel and the bower, though the fact that these rooms were approached through separate doors on the outside is some evidence that there was not. The chapel contains three square-headed windows, and was better lighted than any other room in the building. The upper part of the south-east window, now walled up, retains a part of its tracery. This window served for the east window of the chapel, beneath which an altar may have been placed. On its southern side is a small water-drain, lavatory, or piscina, about a foot square and a foot deep, and nearly two feet from the window. The sill of the south-east window is ornamented beneath by pellet-moulding, exactly like that under the eaves. In the south-west wall is a fire-place, 5 ft. 9 in. wide, which is over the fire-place in the hall below. The fire-place in the chapel [1] may be accounted for by the purposes to which such a room was formerly applied. "We find that when our sovereigns did not attend to public business in the hall, or give audience in their chamber, they used the chapel for that purpose. In the chronicles of the twelfth, and even of the thirteenth century, there are frequent notices of the transaction of secular business in the domestic chapel." [2] There is no reason why the chapel at Padley should not have been used, except in service time, as an ordinary

---

[1] At Heybridge, in Essex, about 1271, there was a "solarium cum capella de constructione Herveii de Borham cum duobus caminis de plastro Paris."—*Domesday of St. Paul's* (Camden Soc.), p. cxix. Here then was a chimney, made of plaster of Paris, in the chapel.

[2] TURNER, *Domestic Arch.*, p. 17, and the authorities there cited.

dwelling room.[1] The roof of the chapel, as well as of the bower, contains a single pair of hammer-beams with one tie-beam in the lath-and-plaster screen which divided the chapel from the bower. In the chapel the ends of the hammer-beams are ornamented by rude figures of angels whose arms support plain shields. In the bower the ends of the hammer-beams are ornamented by plain shields surrounded by cable moulding. No traces of painting or gilding now remain. On the north-east side of the chapel, near the large window, was a doorway leading from the chapel into a long upper room or rooms, which stood on the south-east side of the quadrangle. The south-east wall of this range of buildings yet remains to the height of about twelve feet. In it are very numerous holes for the reception of the beams which supported the floor.

Returning to the outside of the building, there is a pigeon-cote consisting of four rows of pigeon-holes in the gable end above the chapel window. These are part of the original building, and they do not go through into the chapel. Only lords of manors had the right to keep a pigeon-house.[2]

It is probable that the inner walls of the destroyed buildings which surrounded the court were built of wood. This would account for the total destruction of those walls, and the partial preservation of the outer walls. Examples of great houses yet remain in which the walls facing the court are of wood, whilst the outer walls are of stone.

---

[1] At Caddington, in Herefordshire, in 1181, mass was performed three times a week, if required, in the domestic chapel of the manor house.—*Domesday of St. Paul's* (Camden Soc.), p. 147.

[2] ROGERS, *Six Centuries of Work and Wages*, 1884, p. 75.

The outside of the chapel and bower is ornamented just below the eaves by a course of pellet-moulding, reminding us of the *guttae* of a Doric entablature. This is an interesting example of "wooden construction translated into stone," for it represents the ends of the poles or spars which supported the roof. The slates of the roof are modern. The masonry of the outside wall is of large smooth ashlar stones, very well dressed and jointed. At the gable ends, and on the side facing the quadrangle, the masonry is not quite so good, the stones being smaller and less carefully dressed. In the walls are a number of "putlock holes," or *columbaria*, for the scaffolds when the house was being built.

The other rooms or offices, such as the kitchen, brewery, stables, and farm-buildings, were contained in the two sides of the quadrangle which adjoined the hall and buttery.

There are no signs of a moat or any kind of defence, but the house has been completely surrounded by a strong wall which, in some places, is five feet thick. This wall enclosed a quadrangular area of about six acres. It seems to have been a sort of barmkyn, or outer fortification, into which cattle were driven for safety. Quite lately the wall has been sold to a railway company, and the greater part of it removed. The stones in the portion which remains are large; some of the removed stones are said to have been much more so. The outer courses were of stone without mortar. The interior was filled up by grout and rubble.

A little distance up the hill to the east of the house was a small, deep pond, now dry, which may have served for a reservoir to supply the house with water. About 500 yards to the west were the stews or fish-ponds. The railway has gone straight through them.

A house at Charney-Basset near Wantage, in Berkshire, has a hall and buttery on the ground-floor, with a chamber and chapel on the floor above them.[1] In this case the chapel, which is only 12 ft. 5 in. by 9 ft. 10 in., is over the buttery, whilst the chamber, containing a fire-place, is over the hall.

The chapel is separated from the chamber by a stone wall with a small doorway through it. The hall beneath the chamber is 30 feet by 16, and has an original fire-place in it beneath the fire-place in the chamber, and three original windows. It has a door leading into the courtyard. In place of windows the buttery has small loops. As at Padley both the chamber and the chapel have an open timber roof. The chapel, which has two windows, has a piscina and a locker in the wall. As at Padley, too, the entrance to the chamber and the chapel was by steps from the yard.[2] The arrangement of this building, which is ascribed to the end of the thirteenth century, closely resembles the building at Padley in other respects.

A third example may suffice to show that this was a common type of the manor house when built of stone.

---

[1] At Sutton in Middlesex there was "Una aula cum boteleria ad unum caput, cum parva capella ad aliud caput"; and also "unum solarium cum parva capella tegulis coopertum."—*Domesday of St. Paul's* (Camden Soc.), p. cxix.

[2] TURNER, *Domestic Arch.*, p. 153, where see the drawings and plans. Owing to subsequent alterations Turner has mistaken the position of the hall,

In 1464 the manor house of Beaurepaire near Durham is described in an inventory of that date. There was a chapel, an outer chamber (*camera exterior*), an inner or withdrawing chamber (*camera interior*),[1] a hall, a buttery (*promptuarium*), and a kitchen. The outer chamber contained two sheets, two "dormonds," and three bolsters filled with feathers. Its walls and windows were hung with a delicate woollen cloth covered with a tissue of silk. It had a long dining-table with two trestles, a shovel and poker (showing that there was a fire-place), two brass candlesticks, and an iron candlestick fixed to the wall. The inner chamber contained three chests, an old chair, and a stool near the bed (*juxta lectum*). From this we learn that the outer chamber was a women's sitting-room, elegantly furnished and draped, with an inner chamber, *i.e.*, a bed-chamber, adjoining. Such may have been the case at Padley, and possibly also at Charney. The hall at Beaurepaire, which was hung with variegated red say, contained five dining-table leaves (*tabulae mensales*), and four pairs of trestles. There were four long forms and four stools for the high table. As an iron poker is mentioned there must have been a fire-place. The buttery contained four candlesticks, used doubtless in the hall. The kitchen contained a large number of household utensils. In the chapel was a clock with two bells, one of them being larger than the other.[2]

[1] 1567. "The chambre within the greate chambre."—*Richmond Wills* (Surtees Soc.), p. 201. 1444. "Lego eidem optimum bordetbed in le withdrawyng chaumbre... Item lego eidem j lectum plumarium ... in le forchaumbre."—*Test. Ebor.* (Surtees Soc.), ii. p. 101.

[2] *Feodarium Prioratus Dunelm.* (Surtees Soc.), p. 190.

The larger windows at Padley face inwards to the quadrangle or court. Though the country around is very beautiful, the builders of the house did not regard the scenery. Two little windows, 2 ft. 6 in. high and 1 foot broad, in the hall looked outwards, and through them glimpses of the surrounding hills and woods might have been had if the glass were good enough to admit of a view at all. The only view to be had from the bower or women's apartment was through a window which faced a blank wall, or a row of buildings, on the opposite side. Such was the usual way of erecting these houses. Richard Carew, writing of his own county in 1602, says, "The ancient maner of Cornish building was to plant their houses lowe, to lay the stones with mortar of lyme and sand, to make the walles thick, their windowes arched and little, and their lights inwards to the court."[1]

The pleasure of seeing was sacrificed for the advantage of not being seen. Moreover, when glass was rare, or not used at all, country gentlemen could not think of prospects, and they continued to follow the example set by their predecessors. The practice of building in this way was the result of historical tradition. The large Roman villas "at Lydney, Woodchester, Chedworth, and many other places have an extensive cloister or *peristylium*, round all four sides of which the rooms are arranged very like the plan of a mediaeval monastery."[2] The Roman house, with its quadrangle, and its rooms facing inwards, was the type which the builders of such houses as that at

---

[1] *Survey of Cornwall*, ed. 1723, f. 53.
[2] SMITH'S *Dict. of Greek and Roman Antiq.*, i. p. 683.

Padley unconsciously followed, unsuitable as that type was for the English climate. The house at Padley was not expressly built to keep out the sunshine, but it would have served well for that purpose.

It will have been noticed that in the description of the manor houses of Sandon, Kensworth, and Ardleigh nothing is said about upper rooms, and as the descriptions are careful, we may with probability conclude that there were none. At Kensworth the hall was 35 feet long; at Padley it is 32 feet. At Kensworth the hall was 11 feet high when measured to the tie-beams; at Padley it was 12 feet to the ceiling. At Kensworth there was a *domus* between the hall and the bower; at Padley there is an entry or "trance" between the hall and buttery. At both places the relative position of hall and bower was the same, though the bower at Padley was placed over the buttery. It should be noted that the word *búr*, bower, in Old Norse meant buttery. The changes which the word underwent are interesting, for the buttery and kitchen were on the women's side of the house. It is most likely that in early times the word "bower" included the buttery, and was used to describe the whole of the women's side of the house. Even in the thirteenth century "hall and bower" were the essential parts of a manor house, other rooms being mere adjuncts or "appurtenances."[1]

[1] Thus about 1250 the villeins of Blackwell had to provide a wooden house for the Prior of Worcester, built on "forks" or "crucks." "Invenient de suo postes, furcas, ticna, et alia ligna necessaria præter Waldlure ad faciendum aulam, cameram cum pertinentiis, grangiam, boveriam, et coquinam Prioris." — *Registrum Prioratus Wigorn.* (Camden Soc.), p. 65b.

CHAPTER IX.

THE CASTLE AND WATCH-TOWER.

Public character of the English castle—The "keep"—"Toot hills" and the oldest watching-places—Towns built at the feet of castles—The castle at Castleton, Derbyshire, described—Concrete walls of the keep—The angles of the keep directed to the cardinal points—The two rooms of the keep—The concealed roof—Beacons lighted on the summits of towers—Elevated entrance to the keep—The living room of the keep—The garderobe and mural chamber—Curtain rods of the windows—The watchmen employed by the Crown at this castle and elsewhere—No fire-place extant in the keep—The window-like aperture above the concealed roof—Its possible uses—The room in the basement—The cave beneath the keep—The offsets and the lead work—Date of the keep at Castleton—English round keeps compared to Sardinian núraghs—Scottish brocks compared—Church towers used as watch-towers—Elevated position of their doors—"Lanterns" and fire-places in church towers—Church towers used as lighthouses—Church tower at Newcastle controlled by the burgesses—Meaning of " belfry "—Watchmen inhabiting German church towers—Detached bell towers—Circular church towers—Windows facing the cardinal points—Irish and Scotch "round towers" compared—These towers used as watch-towers.

THE public character of an English castle is shown by the fact that it was maintained by a local tax, known as ward-silver, ward-penny,[1] castle-guard, or "waite-fe,". levied on those who dwelt within a defined distance from

[1] *Domesday of St. Paul's* (Camden Soc.), p. lxxviii.—RASTELL'S *Statutes*, 1557, f. 47 b.; *Magna Carta*, s. 29.

its walls. We know that, in one case at least, different tenants contributed towards the maintenance of different parts of the building.[1] It may be noted, by way of comparison, that "Latium was anciently divided into a number of clan-settlements or villages which were an aggregate of dwellings gathered round a central enclosed or fortified space, an *arx* or *castellum*."[2] In England the different villages made separate contributions of castle-guard rent to the castle of their district.[3] A castle was an Acropolis, or place of refuge for the neighbours when plundering enemies invaded the land. It contained a watch-tower, usually known as a keep,[4] and it was always built, if possible, on a hill or rock.

On the tops of many English hills there are enclosures, surrounded by walls of earth, some of which, in early times, were the sites of villages. These are sometimes known as "castles," and they are often called "camps." The ancient inhabitants of Great Britain found that some kind of fortification was necessary for the preservation of their lives and property, and they tried to make themselves safe in pile dwellings or lake dwellings, and, as an alternative to these, on eminences strengthened by art. Like the prehistoric villages in the Po valley, the earth walls of these fortified villages were surmounted by wooden palisades.

[1] See GALE's *Registrum Honoris de Richmond*.
[2] SMITH's *Dict. of Greek and Roman Antiq.*, s.v. *pagus*.
[3] *Notes and Queries*, 8th S., x. 351. In the *Welsh Laws*, ed. by Hubert Lewis, p. 143, the repair of castles is laid down as part of the work of the tenants on a manor.
[4] An old sense of the verb "keep" was to "watch." Compare "He that keepeth Israel shall neither slumber nor sleep."

There were huts within the enclosed villages of the Po valley, and such was the case in Great Britain. As population became more numerous, everybody could not live in an elevated stronghold or in a lake village, and so open settlements in the plain became usual, though people still liked to live within a comfortable distance from their ancient place of refuge. In the end they ceased to inhabit it permanently, but they maintained the earth-walls or substituted stone walls for them, and they threw up a mound, or built a tower, on which the warders kept watch and gave warning of approaching danger. The Roman *oppidum* was the stronghold which commonly overlooked the plain. It was so in ancient Greece. "To detached towers, courts surrounded by masonry were sometimes added as places of refuge for the inhabitants of the neighbouring country and their goods."[1] It was so, too, with the ancient Israelites: "He is my high tower and my refuge." In England the earliest form of watch-tower was an artificial mound known as a "ward-steal," "toot hill," or "touting hill," these words being equivalent to the Latin *specula*, Italian *specchia*, Greek σκοπιά, a watch-tower.[2] Such artificial mounds,

[1] GUHL and KONER, *Life of the Greeks and Romans* (Eng. trans.), 1875, p. 68, where a plan of such a combination in the island of Temnos is given. Compare "*refugium*, geberg," in WRIGHT-WÜLCKER, *Vocab.*, 43, 14.

[2] "*Specula uel conspicilium*, weardsteal."—WRIGHT-WÜLCKER, 180, 3. "*Specula*, a totynghylle,"—*Ibid.*, 797, 20. "Totyng hole or place, or a hyghe hyll to espye all about, *specula*"—HULOET, *Abcedarium*, 1552. The word occurs in German place-names as *spiegel*. Compare the German place-name Wartberg (watch-tower), Spanish *miradéro*, a viewing-place, watch-tower; O. N. *varð-berg*, a "watch-rock"; also O. E. *scēawere*, O. H. G. *scouwa*, watch-tower.

with their surrounding ditches, still exist in considerable numbers. Some are found adjoining enclosed areas or castle yards. Often these mounds are found close to old churches, and then in addition to their use as watching places they were sometimes used as moot-hills, or places on which the moot or local assembly met.

Many English towns are built at the feet of castles. A good example may be seen at Castleton, in Derbyshire, where a castle, anciently known as Peak Castle,[1] protected the neighbourhood for many miles round. Bounded on the west side by a nearly perpendicular abyss, at whose base lies the great Peak Cavern, and on the two remaining sides of a triangular space by steep and all but inaccessible declivities, few strongholds have possessed better natural advantages. Ascending the hill by a zigzag path on the north side next to the town, we enter the triangular area or castle yard by a ruined gateway, on one side of which are some remains of a porter's lodge. The area forms a sloping platform, in whose southern angle stands the watch-tower or keep. The keep is on the highest part of the area, and it is usual for such a building to occupy the highest ground. The wall which still surrounds the area on the north and west sides contains some herring-bone work on the west side. It is a little more than six feet thick, and is now of an average height of nine feet. The wall on the south-east side is modern, and

---

[1] The entry in Domesday is "Terram castelli Will'i peurel in pechefers tenuerunt Gernebern et Hundinc," the words "in pechefers" being written over "castelli." Pechefers may be "Peak forest." The place is called Nordpech in 1173. ("Pipe Rolls.")

seems to have replaced an ancient wall like that on the other two sides, though, for the purpose of defence, a wall on that side would hardly have been necessary. There is no mound or earthwork of any kind within the castle yard, but the ground has been "levelled up" next to the north wall to a height of about eleven feet. Besides the remains of the porter's lodge at the entrance there are some slight remains of a barbican or house on the north wall, as well as of a tower in the north-west angle. It is said that on digging into the area some years ago the "tops of some arches" were discovered.

On the basement floor the walls of the keep are eight feet thick. They are built of concrete made of broken pieces of limestone, which is found on the spot, mixed with mortar. Both the outside and the inside of this concrete wall have been faced with fine and well-jointed blocks of gritstone ashlar, which were brought from a considerable distance. Much of this gritstone facing has been stripped off, or has fallen from two of the outer sides, so that on those sides the concrete is laid almost bare. The concrete is of intense hardness, and holds so well together that little harm has been done to the stability of the building by the removal of its outer facing. We are reminded of the thick Roman concrete walls made of broken stones and lime faced with thin burnt brick. "Walls thus formed were stronger and more durable than even the most solid masonry. Blocks of stone could be removed, one by one, by the same force that set them in place; but a concrete wall was one perfectly solid and coherent mass, which could only be destroyed by a laborious process, like that of quarrying hard stone from its native bed."[1] In the oldest of these walls the concrete was poured into a wooden framework, which was raised as the wall proceeded.

The four angles of the quadrangular keep are directed to the four cardinal points. In other words, if we bisect those angles by two imaginary lines which intersect each other, those lines will point to the north, south, east, and west.

The keep contained two rooms, one above the other. The upper room was surmounted by a roof of good pitch, and, as was usual in rectangular keeps, this roof was concealed by the walls which rose above it. When we consider that these buildings were watch-towers as well as fortresses the reason for this concealment becomes apparent. As the roof was below the rampart walk the watchman's view was uninterrupted, and beacon fires could be more safely lighted, and signals be more easily seen from a distance. Amongst the Romans such fires were lighted on watch-towers to give warning of the approach of freebooters,[2] and the practice was continued through the Middle Ages. In Caxton's *Cronicles of Englond*, printed in 1480, we read "that men shold tende the bekenes that the countrey myght be warned."[3]

The keep was entered not by the opening broken into the lower room on the north-east side (ground

---

[1] Prof. MIDDLETON in SMITH'S *Dict. of Greek and Roman Antiq.*, ii. 188.

[2] "Praedonum adventum significabat ignis e specula sublatus."— CICERO, *Verr.*, ii. v. 35.

[3] In *Hist. Eng. Dict.*, s.v. beacon.

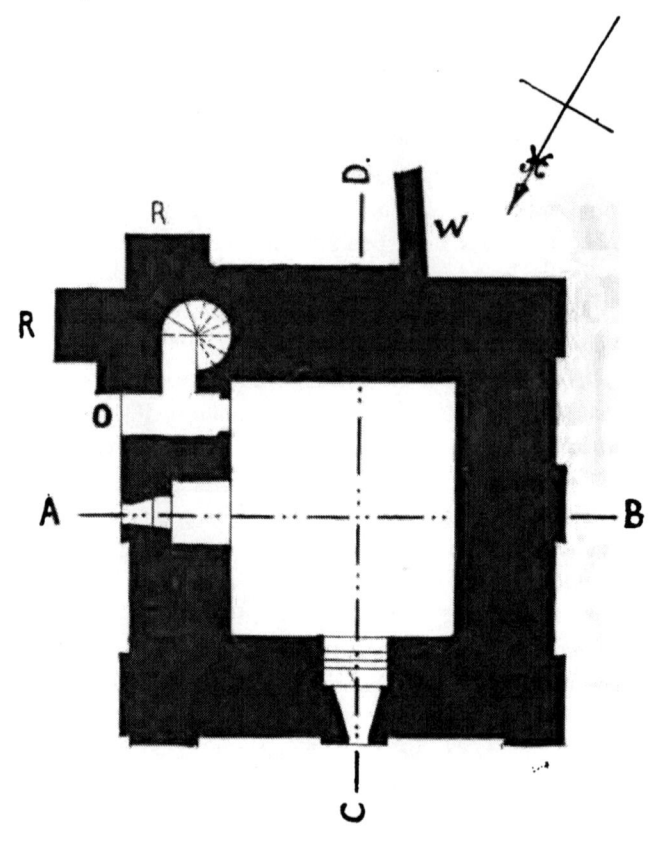

GROUND FLOOR

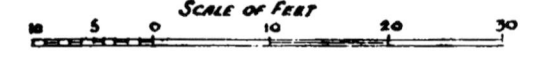

SCALE OF FEET

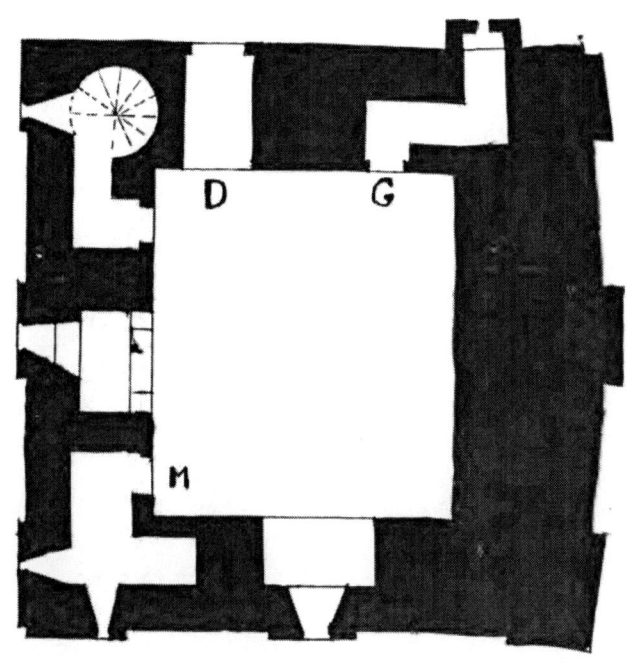

PLAN OF UPPER FLOOR

plan, O), as it is at present, but by an arched doorway (D in the plan of upper floor) opening into the upper room on the south-east side. This doorway, 4 ft. 9 in. wide, is surmounted on the outside by a relieving arch and tympanum. It is 8 ft. 6 in. above the present level of the ground outside.[1] The wall (W) at right angles to the south-east wall seems to be modern.

Passing through the arched doorway we enter the upper apartment or living room. The height of this room was 17 feet to the "square," and 27 feet to the ridge. The length is 22 feet, and the breadth 19 feet. Probably the floor was of wood, but in some castles it is supported by a stone vault. In the thickness of the south-east wall is a gardrobe (G),[2] well concealed from view by a tortuous passage, and having formerly a door at its entrance. The gardrobe projects, like an oriel window without a corbel, over the precipice below, and is lighted by a small window or opening. On the outside it is concealed from view by the later, and apparently modern wall marked "W" on the plan. A narrow doorway, formerly closed by a door, in the north-east wall leads to a mural chamber (M), which has two little windows, one in the north-east and the other in the north-west. It is not known for what purpose this chamber was used, but it would have made a convenient

[1] The entrance to old Scotch houses was "very often by a flight of steps which reaches up to the second story; the floor, which is level with the ground, being entered only by stairs descending within the house."—JOHNSON'S *Journey to the Western Highlands*, ed. 1886, p. 28.

[2] It is engraved in *Arch. J.*, vol. v. 214. An account of this castle by Mr. W. H. ST. JOHN HOPE is given in *Derb. Arch. J.*, xi. 124.

watching-place,[1] bedroom, or store-room.[2] Both the gardrobe and the mural chamber have barrel vaults. The living room is lighted by three narrow windows, the highest of which is in the south-east gable, and ten feet above the floor.

The other windows are in the north-east and north-west walls, and, like the windows in the mural chamber, afford a view on one side of the town beneath, and on the other side of the porter's lodge. The morning and midday sun fell on the gable window, but the other windows are small, and the room was not well lighted. The apertures of the two lower and smaller windows were concealed in the night-time by curtains, for the holes which contained the ends of the curtain rods are there, just below the semi-circular arches which surmount the sides or jambs. There was sufficient room in these recesses to hold beds, but it is more likely that curtains were drawn to make the room warmer by night.

From what has been said it will be seen that this room was intended to be permanently occupied. Fortunately we know from historical records that this keep was used as a watch-tower in the year 1158, and for many years afterwards. The public records show that a porter and two

[1] "Towtynge hoole to look out at in a walle or wyndowe."—HULOET's *Abcedarium*, 1552.
[2] In a description of this castle by Mr. HARTSHORNE in *Arch. J.*, vol. v. 214, it is described as "a small chamber inaccessible," and the plan of it is wrong. The keep has been carefully surveyed by Mr. Edmund Winder, junr., architect, and by Mr. Barton Wells. For their assistance in examining the building at various times the author is much indebted.

SECTION A.B.

SCALE OF FEET
10 5 0 10 20 30

CAVE

SCALE OF FEET

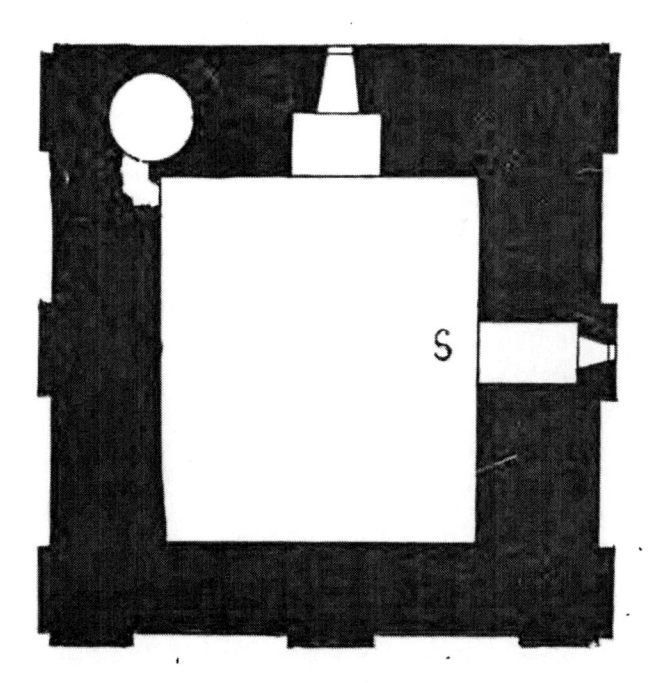

PLAN OF GABLE WINDOW AND WATCHING-PLACE

watchmen (*vigiles*)[1] were employed by the Crown at this place, and received together the yearly salary of £4 10s., which is about £150 of our money. The salaries of the porter and watchmen at other castles are of similar amounts.

At Rockingham Castle in A.D. 1160 a porter and two watchmen got together the yearly salary of £4 11s. 4d. At Worcester in 1163 the only watchman employed received a yearly salary of £1 10s. 5d., and the porter a yearly salary of £2 5s. 7d. At Hanton in 1160 the capellanus, watchmen, and porter got £4 11s. 3d. These salaries were paid to the sheriff of each county out of the Royal Treasury. In 1173 the sum of £45 8s. was paid to twenty knights (*milites*) and sixty foot soldiers at the castles of Nottingham, Peak, and Bolsover, 160 bushels of wheat having been stored at the Peak in the previous year. But this was an extraordinary occasion, and the regular yearly salaries paid to the porter and watchman at Peak Castle—no payments being made to any other persons — show that they were the only officials permanently maintained there.[2] The porter of Peak Castle occupied the lodge at the gate of the enclosure, whilst the watchmen lived in the upper room of the keep. They probably watched in turns, giving signals of approaching danger by hoisting a flag, blowing a horn, or lighting a fire

---

[1] "In liberatione . ii . vigilum et . i . portarii de Pech' iiii . li . et . x . s." *Great Roll of the Pipe* (Pipe Roll Soc.), i. p. 52. Etymologists may consider whether Peche or Pech is cognate with *pagus*, πάγος, in the sense of hill-fort. Compare "beach," cognate with "*fāgus*."

[2] There was a castellan, or constable, but no mention of him is made in the Pipe Rolls.

on the rampart walk. The view from the top is wide and beautiful.

In such a place life would hardly have been bearable in winter without a fire, but there is no trace of either chimney or flue in any part of the building. It will be noticed, however, in the plan (section A B) that the wall on the south-west side of the living room is unpierced by any window, in order, it may be, that a wooden, or perhaps leaden,[1] flue might stand near it. We have already seen in a previous chapter how frequently the flues of ancient fire-places were made of wood and plaster. Such a flue may have been carried through the roof near the opening on the south-west side (S) above the roof which looks so like a window. Unless such a flue existed we are driven to the conclusion that a fire was burnt in an open brazier, thereby filling the room with smoke.

The window-like aperture (S) in the south-west wall above the roof may have been a sheltered watching-place. It may have been what Cotgrave calls "a sentrie, or little lodge for a sentinell, built on high," the origin of our modern sentry box.[2] It will be noticed in the plan that, unlike all the windows below, the floor of this window-like aperture is flat. It is about 6 ft. 5 in. in depth and 4 ft. 1 in. in breadth. The narrow loop-hole at the outer end of the aperture has been crossed horizontally by two iron bars, one at the height of 4 ft. 7 in. above the floor, and the

---

[1] 1507. "To the plommer for casting and working my fummerel of lede," at Little Saxham Hall.—Account in *Prompt. Parv.*, p. 169.
[2] *Dictionarie of the French and English Tongues*, ed. 1632, s.v. *garite*.

other a little above the floor. The adjacent country is highest on this side of the keep, and it was therefore necessary that the watchman should stand, when occasion required, at a greater height than on the other sides, where the country is much more open. It is possible that a cresset light was burnt in this aperture, the flame being protected by a wooden door or shutter kept in its place by the iron bars. The aperture can hardly have been a dormer window.

We may now descend by the circular staircase in the thickness of the wall into the basement or apartment on the ground floor. As usual this basement is at the exterior ground level, whilst the natural slope of the ground within remains unaltered. The height of this room, measured from the highest part of the ground within to the ledges which supported the floor above, was 12 feet, and 17 feet measured from the lowest part of the ground. The entrance to the stairs was closed by a door at the bottom of the staircase, as well as by a door in the living room above. In the basement there are two narrow windows, deeply splayed, "slipped up to," and admitting very little light. Such rooms as this are the rule in keeps of this period, and are regarded by the best authorities as store-rooms.[1] No well has yet been discovered in the basement, as is usual in these buildings, but its pipe may yet be in the wall at the bottom. Strange to say, a small natural cave extends beneath the building, with openings in the cliff on the south-east and south-west sides. A few pieces of zig-

[1] Compare the store-rooms in the basements of many old lofty quadrangular houses in Thessaly, the habitable part being the top story.

zag moulding, which seem to have formed part of some earlier structure, are built into the inner walls of the keep.

There is an offset or ledge on two adjacent sides of the basement, and also beneath the "sentry," not to support a floor, but to diminish the thickness of the wall as it rises. The circular staircase goes from the bottom to the top of the building, so as to supply each floor. At the top it ended beneath a roofed turret, from which a door opened out on the rampart walk. The outer edge of this walk was protected by a wall, now rather less than two feet high. There are no ledges or other evidence of the existence of a story in the roof. The roof itself is entirely gone, but its position is clearly marked by projecting courses of stone or weather-mouldings, which supported the ends of the spars. Remains of the lead which composed the two lateral gutters exist, and it is probable that the roof was made of that material, more especially as lead was found in great abundance in the neighbourhood. Parts of the leaden tube (T) or casing through which the water from the roof was discharged on the north-east side remain in the wall.

The positions of the broad pilaster strips at the angles, as well as in the centres, of the outer facing will be seen on the plans. At each angle of the building was a cylindrical shaft with a neat capital in the Norman style, the shaft at the south angle being very well preserved. Altogether this keep was designed with great ingenuity, and its workmanship is excellent. As a fortress it was impregnable. A few

SECTION C.D

SCALE OF FEET

necessary repairs have been done at the east angle of the keep, the two buttresses (R) at that angle shown on the plan of the ground-floor being new. They are intended to support the building, which seemed weakened by the windows of the staircase and the removal of the outer facing. It appears from entries in the Pipe Rolls that during the years 1172 and 1173 the sum of £113 was spent on works (*operationes*) done at the king's castles of Peak and Bolsover; but the payments made to the watchmen of the Peak at an earlier time seem to indicate that the keep was built before the year 1172. At any rate it cannot be of later date.

Besides the rectangular keep there are in England round keeps, the finest example being that at Conisborough (king's fort), near Doncaster. If we take Mr. Clark's admirable plans and sections of this building[1] and compare them with published plans of those strange round towers, known as núraghs, in Sardinia,[2] the resemblance will be seen to be most striking. These núraghs, like the typical English castle, have walls of great thickness. Their upper stories are reached by staircases in the walls, which wind round the body of the structure as at Conisborough, and "which start either from the ante-room or entrance passage, or from the central hall or chamber." These chambers are "oblong domes"; the lowest room or basement at Conisborough is a "domed vault." As at Castleton and Conisborough, the staircases of the

[1] *Mediaeval Military Architecture*, i. 431 *et seq.*
[2] PERROT and CHIPIEZ, *History of Art in Sardinia*, etc., trans. by GONINO, vol i. pp. 26, 27, 28.

nùraghs lead to terraces or rampart walks on the top, and nearly all the doors point south-east. Such is the case, as we have seen, at Castleton; it is the same at Conisborough. This southern position of the doorways may be a mere chance, and of no importance; but the likeness in other respects is far too strong to be accidental. The Sardinian nùraghs, according to the better opinion, were places of refuge and also watch-towers. From the commanding position of their terraces "the eye could travel over the whole country. At the least sign of danger fires were lighted as signals, which were immediately repeated from one hilltop to another, until the whole country was ablaze with lights."[1]

It is also interesting to compare the thick walls and mural chambers of some English castles with the Scottish "brochs" or "broughs." These are round towers, common in Orkney and Shetland, and also on the adjacent mainland. They have "an outer and inner wall of dry stone, the interstitial space containing little chambers for human habitation, whilst the open central area might be used for cattle."[2] The top is usually reached by a stone staircase which supplies each floor. The tower in the island of Mousa has seven of these chambers, one above the other.[3]

We are so accustomed to regard church towers as bell-

[1] PERROT and CHIPIEZ, *ut supra*, p. 38.
[2] *Hist. English Dict.*, s v. *broch*. The word is from O. N. *borg*, O. E. *burh*, a castle, stronghold. About two miles from Castleton are the remains of a Roman town called Brough.
[3] HIBBERT'S *Shetland;* WORSAAR'S *Danes and Norwegians*, 1852, p. 234.

towers that we are apt to overlook their other uses. They were often used as watch-towers. For example, the imposing tower of Bedale Church, near Richmond, in Yorkshire, "was constructed purposely for defence. As in the keep of Richmond, the enemy might come into the ground-floor by the huge western door, but there they were stopped. The staircase retains its portcullis groove. The existence of the portcullis itself was unknown till it fell, from the effects of a stroke of lightning. All communication with the clock and bells was stopped until it was hacked away. The chamber above is fitted with a fire-place, and even a *templum Clausinæ* (? *Cluacinae*) in stone."[1] In that part of Glamorganshire known as Gower twelve of the sixteen churches "have towers evidently built for defence. The exterior doors, where they occur, are usually insertions."[2] Such towers exist in Lincolnshire and in Cumberland. The church tower sometimes resembles the keep in having its doorway at a considerable height above the ground, so as to be approached by outside steps. Such, for instance, was lately the case at Norton, in Derbyshire, where the doorway, like that of the keep at Castleton, was on the southern side of the tower and six feet above the ground. Under pretence of a "restoration" this doorway has been lately made up, and the outer stairs removed, so that at

[1] LONGSTAFFE'S *Richmondshire*, 1852, p. 56. In the tower of Cockington Church, near Torquay, is a fire-place, etc., on the first floor.
[2] CLARK, *Mediaeval Military Arch.*, i. 114, 117. See also PARKER, *Glossary of Arch.*, 1850, s.v. pele-tower. He says that some church towers were used for habitation and for defensive purposes.

present there is no outer doorway in the tower. The belfry is approached by a ladder as in the Irish round tower, and there has never been a stone staircase. At Royston, near Barnsley, there is a remarkable oriel window in the west side of the tower, a little below the belfry window. It is supported by a long stone bracket or corbel, which gradually dies into the wall, and is surmounted by a similar piece of stone work. Old inhabitants of the village speak of it as "the lantern," whilst others call it a "look-out," and say that a light was burnt in it. About half-way up the tower of Middleham Church, in Yorkshire, "is a stone fire-place, which appears to be of very late date, and is partly composed of ancient tombstones."[1] At Melsonby, in the same county, is a "fortified church tower," which has been described as "a Norman keep in miniature."[1] There is a chimney in the church tower of Thorpe Abbots in the basement on the north side. The flue runs up the wall nine inches square, the smoke escaping from a small loophole,[2] as in the chimney of the crypt at Hornsea, described in the last chapter of this work. The tower of the parish church of St. Nicholas in Newcastle has been repaired by the Corporation of that place from time immemorial.

"It was an acknowledged fact that church bells in the olden times were instrumental in guiding the traveller to his home in the dark nights. The church of St. Nicholas

---

[1] ATTHILL's *Church of Middleham* (Camden Soc.), p. xviii. See other instances mentioned in *Notes and Queries*, 3rd S., xi. 60.

[2] *Archaeologia*, xxiii. 13.

was not only of service in that way, but also as an inland lighthouse. Tennant spoke of the pathless moors of the neighbourhood in the past century, and many a wayfarer who traversed them had reason to bless the lantern of St. Nicholas in the nights of old. History recorded the prominent part which the steeple played during the Civil Wars, when the Scots besieged the town, and the incidents tended to show that the mayor and burgesses had at that time the control, management, and maintenance of the lantern and tower. Again, one of the bells in the steeple was known as the 'common' or 'thief and reever' bell, in consequence of its having been used for the double purpose of summoning the burgesses together for public business, and, it is supposed, of informing thieves, horse, cattle, and sheep stealers on the eve of the annual fairs that they were permitted to enter the town, and that no troublesome questions would be asked. The free burgesses appear to have had some control over the bells and belfry, and they at the present time meet in guild three times in a year, and at their meetings the mayor presides, and is usually accompanied by the sheriff and town clerk. They are summoned to attend the guild meetings by the tolling of the 'common bell,' and on these occasions the ringer is not paid by the freemen, but by the Corporation. The Corporation possess, or did possess formerly, keys to the belfry, and they can require the bells to be rung when they think fit, so long as they do not interfere with divine service. For the use of the bells the vicar and churchwardens have contended, and still contend, that the Corporation are responsible for the keeping in repair of the lantern or steeple."[1]

In Scotch towns the church steeples are often the property of the municipality and not of the church, and the bells in those steeples belong to the municipality.

According to the best authorities the word "belfry" did not originally mean a place in which bells were hung. Its earliest known form is *berfrey*, meaning, "a wooden tower, usually moveable, used in the middle ages in besieging fortifications." Then it came to mean "a tower to protect watchmen, a watch-tower, beacon-tower, etc."[2] Cotgrave defines *beffroy* as "a beacon or a watch-tower from which things may be discerned farre off." In German towns watchmen continued to live in church towers to a late period. "In the fifteenth century," says Beckmann, "the city of Ulm kept permanent watchmen in many of the steeples. In the year 1452 a bell was suspended in the tower of the cathedral of Frankfort-on-the-Maine, which was to be rung in times of feudal alarm, and all the watchmen on the steeples were then to blow their horns and hoist their banners. In the year 1476 a room for the watchman was constructed in the steeple of the church of St. Nicholas. In the year 1509 watchmen were kept both on the watch-towers and steeples, who gave notice by firing a musket when strangers approached."[3] In most, if not in all cities "the town piper, or as we say at present town-

---

[1] *Antiquary*, vol. xxxii. p. 350.
[2] *Hist. English Dict.*; SKEAT'S *Etym. Dict.*
[3] *Hist. of Inventions* (English ed.), 1846, ii. 193.

musician, was appointed steeple-watchman; and lodgings were assigned to him in the steeple."[1]

In some cases the tower, like the Irish and Scotch round tower, was detached from the church. "There are several examples of detached bell-towers still remaining, as at Evesham, Worcestershire; Barkeley, Gloucestershire; Walton, Norfolk; Ledbury, Herefordshire; Chichester, Sussex; and a very curious one, entirely of timber, with the frame for the bells springing from the ground, at Pembridge, Herefordshire."[2] The *clochier* or *campanile* of St. Paul's Cathedral was a separate building.[3] Circular church towers are to be found in some parts of England, as for instance at Little Saxham in Suffolk, and in various parts of Norfolk.[4] These towers are very plain, with the exception of the topmost story, which is usually neatly ornamented. Like the Scotch and Irish round towers, the English towers have four windows in the topmost story facing the cardinal points. As we have seen, the tower of the English castle is sometimes round, like that at Conisborough, which resembles the Irish round tower in having its doorway considerably above the ground.[5]

The construction of the Irish round tower shows that it was primarily intended for a watch-tower, whatever may

---

[1] BECKMANN, *ut supra*, 191. "*Toren bewaerder, toren wachter*, watch-keeper upon a tower, or upon a steeple."—HEXHAM'S *Dutch Dict.*, 1675.
[2] PARKER, *Glossary of Arch.*, 1850, p. 104.
[3] GOMME'S *Primitive Folk-Moots*, 157. The bell of this tower summoned the citizens to the folk-moot.
[4] *Archaeologia*, xxiii., 10 *et seq.*
[5] The distance at Conisborough is twenty feet.

have been its other uses. It is more like a modern lighthouse than anything else. Seventy-six round towers still exist in Ireland. One of the best preserved of these is that on the island of Devenish in Lough Erne. Its height is 85 feet. The doorway is nine feet above the ground. The building is "divided into five stories of unequal height by offsets in the wall, except in the case of the topmost story, which has stone brackets for the support of the floor. ... The upper story has four windows facing the cardinal points, which are each 4 ft. 2 in. in height. ... This tower is a fair representative of the class which exists in Ireland. Their special features are that their average height is from 100 to 120 feet, the average thickness of wall at the base $3\frac{1}{2}$ to 4 feet, and the average internal diameter at the level of the doorway 7 to 9 feet. They taper, and the walls diminish in thickness towards the top. The doorways are mostly at some distance from the ground, as 4, 8, 11, and 13 feet. There are almost always four windows in the upper story facing the cardinal points, and there is never more than one aperture in each of the stories underneath."[1] There are several round towers of exactly similar construction in Scotland. Either they are bonded into a church, or are close to a church. When they form part of a church the entrance is not on the outside, but by an opening in the west gable of the nave.[2] In all these towers, whether

---

[1] ANDERSON, *Scotland in Early Christian Times*, 1881, p. 46. The chief authority on the Irish round tower is PETRIE'S *Inquiry into the Origin and Uses of the Round Tower of Ireland*, 1845.
[2] ANDERSON, *passim*.

English, Irish, or Scotch, the most important part of the building, and the one on which the builder has bestowed the most pains, is the topmost story with its four windows. Every other part of the building is ancillary to this room, in which the watchman could sit and watch.

CHAPTER X.

THE CHURCH OR LORD'S HOUSE

Absence of "municipal buildings" in the Middle Ages—Such buildings in churchyards—Local councils held in the open air—Local councils meeting in churches—The English church known as a basilica in early documents—Secular uses of churches—Courts of justice sitting in ancient Welsh churches—The jurisdiction of ecclesiastical courts—Local councils in north-western Spain—Gradual decline of the secular uses of the church—"Squints" in churches—Schools kept there—A new church involved the establishment of a new free community—The church was the "house" of the lord of a community—The "parish" and the "hreppr"—The rector and his deputy—Chancels owned by lords of manors—Striking resemblance between the crypt in the basilica at Pompeii and the crypts of some English churches—Crypt at Hornsea with a fire-place—Causes heard in the *secretarium* behind the high altar—The form of the open-air court.

THE buildings known as churches will here be considered in their character as basilicas or town-halls, in other words as places where public business was done and justice administered, though it is not denied that they were also temples of religion. These buildings will gain a new interest, or even a new charm, when we see them as they once were—the centre-pieces of the old social life. To understand their structure it will be necessary to glance at their history.

A good authority on architecture has said that "one of the most remarkable characteristics of English architecture, though it is but a negative one, is the almost total absence of any municipal buildings during the whole period of the Middle Ages. The Guildhall of London is a late specimen, and may even be called an insignificant one, considering the importance of the city. There are also some corporation buildings at Bristol, and one or two unimportant town halls in the cities, but there we stop."[1] It was the same in Belgium, where the municipal buildings surpass those of any other country. But "none of these are very old."[2]

When we first meet with "municipal buildings" in England they are usually in a churchyard. According to Anthony à Wood, the old portmoot of the burgesses of Oxford was held in St. Martin's churchyard in and before the time of Henry II.[3]

Before local councils or courts made use of roofed buildings they sat on artificial mounds in the open air. For example, at Stoneleigh, in Warwickshire, the court of the sokemen used to be held on a hill called the Mootstow-hill (*i.e.*, assembly-place hill), near that town. It was so called because pleading was done there. But after the abbots of Stoneleigh had acquired the said court and liberty for the easement of the tenants and suitors, they made a court-house in the midst of the town of Stoneleigh.[4]

---

[1] FERGUSSON, *Hist. of Architecture*, ii. 413.
[2] *Ibid.*, ii. 199.   [3] *Archaeologia Oxon.*, i. 274.
[4] "Curia de Stonle ad quam sokemanni faciebant sectam solebat ab antiquo teneri super montem iuxta villam de Stonle vocatam Motstowehull, ideo sic dictum quia ibi placitabant sed postquam abbates de

There seems to be no evidence of the existence of a town-hall at Stoneleigh, and it is likely that the "court-house" was the church. To pass in another case from likelihood to certainty we find that as late as 1472 the parishioners of two parishes in Yorkshire are reported to the Archbishop of York for holding their local council in the church and churchyard.[1] The practice had been forbidden two centuries before,[2] but customs die hard, and it is not surprising to find the old practice lingering on even in the fifteenth century.

"One of the canons of the Scots church," says Mr. James Logan, "prohibited the laity from holding courts in churches. This injunction was unnecessary, if meetings had not been at first held in them which were inconsistent with their sacred appropriation. From this, and some other reasons I shall adduce, I have formed an opinion that moothills were first raised for such purposes as churches were considered unfit for."[3] The truth is that moothills were the original seats of assemblies afterwards held in

Stonle habuerunt dictam curiam et libertatem pro aysiamento tenencium et sectatorum fecerunt domum curie in medio ville."—*Stoneleigh Reg.* f. 75 in VINOGRADOFF's *Villainage in England*, p. 367. The council of sokemen usually consisted of twelve men as in the "Twelve Men" of St. Austell's in Cornwall, the Twelve Feoffees of Hornsea, the Twelve Capital (or Church) Burgesses of Sheffield, the Twelve Lawmen of Stamford and Lincoln, etc.

[1] "Dicunt quod omnes parochiani ibidem tenent plebisitum, et alias ordinaciones temporales, in ecclesia et cimiterio."—*York Fabric Rolls* (Surtees Soc.), p. 256.

[2] INDERWICK, *The King's Peace*, p. 13.

[3] *Archaeologia*, xxii. 200. SKENE'S *Acts of Parliament of Scotland*, 388.

churches. Mr. G. L. Gomme has given instances of courts held in English churches, and he cites Ritson on *Court Leets*, who says that "the stewards or bailiffs of a leet would, in bad weather, occasionally hold courts in the church, where, notwithstanding a canon, it is in many places still held."[1]

The English parish church was known as a basilica at least as early as the seventh century,[2] and it had not ceased to bear that name in the Latin documents of the fifteenth century.[3] It was habitually used not only as a court of justice, but as a place in which most kinds of public business could be lawfully done. The evidence on this point is abundant, but only a brief epitome can be given here.

At Exeter in 1358 public banqueting and drinking in the church, especially in the choir, were forbidden.[4]

Grosseteste, bishop of Lincoln, directed that "markets were not to be held in sacred places, seeing that the Lord cast out those who bought and sold from the temple."[5]

---

[1] *Primitive Folk-Moots*, 53, 59, 115.

[2] An authentic inscription recording the dedication of Jarrow church in 685 contains the words, "dedicatio basilicae Sancti Pauli."—*Inventories, etc., of Jarrow and Monk-Wearmouth* (Surtees Soc.), p. xxvi.

[3] 1458. Commission to John Bishop of Philippolis "ad consecrandam basilicam infra villam de Colthorp . . . . . . cum cimiterio."—*York Fabric Rolls* (Surtees Soc.), p. 240. In 1480 there was a commission to the Bishop of Dromore to consecrate "basilicam, et cemiterium in villa de Lamley de novo constructam."—*Ibid.* p. 241.

[4] *Archaeologia*, xviii. 412.

[5] "Praecipimus etiam firmiter auctoritate Evangelica et etiam de speciali indulgentia apostolica ne in locis sacris habeantur mercata; cum Dominus ementes et vendentes de templo ejecerit."—*Roberti Grosseteste Epistolae*, ed. LUARD, p. 161.

In 1275 deeds were kept in a chest behind the high altar of St. Paul's Cathedral.[1] In 1409 we read of men and boys making an uproar and playing in York Cathedral, even whilst mass was being said. And it was complained that the sacristans did not thrash mad dogs (*furiosos canes*) and those who disgraced themselves or did business in the church.[2] In 1504 the accounts of certain executors were to be audited yearly in St. Mary's Church at Bury St. Edmunds.[3] Marriage settlements were executed and serfs manumitted at the church door. In 1510 pedlars sold their wares on feast days in the church porch.[4] In 1601 mortgages were paid off in the south porch of Ecclesfield church in Yorkshire.[5] In 1665 bread was stored in churches. The "walks in Paul's" are mentioned by the Elizabethan dramatists, and the nave of the cathedral was used, like a Roman basilica, as an exchange mart. "Perhaps the most remarkable survival of Roman institutions in Britain was the practice of the old order of serjeants-at-law who assembled in the nave of old St. Paul's Cathedral, each serjeant having been allotted a special pillar in the cathedral at his appointment, where he met his clients in legal consultation, hearing the facts of the case, taking notes of the evidence, or pacing up and down."[6] Bishop

---

[1] *Household Roll of Bishop Swinfield* (Camden Soc.), p. cxxx.
[2] *York Fabric Rolls* (Surtees Soc.), p. 244.
[3] *Bury Wills* (Camden Soc.), p. 97.
[4] *York Fabric Rolls, ut supra*, p. 271.
[5] Court Rolls in the possession of the Duke of Norfolk. On the Sunday before Candlemas, 1318, the execution of a deed relating to land was witnessed in Felkirk church near Barnsley by all the parishioners.—*Yorkshire Arch. Journal*, xii. 257.
[6] G. L. GOMME in *Contemp. Review*, May, 1896, p. 694.

Bonner in 1552 forbade any manner of common plays to be played, set forth, or declared in churches or chapels. As late as the seventeenth century Yorkshire people danced in their churches at Christmas.[1] Notice of the holding of the Court Baron of the manor was published in Hathersage church in 1656.[2] At Ashburton in Devonshire, "the annual court leet and court baron of the manor lords is held alternately by their stewards in the chapel of St. Laurence."[3]

The ancient Welsh laws show that churches were regularly used as courts of justice. Theft was denied by the defendant at church upon a relic. "Let the judge," it is said, "require of him his oath, with that of two men nearest to him in worth; and that in a week from the succeeding Sunday, at the church where his sacramental bread and holy water shall be."[4] If a man made a false appraisement the church proceeded against him for perjury.[5] If a man did not pay a fine which he had been ordered to pay, then "let the church proceed against him and let him pay the debt in full."[6] Relics, we are told, were not necessary "in causes carried on in the churchyard, or in the church; because it is the place of the relics."[7] In a case of debtor and surety judgment was given in the church.[8] In many other places in the Welsh laws churches are incidentally referred to as courts of justice. But

---

[1] AUBREY'S *Remaines of Gentilisme*, pp. 5, 213.
[2] MS. in the Author's possession.
[3] A. J. DAVY in *Notes and Queries*, 8th S., xii. p. 32.
[4] *Welsh Laws*, ii. 235.   [5] *Ibid.*, ii. 35.
[6] *Ibid.*, i. 135.   [7] *Ibid.*, ii. 37.   [8] *Ibid.*, i. 115.

litigious business was transacted on weekdays and not on Sundays.[1] Inquisitions, however, by the king's sheriff were held in England as late as the thirteenth century on Sundays.[2]

The Welsh practices just referred to belong to the ninth or tenth century. The jurisdiction of English churches in matters of civil and criminal law extended to a much later period. At Ripon, for example, in the fifteenth century we find the chapter of the collegiate church there dealing with a great variety of questions which now are only within the cognizance of non-ecclesiastical courts of law. The chief matters with which they dealt were testamentary cases, and next to these in point of number came actions of debt. They also dealt with acknowledgments of tenure, affiliation, defamation of character, matrimonial cases, and breaches of promise of marriage, perjury, theft, etc.[3] This judicial process was similar to the practices of other ecclesiastical courts. It does not appear in what part of the collegiate church of Ripon the court sat. At Durham it sat in the galilee of the cathedral.

If we turn to north-western Spain we shall see how these earlier usages of the church have survived to modern times. The local government there "has been purely democratic; the council, which consists of all the *vecinos* (neighbours), assembling on Sundays at the summons

---

[1] *Welsh Laws*, ii. 70.

[2] *Yorkshire Inquisitions* (Yorkshire Arch. Soc.), *passim*.

[3] Acts of Chapter of the Collegiate Church of SS. Peter and Wilfrid, Ripon, A.D. 1452 to A.D. 1506 (Surtees Soc., 1875).

of the church bell."[1] It was the lord's day, *dies dominicus*, as our old charters have it, and in Spain his council met on Sundays. This Spanish case is only an accidental survival of what was once the universal practice in Western Europe. Traces of secular uses of the churches may be seen everywhere.[2] The history of the Christian Church has been, in a large measure, a history of the decline of her secular power. The transition from the basilica-temple to the temple has been going on for a very long period, and the change is not yet fully carried out, even though the royal arms have been removed from every parish church in England.

The fabrics of our churches still continue to puzzle the antiquary. Who, for instance, can explain those strange apertures, known as "low side windows," which are found in the chancels of so many of these buildings? Nor is it easy to say what is meant by the very numerous oblique holes known as "squints." In this case, however, we have a clue which may lead to the truth. The greatest number of squints are in the wall adjoining the south side of the chancel arch, and they point directly to the south door or main entrance to the building, in such a way that a person standing at the door can see straight through the hole to the place now occupied by the altar or communion table. "In Bridgewater Church, Somerset, there is a series of these openings through three successive walls, following the same oblique line, to enable a person standing in

---

[1] *Quarterly Review*, vol. clxxxii. p. 484, where much valuable information on this subject is given.
[2] See some examples in GRIMM's *Rechtsalterthümer*, p. 805.

the porch to see the high altar."[1] Thus wrote a good authority on church architecture. But in ancient times "the altar was placed at the end of the nave, on the chord of the apse."[2] It stood directly under the chancel arch, so that "squints," if they existed in early times, cannot have been intended to enable people to see the elevation of the Host at the altar. The object of the opening seems rather to have been to enable a man standing within the door of the porch to see the high seat occupied by the president of an assembly sitting in the chancel. That man must have been a door-keeper, as in an old English poem written about 1330:—

"In the ealde lawe dore-ward
Lokede dore and yate.

* * *

"So doth thes dore-wardes eke
In holy cherche nouthe."[3]

The *ostiarius* or door-ward is described by Shoreham as the first of the seven orders of the church, though the lowest in rank. It is remarkable that in the serio-comic language of the Edda a door-keeper or usher kept watch over the entrance to the hall of the gods, tossing up seven short swords at once, and from this we may perhaps infer that in public ceremonies a door-keeper with a drawn sword kept the door of an old northern hall or palace. In the church it is likely that the door-keeper stood in such a position that he could see the face of the president

[1] PARKER'S *Concise Glossary of Architecture*, 1875, p. 258.
[2] FREEMAN'S *Architecture*, p. 155.
[3] *Poems of William de Shoreham*, ed. WRIGHT (Percy Soc.), p. 46. Perhaps we ought to read "mouthe."

through the "squint," and be able to take orders from him either directly, or indirectly through the medium of an official sitting near the inner opening of the "squint."

The "usher" of a school, not unlike the Usher of the Black Rod in the House of Commons, was originally an *ostiarius* or door-keeper. He was so called because, in addition to keeping the door of a church, he taught his pupils in the porch. A reminiscence of this practice may be found in the form of "*testamur*," which is given by the "masters of the schools" at Oxford to an undergraduate who has passed "responsions," and in which it is certified that the candidate "*quaestionibus magistrorum scholarum in parviso pro forma respondit.*" Here "*parvisus*" is the "parvis" or porch of a church or other building. The practice of teaching in the porch of a church was borrowed from the Romans; there was direct continuity between the Roman and the English method. Amongst the Romans "the elementary schools and those of the *grammatici* were usually held in a verandah partly open to the street, and the schoolroom is accordingly called *pergula, taberna,* or *porticus.*"[1] The stone seats so often to be seen in the porches of churches may have been the benches on which children or catechumens once sat whilst they were under the instruction of the "usher," and before their admission to the full privileges of the church. Evelyn, in his *Memoirs*, says "that one Frier taught us in the church porch at Wotton."[2]

[1] SMITH's *Dictionary of Greek and Roman Antiq.*, ii. 97*a*, and the authorities there cited.
[2] *Memoirs*, 2nd ed., 1819, vol. i. p. 3.

A tradition exists amongst some of the villages in the High Peak of Derbyshire, such as Hope and Tideswell, that school was held in the church porch. Some church porches have rooms over them, others have inner galleries approached by inner staircases.[1] At Hornsea, in East Yorkshire, school was held in the south aisle of the nave down to about 1850.

The ancient Welsh laws declare that "if a town have leave from the lord of the country to build a church and to bury the dead in its cemetery, then that town becomes free, and all its inhabitants (*homines*) are thereafter free."[2] To build a church for the first time in a town was to create a new "liberty." In England there are many ancient divisions known as liberties, and at Ripon invasion of the liberty was a complaint frequently brought before the ecclesiastical court.[3] A new church, then, was the nucleus of a new liberty or free community. Such a church was the "house" or public hall of a new lord, who presided over that community. It was the "house" of the village chief, or, to adopt the modern term, of the lord of the manor. Now the word "church," according to the best modern scholars, is derived from κυριακόν, the lord's house. The Latin word *dominicum* and the Irish *domhnach* are used in the same sense. In the same way basilica is βασιλική, the king's house, lord's house,[4]

---

[1] See description in *Notes and Queries*, 8th S., x. 396, xi. 9.
[2] "Si villa habeat a domino patrie licentiam eclesiam edificare, et in cimetirio ejus corpora sepelire, tunc villa libera fit, et omnes homines postea sunt liberi."—*Welsh Laws*, ii. 873.
[3] *Ripon Chapter Acts* (Surtees Soc.), *passim*.
[4] Lange shows that in Plato's time the Athenian "king's hall" was called βασιλική.—*Haus und Halle*, 97, 153.

so that church and basilica are virtually identical terms. Judging from the Spanish evidence the court held in the church seems to have been originally analogous to the old Greek *ecclesia*, the assembly of citizens summoned by the crier, as in Western Europe it was summoned by the church bell or by the "moot horn."

The district attached to the new "liberty" was the parish, παροικία, a word which in the later civil law was applied to a rural commune, or community of peasant farmers.[1] The word was sometimes used in the sense of a judge's district.[2] The English parish had some resemblance to the Old Norse *hreppr*, or poor-law district. "It is ordained in our laws," says the compiler of Grágás, "that we have lawful villages (*hreppar*) in our country. That is a lawful village in which twenty or more husbandmen (*böndr*) dwell. It is lawful for them to divide the village into five or four divisions for distributing food, and for apportioning the tithe."[3] Such divisions seem to be identical with the districts known in some parts of England as byrlaws. At Ecclesfield, in Yorkshire, the four byrlaws into which the parish was divided made separate contributions to the church. Each byrlaw had its own collectors.[4] The rector of a parish was formerly known as the "town

---

[1] Smith's *Dict. of Christian Antiq.*, ii. 1554*b*.
[2] See *parochia* in Maigne D'Arnis. In Iceland, during the heathen times, a new temple became the nucleus of a new community or goðorð.
[3] *Grágás*, i. 443.
[4] Gatty's *Ecclesfield Registers*, 153 *et seq.*

reeve" or "person."[1] Whether we call him villicus, agent (*actor*), curator, procurator, rector, town-reeve, parson, or bailiff, he was still the fiscal officer of his district, and as such responsible only to his master the bishop.[2] He was entitled to the chief seat in the chancel.[3] As such he was a man of dignity, "the person," or, as we should say, "your Honour," or "your Reverence."[4] A curious proof of the way in which the rector was regarded as the owner of the chancel may be seen in an order of council of the year 1307 when rectors of churches were ordered not to presume to cut trees down in churchyards, except when the chancel required repair.[5] In a recent case, where the Duke of Norfolk claimed the ownership of the chancel of the parish church at Arundel, it was held that the evidence showed that the chancel "had always been the property of the Duke and his predecessors in title."[6]

The chancel was the tribunal ($\beta\hat{\eta}\mu\alpha$)[7], and was the plat-

---

[1] "*Uillicus, uel actor, uel curator, uel procurator, uel rector*, tungerefa."—WRIGHT-WÜLCKER, *Vocab.*, 111, 13. "*Hic rector*, a person."—*Ibid.*, 680, 38. "Túngeréfa, rector pagi vel pagelli."—GRIMM'S *Rechtsalterthümer*, 757.

[2] LAPPENBERG, *England under the Anglo-Saxon Kings*, ii. 328.

[3] PHILLIMORE'S *Eccl. Law*, 1873, p. 1807.

[4] "Laicus quidam magnæ personæ ad nos veniens dicebat," etc — MAIGNE D'ARNIS, s.v. *persona*.

[5] RASTELL'S *Statutes*, 1557, f. 56. It seems that the *culacium* or *colacium* of an ox-house was sometimes built by the lord, whilst the tenants built the ox-house itself. See *Domesday of St. Paul's* (Camden Soc.), p. 48.

[6] 49 *Law Journal Reports*, C.P., 782.

[7] PHILLIMORE'S *Eccl. Law*, p. 1777.

form from which the speaking was done. The chancel screen was the lattice of open work behind which sat the lord and his assessors. It was the presbytery or seat of the elders, and it does not appear to have been known in

SECTION OF CRYPT, POMPEII
(From Lange)

England as the "choir" till the end of the thirteenth century.[1]

One of the strongest proofs that the oldest English churches were true basilicas is to be found in certain crypts

[1] The earliest quot. in the *Hist. Eng. Dict.* is of the year 1297. The word πρεσβύτερος was sometimes applied to the "headman" of a village. See authorities in SMITH'S *Dict. of Christian Antiq.*, ii. 1699a.

which still exist under the floors of churches. These crypts have such a striking resemblance to the subterranean chamber beneath the tribunal of the basilica at Pompeii, that they must all have been intended for the same purpose.

"At the west end," says Dr. Lange, "of the great hall" of the Pompeian basilica, "are three rooms. The middlemost of these is the tribunal, which is raised 5½ feet above the floor of the great hall, and is 32 feet broad and 18 ft. 2 in. deep. On the sides of the tribunal are two side rooms about 18 feet broad, such rooms being separated from the tribunal by two small staircases, and their floors being on a level with the side aisles. Their back walls are in a straight line with the back wall of the tribunal. The anterior enclosing walls of the staircases end towards the side rooms in three-quarter pillars. From the side rooms small doors lead into the staircases in which stairs, divided into two, four, and again two steps, lead into a subterranean chamber lying 11 feet beneath the tribunal. This chamber, lighted up on its hind wall by two small cellar windows,[1] is connected with the floor above by two irregular holes (A A) whose ancient origin is probable, but not certain. As the doors of the subterranean chamber could not be locked, the hitherto prevailing opinion that it was a prison or treasure room is untenable. Probably it served for depositing objects

---

[1] Beneath the present east window of Middleham church, in Yorkshire, "are two low plain square windows (now blocked up), which have been considered by some to have been the windows of a former crypt."—ATTHILL's *Church of Middleham*, p. xvii.

which were required in proceedings at law."[1] The basilica was built about 93 B.C.

Let us put the plan of this subterranean chamber and that of the crypt at Repton in Derbyshire side by side. The only material difference between the two crypts lies in the fact that at Repton the back walls of the "side rooms," otherwise the aisles, are not, as in the Pompeian basilica, flush with the east wall of the chancel. In some churches, however, as, *e.g.*, at Sheffield, where there is a crypt,[2] the back or east walls of the aisles of the chancel are flush with the back or east wall of the chancel. "In the western angles [of the crypt at Repton] are two passages communicating by flights of steps with the church above."[3] This crypt was discovered in the last century by an accident. A workman preparing a grave in 1779 for Dr. Prior, the deceased headmaster of the school, was suddenly precipitated into it.[4] "In the south-west division is the repair of a hole broken through the vault."[5] Similar holes are found in other crypts. At Hexham, "nearly in the centre of the vault, which shows some traces of the characteristic Saxon dressing, are traces of a small rectangular opening, like one in a similar position in the crypt at

---

[1] LANGE, *Haus und Halle*, p. 352.

[2] In this crypt there was a staircase on each side of the tribunal, that on the south side being now covered over, but used for gaining access to a vault. There is also a "cellar window" in the east wall as at Repton.

[3] Cox, *Churches of Derbyshire*, iii. 434.

[4] Cox, *ut supra*.

[5] *Derb. Arch. Journal*, v. p. 170. The opening at Ripon is covered by a stone slab. It resembles a "manhole."

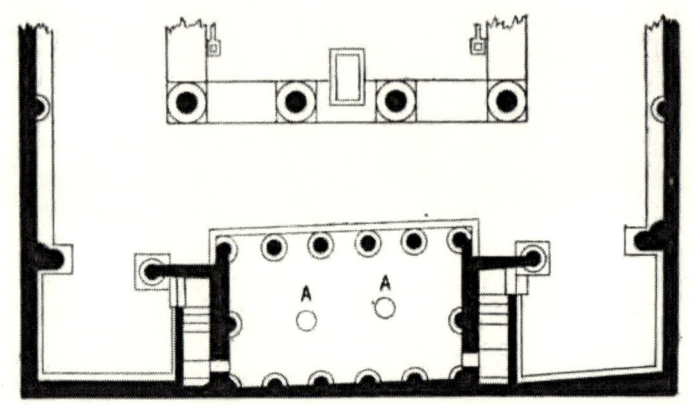

TRIBUNAL OF POMPEIAN BASILICA
(From LANGE'S *Haus und Halle*)

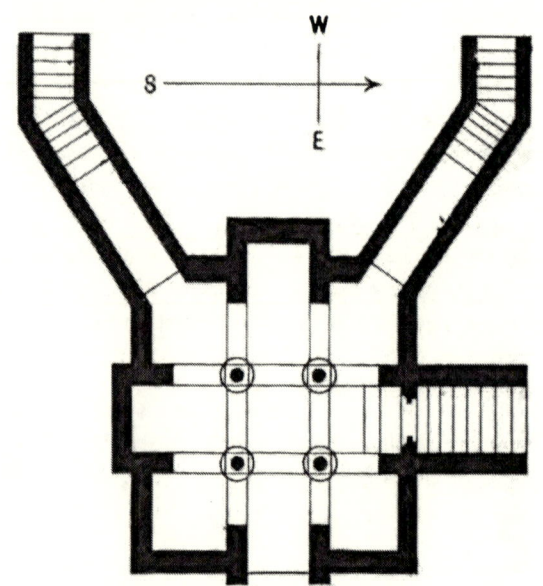

PLAN OF CRYPT AT REPTON
(From LYSONS' *Derbyshire*)

Ripon; but for what purpose it has been used (the coincidence inclining me to think it is not merely accidental) it is not easy to conjecture."[1] "The area of the crypt [at Repton] is nearly 17 feet square. The roof, of vaulted stone, is supported by four spirally-wreathed columns, with plain square capitals, and by eight fluted responds

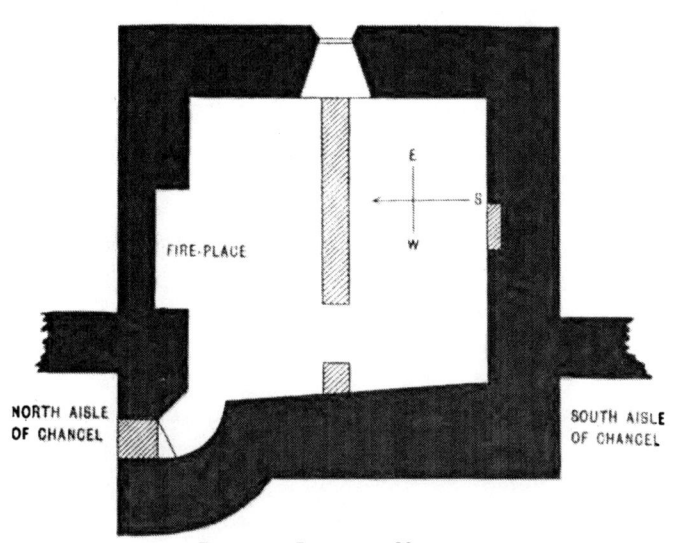

PLAN OF CRYPT AT HORNSEA

against the walls."[2] In the east wall, under the chancel window, is a window for admitting light to the crypt. The entrance on the north side is of later date than the rest of the building. It is not, therefore, an original entrance, and it is in the position occupied by the fire-place of the

---

[1] RAINE'S *Hexham Priory*, ii. p. xxxix.   [2] COX, *ut supra*.

crypt at Hornsea to be presently described. The roof is plastered, and there are remains of coloured decoration on the capitals of the pillars. The stones are smooth, as though they had been polished with sand. The architecture is Roman, or Romanesque. Brixworth church, Northamptonshire, built chiefly of Roman bricks, has an apse surrounded by a corridor or crypt entered by steps from the chancel.[1]

A crypt under the east end of the chancel of Hornsea church in East Yorkshire differs from that at Repton in having a fire-place, 6 ft. 2 in. wide and 3 ft. 2 in. high, on its north side, and only one staircase, viz., in the north-west corner. It is probable, however, that there was a corresponding staircase in the south-west corner. The tomb of Anthony St. Quentin, the last rector, who died in 1430, stands above that corner, so that the entrance to the staircase may have been built up. In shape the crypt approaches to a square measuring 15 ft. 5 in. from north to south, and, in the north compartment, 14 ft. 2 in. from east to west. In the south compartment the measurement from east to west is about a foot less. In the east wall is a window splayed inwardly to a width of nearly 4 feet, and diminishing to 1 ft. 8 in. in the narrowest part. The crypt is at present approached by a ladder under a trap-door over the staircase in the north-west corner, and near the modern altar steps. In 1840 we are told that "there is a vaulted crypt beneath the chancel; the entrance is by a flight of steps under the farthest arch."[2] The width of the staircase

[1] SMITH's *Dict. of Christian Antiq.*, i. 386, where see a plan There appears to be a staircase on each side.
[2] POULSON's *Holderness*, i. 330.

so far as it can now be traced is 2 ft. 7 in., and the lowest of the old stone steps is yet in its place. The steps led into the north "side room," or aisle, of the chancel, the approach being now closed by a modern wall. The chancel has aisles, in three small bays, on the north and south sides. There are holes in the jambs of the fire-place, as if for the insertion of iron bars, and both the jambs and the mantel-piece are rebated on the inner edge to the depth of an inch and a half, either for ornament or to hold a chimney-board when the fire-place was not in use. The tapering flue of the chimney goes up the wall to the height of six feet above the level of the ground outside, when it is turned out by a neat curve, the aperture being a horizontal hole, like a small loop-hole laid on its side, immediately under the sill of the large north window above. The hole measures 10 inches horizontally, and $3\frac{1}{4}$ inches vertically, and its edges, as well as the adjoining sill of the window, are much blackened by smoke. Besides the great east window of the chancel there are two side windows adjoining, one in the north and the other in the south, all three being supported by the walls of the crypt, and the space included by them forming a kind of apse. The walls of the crypt, as inferred from their thickness in the small east window, are three feet thick. They are built of sea cobbles, and the crypt seems to have been plastered within. The little window is protected by iron bars. There seems to have been a niche or cupboard in the south wall. It is now built up, and only the topstone or head-piece remains. The outside walls above the crypt are built of excellent masonry. The roof of the crypt is unhappily of modern brick, and has been raised about a foot to give height to modern altar steps. This is much to be regretted, as the old church floor was flat. A brick wall, with a foundation of sea cobbles, now divides the crypt into two parts, and excludes much of the light which once shone through the window. From the top of this wall two modern brick barrel arches spring, their opposite sides resting on the north and south walls of the crypt. The extreme height of the arches is 6 ft. 10 in. There is a legend in the village that, once upon a time, the crypt was inhabited by a being called Nanny Cankerneedle. Possibly "cankerneedle" refers to the hot iron rod which caused a "canker" in the hands of the guilty after the ordeal by fire. The name will remind the reader of St. Wilfrid's needle in the crypt at Ripon. There was a church at Hornsea in 1086,[1] but the present building does not seem older than the fourteenth century. The crypt, however, may have been built before the Conquest.

Under the east end of a Coptic church at Cairo is a crypt eight or nine feet below the surface of the church. It measures about 17 by 20 feet, and is approached by two flights of steps. In the north wall is a recess corresponding in position to the fire-place at Hornsea. In the opposite or south wall is a corresponding recess, as at Hornsea. There is also a recess in the middle of the east wall where the window should be, and where an altar now stands.[2]

In the old English church the altar did not stand at the

---

[1] *Domesday Book.*
[2] MICKLETHWAITE in *Archaeologia*, xlviii. 405, where plans, etc., are given.

east end of the chancel, but the apse, anciently known as the "shot," was behind the altar.[1] Such, probably, was the case at Repton and Hornsea. Amongst its other names the English chancel was known in mediaeval Latin as *secretarium*. Now "from the fifth century causes were exclusively heard in the *secretarium* or *secretum*. The public was shut off by *cancelli* and curtains (*vela*), which in exceptional cases were drawn aside."[2] The "side rooms" or aisles of numerous chancels resemble those at Hornsea, and these "side rooms" were commonly divided from the central room of the chancel by lattices or open wooden screens, many of which still remain. Elyot, in his Latin Dictionary, 1542, says that "*cinclidæ*[3] are bayes or parclosis made about the places of judgment, where men not being sutars may stand, beholde, and here what is done amonge the juges and pledours. Such a lyke thing is at Westminster Hall about the common place, and is called the bekens."

We have just seen that pleading was done on the Moot-stow-hill at Stoneleigh. Some of these open-air courts still remain in a more or less complete form, and they are often near old churches. In such an open-air court the judge sat on a round mound. Below on the left-hand of the judge sat the plaintiff; on his right hand sat the defendant.

---

[1] A vocabulary of the tenth or eleventh century has: "*Propitiatorium, uel sanctum sanctorum, uel secretarium, uel pastoforum,* gesceot bæftan þæm heahweofode." — WRIGHT-WÜLCKER, *Vocab.*, 186, 20. "Chamber wherin a sexten of a churche or like churche keper doth lye—*Pastophorium*."—HULOET's *Abcedarium*, 1552.

[2] SMITH's *Dict. of Greek and Roman Antiq.*, i. 248.

[3] That is κιγκλίδες.

According to the ancient Welsh laws "the lord is to sit with his back to the sun or wind, lest he be incommoded by the sun, if powerful, or by the wind, if high. And the judge is to sit before the lord, so that he may hear and see each of the two parties to the suit. And the defending party is to sit on the lord's right hand, and the claiming party on the left; because the right is to support, and the left to claim."[1]

This description can only apply to an open-air court, and, as the court was held in the morning, the lord must have sat in the east, with his face to the west. In this respect the indoor court was a copy of the outdoor court.

[1] *Welsh Laws*, ii. 203. The Continental practice, as in the Pompeian basilica, was for the judge to sit in the west. On this point see the quotation in GRIMM's *Rechtsalterthümer*, p. 807. Italian churches are not oriented.

SUMMARY

THE main results attained in the foregoing pages may now be given in a brief summary.

The earliest remains of houses, properly so called, in Great Britain are of a round shape, with a central open hearth. They were built of wood or basket work. Light was admitted by the door, or by the aperture in the roof which formed a vent for the smoke. Such houses were made wind-and-water tight by a plastering of mud-clay. They appear to have been thatched with reeds or heather. The so-called beehive houses are imitations in stone of these round houses. Many prehistoric round houses were probably built of mud.

Holes in the earth and cave-dwellings are older than the round houses just mentioned. They belong to a very remote antiquity, and can hardly be called houses at all. They are little better than the burrows of the rabbit or fox.

The beehive houses show a tendency towards a rectangular form. The rectangular house, however, was not evolved from the round house, but from the temporary booth or tent built by shepherds for their summer residences on the mountains or summer pastures. Such a booth was erected by placing two wooden "forks" or "crutches" at a convenient distance apart, and extending a ridge-tree from the apex of one "fork" to the apex of the other. The framework so made was covered with whatever material was most suitable for use.

The rectangular house was evolved from such a booth or tent. The way in which this was done can be well illustrated by noticing how children build houses with packs of cards. First they incline a pair of cards towards each other so as to make a kind of tent, and then they adjust the cards all round the tent in such a way as to make the outer walls upright and to leave the sloping tent within. In these toy houses the whole tent stands within; in the rectangular house of real life only the triangular wooden framework of the tent stands within.

The booth which was supported by a couple of "forks" might be extended to any length by adding other pairs of "forks" at the ends. The space included between any two pairs of these "forks" was known as a "bay." As the "bays" were of uniform length, the practice arose of speaking of a building as containing so many "bays."

The normal length of the bay was sixteen feet. Its length was therefore the same as that of the rod or perch in land measurement. Both buildings and acres were measured by the rod of sixteen feet. The length of this rod was determined by the standing-room required by the "long yoke" of oxen, whether standing in the stall or the plough-team.

Just as the booth or tent supported by a pair of "crutches" could be extended in the direction of its length, so it could be widened at its sides. This was done by affixing aisles, or, as they were called, "outshots" at the sides. A building so framed consisted of a nave with an aisle on one or both sides. These "outshots" were sometimes formed by a complex wooden framework affixed to the "crutches," as in the example from Bolsterstone (p. 75). Usually, however, upright pillars took the place of the "crutches," and then the form of the building was like that of the typical parish church in which the nave is separated from the aisles by two parallel rows of pillars.

The typical dwelling-house contained a hall and bower, and a buttery or store-room. The hall was the men's apartment, but, as it contained the fire, the food was cooked there. The men slept in the hall, and the bower was the women's apartment.

As was the case in other countries, it is probable that in the largest form of dwelling the cattle were housed in the aisles of the fire-house or hall, the men sleeping in a loft over the horses, and the women in a corresponding loft over the cows. In such cases there was an exedra at the end for the use of the master of the household and his family. In form such a building resembled a church, with nave, aisles, and chancel.

The bower was sometimes called "the woman house." It corresponds to the *stofa* of the Norsemen and the *gynaeconitis* of the Greeks.

In ancient cities the forms of the houses and the arrangement of the streets were modified by foreign influence. The space available for building purposes was limited by the walls or ramparts, and this limitation of space caused the houses to be built to a greater height than in the country. The chief apartment was on the upper floor, and the basements, and even the cellars, were occupied as shops. The upper stories projected over the basements. Most of the streets were too narrow to permit the use of carriages or vehicles in them. The two main streets, which intersected each other at right angles and passed through the four gates, were used for carriage traffic.

Usually the chimney or flue which carried the smoke was built of wood, plastered with mud-clay. The perishable nature of such a structure, together with the confusion which has arisen from the use of the word "chimney" in various senses, has led to the belief that chimneys were not in early use. It seems, however, that a "cover," or wood-and-plaster hood, stood over the hearth, whereas some authors understood a "chimney" to mean only a stone flue, built into, and forming part of, an outer wall.

In ancient buildings of every kind the frequent use of colour-wash, both on the inner and outer walls, has to be noticed. Wall-painting was much used. The interiors of houses, including churches, were whitewashed and decorated with mural paintings. Often their exteriors were covered with colour-wash.

In the great country house of the Middle Ages, or manor-house as it may be conveniently called, the chief rooms were the hall, or men's apartment, which corresponded to the Greek *andronitis*, and the bower or chamber, which corresponded to the *gynaeconitis*. A chapel was frequently added. To these chief apartments other rooms, such as a kitchen, brewhouse, washhouse, stables, etc., were often annexed, and then the whole range of buildings were usually grouped round a quadrangular area. When the chapel, hall, or bower were on an upper floor, access to them was obtained by outside stairs. In many of these buildings distinct traces of Greek and Roman influence may be seen. The chief windows opened into the quadrangle.

The castle, properly so called, was a stronghold used for the defence of a particular district. It was supported by taxation, and its officers were appointed by the Crown. Frequently it occupied the site of a prehistoric fortified village, and the Old English *castel* meant "village." The most characteristic of its buildings was a watch-tower or keep, which often occupied the site of an earlier toot-hill or specular mount. From this keep watch was kept over the surrounding country, and signals of approaching danger given. Church towers, like the Irish and Scotch round towers, were often, perhaps generally, used as watch-towers. In many cases they belonged to the municipality, and in form and construction resembled the watch-towers found in castle yards.

Modern scholars have shown that the word "church" means "lord's house," and the evidence which we have given proves that this "house" was the public hall, town hall, or basilica of a district or community. It was used both as a temple and a court of justice. It was also the place where the local council met. The forms of these buildings are identical with the forms of the heathen basilica. This identity is especially apparent in the striking correspondence between the crypts found in some English churches and the crypt of the basilica at Pompeii. The double staircases, the holes in the roof, and the small "cellar-windows" are found as well in the Pompeian crypt as in crypts of English churches. There are, besides, other points of resemblance.

The progress of man in the arts can be measured by the difference between the cave-dwelling and the cathedral. The first links of the long chain of evolution which extends between the lowest and the highest forms of human dwellings were forged by the men who tilled the land and watched the flocks. It was they who fashioned and maintained the shapes which for so many ages prevailed both in the cottage and the palace.

EXCURSUS I.

Contract for Removing and Refixing a Hall and Chamber, A.D. 1321.

THE document is in the British Museum, Add. MS. 6670, p. 293. It is entitled, "A Copie of the Byll for the removinge the Hall Rogeri Columbell de Darley arm." The copy contains some misreadings, but it is here faithfully reprinted as it stands in the MS.

"Ista indentura testatur quod die sabbati proxima ante festum invencionis scē Crucis Anno Dnī 1321 Ita convenit inter Joñem de Derlegh ex una parte et Wiłłm de Keylstedis cementarium ex altera vidz. quod dictus Wiłłmus concessit et fide mediante fideliter manucepit se removendam Aulam et Cameram Joñis de Derlegh et illas reparandas in quodam loco qui vocatur Robardyerd: Aulam vidz de eadem mensura sicut steterat in antiquo loco et duas fenestras in Aula quaque fenestra de duobus luminaribus et duas gabeles tabulatas sep Aulam longitudo Camē. vidz. quadraginta pedum inter parietes. latitudo. vidz. Sicut meremiū antiq̄ Camē dcē postulat cum tribus fenestris quaque fenest de duobus luminaribus et una fenestra de uno luminare et uno Chimino de meremio usque le baas cum ij gabelis tabulat^s. cum uno Warderobe et uno oriell predicte [camer]e pertinente cum novem hostiis de petris aule et camere pertinente et predict⁸ Wiłłm⁸ debet ponere . . . . singultum sup Cameram quod fuit sup Aulam. Ad quā quid̄ Convencoē fidelitʳ. faciend̄ dictus Wiłłm⁸. . . . . se heredes ex executor̄ suos et oĩa bona sua ad districtione cujusq̄ Judic̃ Ecc̃astia veḷt . . . . Et dict⁸. Joh̃es concessit pro se et hered̄ suis dare dc̃o Wyłło pro dc̃a op̄acōe octo marcas . . . . pro vicus Sicut opus suū opavʲit et unam robam servient̄ . . . . ip̄ius usual̄. In cujus . . . . datum apud Derl . . . . (cetera desᵗ.).''

EXCURSUS II.

Extracts from "A Survey of Lands belonging to the Mannor of Sheffield, 1611."

From the MS. collections of John Wilson, Esq., of Broomhead Hall, now in the possession of his great-grandson, Charles Macro Wilson, Esq.

"Tennamentts and Landes surveyed by Mr. Will'm Leighe, Baylyffe of Sheffeld.

"SHEFFELD TOWNE.

"*Gilbert hauldsworthe.* One dwellinge house 2 baies, 2 chambers, one parler, one kitchen, one stable 2 baies, one hey house 2 baies, one beast house 2 baies, one barne 2 baies, one swinehouse.

"*James hill.* One dwellinge house 2 baies, 2 chambers, one barne 2 baies, one parler with a chimney, one kytchen, one warehouse.

"*Franncis horner.* One dwelling house 2 baies, one parler, one kitchen 2 baies, one chamber, 2 stables, one slaughter house 2 baies.

"*haulecar farme.* One dwelling house 4 baies, one corne barne 4 baies *et di.*, one hey barne 2 baies, beast houses 3 baies, 2 outshutts.

"*R. Hadfeild farme.* One dwelling howse   baies, one kitchen   baies, two corne barnes   baies, one hey barne   baies, one kilne house with mault chambers, two stables, two beast houses   baies, one shepe house   baies, one cottage, one wainehouse.

"*Simon heathcote farme.* One house 2 baies, one parler, one chamber, one houell to set beast in corne barne made of poules very badd.

"*Vid. Sikes farme.* One house 2 baies, one beast house one bay, one cottage one bay, one parler, one litle house of the comen.

"*Laurence Eyre farme.* One house j bay slated, j part couered with thack 2 baies; j barne couered with thacke one bay, one fald.

"*Christopher Limer farme.* One house 4 baies, one parler, one chamber, one beast house with a chamber ouer yt, one smethey j bay, one barne 3 baies, one outshutt at the end.

"*Edw. Hill.* One house j bay, one chamber, one beast howse 2 baies.

"*Robert Taylior.* One house 2 baies, one parler, one barne 2 baies.

"*Christopher Hawksworthe.* One house 4 baies, one parler, one beast house one bay, one chamber, one outshutt, one barne 3 baies.

"*Steel farme.* One house j bay, one chamber, one parler, one chamber ouer the kytchen, one barne 2 baies, one outshutt, one wainehouse one bay, one beast house 2 baies, with a chamber ouer yt.

"*John Lansdale.* One house 3 baies, one parler, on chamber.

"*John Smithe farme.* One house 2 baies, one barne 2 baies, one outshut.

"*Robert Hauksworthe farme.* One house 3 baies, one parler, one barne 2 litle baies, one other barne j bay, one beast house j baye, one kilne in the well close, one ould house to sett beast in 3 baies, 2 other ould howses to put fuell in.

"*Vid. Hoyland farme.* One house 4 baies, one turfe house j bay, two parlers, one barne 4 baies, one beast house 2 baies, one beast house j bay, one swine coate.

"*Geo. Morrey farme.* One house 3 baies, one parler, 2 chambers, one beast house, one barne slated 3 baies, one beast house 2 baies, one kilne house.

"*Thom. Unwin farme.* One house 3 baies, 2 parlers, one chamber, one cowe house 2 baies, one barne 2 baies, one outshutt, one turffe house 2 baies.

"*John Fearneley farme.* One house one bay, one chamber, one kitchen one bay, one parler, one parler with a chimney, one chamber ouer the same, one beast house 2 baies, one hey house 2 baies, one barne 2 baies, one waine house, one tann house.

"*Vid. Moore farme.* One house 3 baies, one chamber, one parler, one barne of one of the 3 baies, one outshut at the end of the said house for catle.

"*Nich. Sampson farme.* One house one bay, one parler aboue the house, 2 baies beneath the house for beast howses, 2 parlers newly builded, 2 chambers ouer the parler, one barne 4 baies, 2 outshutts, one beast [house] 2 baies, j hay house 2 baies.

"*James heaton.* One house j bay, j barne one bay.

"*Will'm Brodhead farme.* One house j bay, 2 parlers 2 baies, beast houses 2 baies, one hey barne one bay, one

P

corne barne 4 baies, one ouen house j bay, beast houses 3 baies.

"*Richard Wilson farme.* One house 7 baies, one corne barne 3 baies, one hey barne 2 baies, beast houses 4 baies, a swinehull, one kilne house j bay, one wainehouse 2 baies.

"*Robert Beard farme.* One dwelling house ij baies, one parler, one ouen house j bay, one smythey j bay, one barne 2 baies & 2 outshutts for cattle, one swinehull.

"*Robert Carr farme, Butterthwayte.* One house 3 baies, one parler with a chimney, 3 chambers, 2 chambers with chimnies, one kitchen one bay, one cowe house 2 baies, one hey howse, one stable one bay, one barne 3 baies, one outshutt for beasts, one oxehouse j bay, one hey barne 2 bay, one bay of hey couered with brome, one backe house 2 baies.

"*John Wilson farme.* One house 2 baies, 2 chambers, j parler, 2 cott. 2 baies, 2 chambers 4 baies, one barne 2 baies, one stable.

"*Christopher Wilson farme,* vocat. Pogges. One house 3 baies, 2 parlers, j chamber, one barne 3 baies in decay, one hay house j bay in decay, and other house fallen downe."

EXCURSUS III.

Length of Yokes and Bays.

ACCORDING to the *Welsh Laws* there were 8 feet in the field yoke and 16 feet in the long yoke. (i. 187.) "There are sixteen feet in the length of the long yoke." (i. 539.)

"Sexdecim pedes et dimidium iugum faciunt longum, id est, hẏrẏeu." (ii. 784.)

"Pedes xv. et dimidium faciunt longum jugum." (ii. 852.)

The *Welsh Laws* also speak of "a rod, equal in length to that of the long yoke, in the hand of the driver." (i. 187.)

1396-9. "In vaccaria insuper de Felsa unam novam domum vaccariæ, lxxx pedum in longitudine; fecit de novo ædificari." *Chron. Monast. de Melsa* (Rolls Series), iii. 242.

This was exactly 5 bays of 16 feet each. On the next page we have a berchary 160 feet, *i.e.*, ten bays, in length.

SOME BOOKS CITED.

THE chief literary sources of information about the early English house are old surveys, deeds, court rolls, building accounts, and building contracts, monastic inventories and cartularies, chronicles, old dictionaries, and ancient laws, together with numerous public records, printed or unprinted. To these may be added occasional references or descriptions in old poems, such as *Beowulf*, *Piers Plowman*, and the *Canterbury Tales*. The Icelandic Sagas are also useful, but this source of information must be treated with caution. The number of books and journals relating to architecture, topography, and British antiquities, is very great, and it need hardly be said that many valuable facts are scattered about in them.

Anderson, Joseph. *Scotland in Early Christian Times.* Edinburgh, 1881.

Ancient Laws and Institutes of Wales (Record Office Publications). 2 vols. 1841.

Clark, G. T. *Mediæval Military Architecture in England.* 2 vols. London, 1884.

Fergusson, James. *A History of Architecture in all Countries.* 4 vols. London, 1874-76.

Guest, Edwin. *Origines Celticae, and other Contributions to the History of Britain.* 2 vols. London, 1883.

Hale, William H. *The Domesday of St. Paul's of the year MCCXXII.* Camden Society. 1858.

The leases of manors during the 12th century, printed at the end of this volume, some of which contain descriptions and measurements of buildings, are very useful.

Lange, Konrad. *Haus und Halle: Studien zur Geschichte des antiken Wohnhauses und der Basilika.* Leipzig, 1885.

Meitzen, August. *Das deutsche Haus in seinen volksthümlichen Formen. Seperat-abdruck aus den Verhandlungen des deutschen Geographen-tages.* Berlin, 1882.

Meitzen, August. *Wanderungen, Anbau, und Agrarrecht der Völker Europas nördlich der Alpen.* Berlin, 1895.

This work contains, amongst other valuable matter, an essay on "Das nordische und das altgriechische Haus."

O'Curry, Eugene. *On the Manners and Customs of the Ancient Irish.* Edited by W. K. Sullivan. 3 vols. London, 1873.

Riley, H. T. *Munimenta Gildhallæ Londoniensis* (Record Office Publications). 1859–62.

Seebohm, Frederic. *The English Village Community.* London, 1883.

See pp. 187, 194, and 239 of Mr. Seebohm's book.

Turner, T. Hudson. *Some Account of Domestic Architecture in England from the Conquest to the end of the Thirteenth Century.* With numerous illustrations of existing remains from original drawings. Oxford, 1851.

This was followed by three more volumes, edited by J. H. Parker, and bringing the subject down to the reign of Henry VIII. It is an excellent work.

Violet-le-Duc, M. *Dictionnaire Raisonné de l'Architecture Française du XIe au XVIIe Siècle.* 10 vols. Paris, 1858.

Wright, Thomas. *The Homes of Other Days: A History of Domestic Manners and Sentiments in England from the earliest known period to modern times.* London, 1871.

INDEX

Aitch = mantel-piece, 46.
Ambry, or locker, 137, 146.
Angiportus, 99.
Appentices, in streets, height of, 101.
Arch, semicircular wooden, 73.
—— Gothic, origin of, 17, 29.
Archil, colouring of walls by, 67, 71, 91, 123.
Argillae, 13.
Ashlar, its use in costly buildings, 145.
Autumn house, how made, 35.

"Balk," 82, 83.
Barns, of great size, 67 *n.*, 132.
—— stacks built in, 133.
"Barton," 38.
Basilical form of house, 72, 88, 89.
Basing = foundation, 13, 108.
"Bay," defined, 17.
—— = gulf, 33.
—— normal length of, 17, 18, 33, 66, 72, 75.
"Bay," an architectural unit, 17, 66.
"Bay," half of a, 207.
—— a standard of measurement, 32.

"Bay," buildings sold by the, 33.
—— exceptions to normal length of, 20, 33, 64.
"Bay," house of one, described, 19 *et seq.*
"Bay," its length the space required for two pairs of oxen, 66.
"Bay," its length equivalent to the perch or rod, 68.
Bay of hay, 33, 210.
"Bays," building in, 17 *et seq.*
—— and yokes, 210.
—— forming aisles (*see* "Little Bay").
"Bays," little, 33, 74.
—— or parcloses, 197.
—— mentioned in 1321(?), 205.
Beds, of rushes, etc., 78.
—— in the hall, 78.
—— in chests, 80.
—— over ox-houses, 81, 82.
—— in alcoves, 85.
"Beehive" houses, 11.
—— —— double cells of, 12.
Bekens, 197.
Belfry, meaning of, 172.
Blue, a favourite colour for walls, 123.

Booth, 22.
—— copied in stone, 22, 26.
—— = "summer-house," 27.
—— = shop, or stall, 101.
Bordarii, 37 *n*.
Bostar, 74 *n*.
Bower, or women's room, 44, 60, 63, 130, 131, 133, 134, 146, 149.
Bower, amongst the Norsemen, 62.
Brandreth, 63.
Brick, earliest buildings of, 110.
—— the word not found in Old English, 110.
Brick, disuse of, improbable, 111.
Brocks or boughs, 168.
Buffet, 45, 133.
Buttery, north-west position of, 20, 48, 52, 53, 137.
Buttery, in Norse houses, 62.

Camera, 74 (see "Chamber").
Camera ima, 61 *n*.
Caminata, 60.
"Cankerneedle," 196.
Carcass of a house, 108 *n*.
Cardinal points in keeps or watch-towers, 155.
Castle, public character of the, 150.
—— a place of refuge, 151.
—— keep or watch-tower in, 151.
Cellars used as shops, 95.
Chambers, adjoining the house-place, 46, 48 (see "*Camera ima*").
Chambers, divided by a brattice, 46.
Chambers, women's apartments, 62, 133, 142, 146.
Chambers, before the "front" of a house, 74 *n*.

Chambers, great and little, 104, 105, 142.
Chambers, outer and inner, 147.
—— furniture of, 147.
Chancel, the property of the lord, 188.
Chancel, the tribunal, 188.
—— called "shot" (*see* "Out-shut").
Chapel, in a manor-house, 140, 141, 146, 147.
Chapel, fire-place in, 143.
—— business done in, 143.
—— communicating with "chamber," 146.
—— clock in, 149.
—— Court Leet held in, 181.
Charcoal burner's hut described, 3.
Chimney, 2.
—— of wood and plaster, 38, 40, 48, 112, 117–120, 163.
Chimney, early use of, 117.
—— curious hole in, 39.
—— in Greek and Roman houses, 119.
Chimney, curved, 46.
—— none in old German houses, 84.
Chimney, evolution of, 111.
—— central, 111, 115, 120.
—— "rooms" in, 112, 117.
—— against walls, 112.
Churches, thatched, 128.
—— whitewashed, 126, 128.
—— their secular uses, 176 *et seq.*
Churches, courts held in, 178 *et seq.*
—— called *basilicae* in old documents, 179.
Churches, drinking in, 179.
—— banqueting in, 179.

INDEX

Churches, markets held in, 179.
— deeds kept in, 180.
— accounts audited in, 180.
— pedlars' wares sold in porch of, 180.
Churches, mortgages redeemed in porch of, 180.
Churches, lawyers' consultations in, 180.
— deeds witnessed in, 180 *n*.
Churches, plays acted in, 181.
— dancing in, 181.
— pleading in, 181.
— judgment in, 181.
— testamentary cases in, 182.
Churches, legal business in, 182.
— "low side windows" in, 183.
Churches, "squints" in, 183.
— doorkeeper in, 184.
— schools held in, 185, 186.
— the nucleus of fresh communities, 186.
Churches, the "houses" of manorial "lords," 186.
Churches, rectors of, their duties, 188.
Church towers, used as watchtowers, 168 *et seq.* (*see* "Watchtowers").
Church towers, fire-places in, 169, 170.
Church towers, garderobes in, 169.
Church towers, resemble keeps, 169.
Church towers, "lanterns" in, 170, 171.
Church towers, belonging to municipalities, 170, 172.

Church towers, as inland lighthouses, 171.
Church towers, bells in, guide travellers, 170.
Church towers, watchmen in German towns, 172.
Church towers, detached from churches, 173.
Church towers, circular, 173.
— — cardinal points in, 173.
Circles, decoration of hearths with, 125.
"Clam staff and daub," 32, 44, 46, 49, 51.
Clunch, building with, 110.
Cob walls, 41 *n*.
"Coit," description of one, 69.
— aisles of, 72.
Colacium, culacium, 188.
Cold Harbour, 128.
Combined houses and barns, 61, 62, 75, 77, 85.
Concrete, walls of, 154.
Conical house, 2, 3.
Conservatism in architecture, 32.
Couples (*see* "Crucks").
"Cover," canopy over fire, 112, 115.
Croiche, 60.
"Crucks," "croks," "crutches," buildings supported by, 17, 19, 44 *et seq.*
"Crucks," identical with "forks," 27.
"Crucks," known to the Romans, 28.
"Crucks," plinths or stylobats for, 31, 53, 72.
"Crucks," often older than the walls, 32.
"Crucks," holes near feet of, 78, 108.

Crypt, its significance in church history, 190.
Crypt, in Pompeian basilica described, 190.
Crypt, English, compared to Pompeian and Coptic, 190 *et seq.*
Crypt, holes in roofs of, 190, 191.
—— double staircases in, 190, 191, 194, 196.
Crypt, "cellar windows" in, 190, 191 *n.*, 193, 194, 196.
Crypt, use of, 190.
—— coloured decoration of, 194.
—— fire-place in, 194, 195.
—— legends about, 196.
Culina, 86, 88 *n.*

Dawbing, 108, 126.
Domus = fire-house or *atrium*, 44.
—— = entry, 130.
Doors, sloping jambs of, 2, 3, 11, 25.
Doors, facing south, 20.
—— winnowing, 73.
—— in gable ends, 19, 20, 22, 23.
Doors, of harden (sack-cloth), 41.
—— posts before, 46.
—— arched wood, 49.
—— for oxen, 61.
—— of "coits," 72.
—— separate, for men and women, 141, 143.
"Dovet," turf for thatching, 127.
Duns and raths in Ireland, 14.
"Dung" or "tunc," a winter-room or underground room, 15.

Eaves, spars under, represented by pellet-moulding, 145.
Enclosure of manor house, 145.

Enterclose, 46.
Entry, what it was, 61, 62.
—— building divided by, 61, 137.
Entry, barred by pole, 138.
Estland boards, 109 *n.*

Fenestrals, 123 (*see* "Harden").
Fire, in nave or central division, 78, 80, 84.
Fire, continually burning, 84.
—— protection against, 104.
Fire and flet, fire and lodging, 61 *n.*
Fire-house or hall, 59, 60, 61 *n.*, 62, 63.
Fire-house or hall, its central position, 60.
Fire-place, position of in tent-shaped house, 20.
Fire-place, built outside the "crucks," 53.
Fire-place, in chapel, 140, 143.
Fish-ponds, attached to great houses, 146.
"Flet," 82 *n.*
"Floor" = threshing-floor or main entrance, 60, 83.
"Floor," in Saxon house, 79.
—— in North German house, 83, 85.
Floors, of clay, 46, 51.
—— decoration of, 124 *et seq.*
—— washed with milk, 124.
Fodderum, 70.
"Forks," 17, 27, 149 *n.* (*see* "Crucks").
"Forks," known to the Romans, 28.
Framework of house set up first, 108.

INDEX

Fresco-painting, 126.
Frisian house, 82.
"Front" of house, 22, 74 *n*.

Gable end, the "front view" of a house or booth, 22.
Gable end, door in, 19, 20, 22, 23.
Gables towards the street, 104, 109.
Galilee, 29 *n*.
"Galing," "goaling," a passage or alley, 99.
Gardrobe, 158 (*see* "Warderobe").
Garret, 103.
Gavels, gavelforks, 17, 59.
Glass, dearness of, 120–122.
Glassby, 123 *n*.
Glass windows, early use of, 122.
—— —— tenants' fixtures, 122.
Glastonbury, houses in lake village near described, 4 *et seq*.
Glastonbury, rectangular house there, 6.
Gothic arch, origin of, 17, 29.
Grange, 59 *n*.
Grass-houses and grassmen, 37.
Greek peasant's house described, 88, 89.
Gulf = bay, 33.

Half a bay, 207.
Half-hall, 71.
"Half-timbered," a misleading phrase, 109.
"Hall," or house-place, 59.
"Hall" = fire-house, 60.
—— in manor house, 140, 146, 147.
"Hall-house," 59.
Hall and bower, 12, 130 (*see* "Bower").

Hall and bower, the essential parts of a manor house, 149.
Hallan, halland, 45.
Harden, windows and doors of (*see* "Fenestral").
Hazel rods, building with, 109.
Hearth, next to threshing-floor, 62, 63.
Hearths, superimposed on each other, 8, 125.
Hearths, decorated with circles, 125.
Hecks, 70.
Height of rooms in old houses, 8, 38, 44, 48, 53, 72, 103, 104, 130.
"House" = fire-house, house-place, or dwelling-house, 44, 59, 208.
"House" = entry, 130.
"House-part," 44 *et seq*. (*see* "House").
"House-part," open to the roof, 49, 50.
"House-part," usually in centre of building, 52.
Houses combined with barns, etc., 61, 62.
Hulk, 29 (*see* "Ship-shaped House").

Ireland, oblong houses in, 78.
Irish houses, lengths of old, 63, 64.
Insulae, 101, 102.

Jetties, projecting stories, 101.
"Jennel," 99.

Keep (*see* "Watch-tower").
Kell = cell, 74.

Lady's bower, 15.
Lantern, where placed, 87.

"Lanterns" in church towers, 170, 171.
Leaves and flowers, decoration by, 124, 125.
Lesche, 128.
"Little bay," 33, 74.
Locker or ambry in wall, 137, 146.
Loop-hole, meaning of, 121.
Louvre, 11, 115, 116, 121.
"Low side windows," 183.
Lucken Booths, 101.

Manor house, rooms in, 129.
—— —— halls in, dimensions of, 149.
Manor house, pigeon-cotes in, 144.
—— —— hall and bower the essential parts of a, 149.
Mantellum camini, 116.
Mantel-tree, 38, 46, 49, 115 *n*., 116 (*see* "Aitch").
Mapalia, 27, 28.
Meremium, timber for building, 107 *n*.
Mossing of houses, 108, 126.
Moot hills, 153, 177, 178, 197, 198.
Mud house in East Yorkshire described, 38.
Mud houses, 110.
—— walls, method of building, 40.
"Municipal buildings," absence of early, 177.
"Municipal buildings," in church-yards, 177.

Narrow streets, preference for, 97.
"Nave," in architecture, 29, 43 (*see* "Ship-shaped House").
"Nave," without aisles, 72.

Nave and aisles in domestic buildings, 72, 78, 88, 89.
Noggin houses, 126.
Norse house, typical, 62, 63.
Nubilaria, 133.

Oriel, 206.
Orientation, 10.
"Outshuts," "outshots," 20 (*see* "Little Bay").
"Outshuts" described, 43 *et seq*.
Oval houses, 6, 11, 16.
—— —— difficult to build, 11, 16.
Oven house, 210.
Ox-house, 75, 84, 130.
—— English and Roman, 67.
Ox-house, loft above, 75, 83.
—— in barns, 76.
—— living in, 82.
Ownership, divided, of the same house, 103.

Pairs of principals, late introduction of, 32.
"Pan," or "pon," 8, 29, 30.
Parclose, 46, 105, 197.
"Parging," or "sparging," 110.
Parish, what it was, 187.
"Parpoint" walls, 111.
Party-walls of freestone, 103.
Passages connecting adjoining huts or cells, 12.
"Pennpits," 15.
Pergula, 94, 97.
Piscina, 143, 146.
Pit dwellings, 12.
Projecting stories, object of, 102.
Prospects from houses, disregarded, 148.
Putlock holes, 145.

INDEX

Quadrangles, building in, 132, 135.

Raths and duns, in Ireland, 14.
"Reared house," 107.
Rearing a house, what it was, 107, 108.
Rectangular house, origin of its form, 17 *et seq.*
Rectangular house, in Glastonbury lake-village, 6.
"Rent," passage between houses, 99.
Reredos, 115.
Rood for measuring land, how its length was ascertained, 68.
Roof, common, 77.
Roofs, covered with lead, 18.
—— thatching of, 20, 47, 126, 127.
Roofs, rounded at the gable ends, 47.
Roofs, great extent of, 72.
—— mossed, 108.
—— of turf and heather, 127.
—— concealed, 155.
Roman villas, 148.
—— —— copied in manor houses, 148.
Rooms, upper, absence of, in old houses, 149.
Rotten Row, "ruinous street," 105.
Round house, 1 *et seq.*
—— —— early disuse of, 92.
Round Towers (*see* "Watch-towers").
Rows, 94, 98, 99.

Saxon house, 80.
"Scaffold" = hay-chamber, 86, 87.

Sconce, 45.
Secretarium, 197.
Selda, 101.
Sentry, 163.
"Set," in place-names, 35.
Shielings in Iceland, 19.
Ship-shaped house, 26–29.
—— —— strange to the Romans, 28.
Ship-shaped house, how its walls became vertical, 29.
Shippon, 69 *et seq.*
—— combined with house, 69, 72, 77, 85.
"Shooting," the process of, 109.
Siles, sÿles, 18, 59.
Singultum (?), 206.
Skell-boost, 70, 71.
Sod houses, 110.
Solar, 48 *n.*, 132.
—— its meaning and origin, 102.
—— the chief living room in town houses, 103.
"Sparging," process of, 110.
Specula, 152.
Speer, 38, 45, 49, 54, 61.
Spinning house, 58 (*see* "Weaving Room").
"Squint" in churches, 183.
Stable, 84.
Stair, originally a ladder, 39, 49, 55, 57.
Stair, perpendicular, 57.
—— hole for, 56.
Staircase, evolution of, 55.
Stair-head, 56.
"Stair-hole," 56.
Stairs, outside the house, 140, 146, 158 *n.*
Stalls for goods, 101.

Stone, early use of, in great buildings, 109.
Streets, reasons for narrow, 97, 98.
—— for foot-passengers only, 98.
"Stud and mud," building with, 32.
Sudes binales, 27.
"Summer house," how it was built, 27.
"Summer house" = *bourde portable*, 34 *n*.
"Summer house," place-names referring to, 34.
"Summer house," sometimes permanently occupied, 35, 36.
"Summer house" amongst the Romans, 35.
"Summer house," widespread use of, 36.
"Summer house" used by nomadic tribes, 36.
"Summer house" compared to the winter house, 65.
"Summer house," sometimes built of sods, 110.
Sun-chamber, 132.

Tabernae, 94.
Table, uses of, 58.
—— forms for, 147.
—— precedence at, 58.
—— with trestles, 147.
—— round, place of honour, 58, 84.
Table dormant, 54 *n*.
Tacitus, his description of German houses, 90, 91, 123 *n*., 126.
"Taverns," underground shops, 94 *n*., 95, 101, 109.
"Tavern stairs," 95.
—— —— obstructions caused by, 96, 97.

Thatch of rye straw, 47.
—— heather, 82, 127.
—— rushes, 127.
Threshold = threshing-floor, 61, 62.
—— none where no barn, 61.
—— buildings divided transversely by, 61.
Threshold, serpentine marks on, 125.
"Threskeld," 61 *n*.
Tie-beam and king-post, gradual introduction of, 32.
Tiles, the old name for bricks, 111.
Toft and croft, 91.
Toot hills, 152.
Town house, description of one, 104.
Town houses, 93 *et seq*.
—— —— height of, 103, 104.
Trades, in different quarters of towns, 100.
"Trance" = entrance, described, 139.
"Trap hetch," or "throp hetch" (trap door), 39, 56.
Trisantia, 139.
Turf house, 209.
Turf nook, 83.
Turnpikes, 99.
"Tunc" or "dung," a winter-room or underground room, 15.

Underground dwellings, 12–15.
—— —— warmth obtained in, 14, 15.
Underground passages, 13.
Upper rooms, absence of, in old houses, 149.

"Waldlure," 147 *n*.
Walls, outer, built after the house had been set up, 30, 31.

INDEX

Walls, decoration of, 122 *et seq.*
—— materials for, 32.
—— party, of freestone, 103.
—— surrounding manor house, 145.
Walls of concrete, 154.
—— thick, in castles, 154.
Warderobe, 206 (*see* "Gardrobe").
Washing room, 84, 129.
Watch-towers (see "Church Towers").
—— cardinal points in, 155, 173, 174.
Watch-towers, rooms in, 155.
—— concealed roof of, 155.
Watch-towers, beacon fires on, 155.
Watch-towers, raised doorways in, 157.
Watch-towers, living room in, 158.
—— rooms in walls of, 158, 168.
Watch-towers, watchmen for, 162.
—— fire-place for, 164.
—— circular, 167.
—— compared to Sardinian núraghs, 167.
Watch-towers, position of outer door of, 168.
Watch-towers, attached to churches, 168.
Watch-towers ascended by ladders, 170.
Watch-towers, Irish and Scotch, called "round towers," 173, 174.
Watch-towers, watch-room in, 175.
Water, supplied from reservoir, 146.
Wattles, or rods, building with, 3, 12, 18, 21, 27, 28, 30, 32, 44, 109

Wattles, substitutions for, 32, 46, 49, 51.
Weaving room, 57, 84 (*see* "Spinning House").
Wells, in and near houses, 41, 81.
White dwellings, 123 *n.*
Whitewash, early use of, 126.
—— a protection against fire, 126.
Whitewash, applied to church walls, 126.
Whitewash, of chimneys, 116.
Wicker house, 2, 123.
Wind-braces, 17, 20.
Windows, evolution of, 11, 25.
—— of harden (sack-cloth), 41.
Windows, smallness of, in old houses, 109, 120.
Windows, facing inwards, 140, 141, 148.
Winnowing door, 61, 62, 73.
Winter house, 34; 69.
—— form of, 65, 69.
"Wints," "wynds," "wents," 99.
Wood, building in, 91, 104, 106 *et seq.*
Wood, brought from Norway, 107 *n.*
Wood-carving, ancient, 104.
"Woman house," 131.
Women's apartments (*see* "Bower").
"Worth," in English place-names, 14, 15 *n.*
"Wrastlers," 76 *n.*

Yellow, a favourite colour for walls, 123.
Yokes and bays, 211.